Ruby Parker's Last Orders

James Ward

COOL MILLENNIUM BOOKS

2

Copyright © James Ward 2020

James Ward has asserted his right to be identified as the author of this Work in accordance with the Copyright, Designs and Patents Act 1988.

This is a work of fiction. All names, characters, and events are the product of the author's imagination, or used fictitiously. All resemblance to actual events, places, events or persons, living or dead, is entirely coincidental.

First published in KDP 2020.
This edition published 2021.

A CIP catalogue record for this book is available from the British Library.

ISBN: 978-1-913851-18-7

Cover picture shows the view from 20 Fenchurch Street towards Canary Wharf.

This novel was produced in the UK and uses British-English language conventions ('authorise' instead of 'authorize', 'The government are' instead of 'the government is', etc.)

To my wife

Chapter 1: Plucked from Obscurity

Pavel Nikolayevich Alikhanov was a quiet young man, and for a long time, his only ambition in life was to be a serial killer. Growing up in Noyabrsk, in the northern Russian district of Yamalo-Nenets, he first noticed that he was nothing like his peers just after his fourteenth birthday. For example, he experienced inexplicable hatreds for his classmates; he had a strong sense of his own superior uniqueness somehow inseparable from the urge to destroy other, less worthy lives, even those of passing strangers; he strongly preferred his own company; he continually fantasised about killing young women.

After a few years, and an increasingly focussed programme of reading and surfing the internet, he realised others had trodden the same dark path before him. Not only his mental outlook, but also his upbringing - he was an only child, his mother had left home when he was five, his father was an alcoholic, subject to random fits of extreme violence - matched the blueprint: he was a budding repeat-murderer, someone very like Ted Bundy and Jeffrey Dahmer. His relief was so strong, he almost cried. After all, lots of people grudgingly admired serial killers: they bought and read books about them, they spent hours watching documentaries about them, they made movies about them, they even paid to go on 'tours' themed around particular perpetrators. He had a vocation and, at least in terms of forebears, he wasn't alone.

He travelled twenty miles from home for his first killing – of a shop assistant from Labytnangi called Anna Klimova – when he was just eighteen. He'd never been to that part of Noyabrsk before, and he had no idea he was going to commit murder until the victim appeared from around the corner of a concrete warehouse by the Ob River. The conditions were perfect: the melancholy orange of the sunset, the thick falling snow, the comprehensive wistful solitude. He strangled her with intensity and vigour and dumped her body in the reeds. On the way home, an hour later, he felt elated. The whole thing seemed like a work of art.

He used knives for his next three murders, and by the third, he'd begun to tire of killing young women relatively spontaneously. To evolve, he needed to add kidnap and torture, and possibly throw in the odd male, just to confuse the investigators.

Such was his development-plan at the time the police intervened. The way they caught him – storming the building in the middle of the night while he was asleep – was unfair enough to verge on the obscene, especially since he was only twenty-two and his career had hardly begun. And as the papers commented, he didn't look like a brute, nor even as if he had sufficient strength to kill a person: he was thin and gangly with the hollow cheeks, sunken grey eyes and anaemic skin of an artist fallen on hard times.

It transpired that he hadn't been particularly careful about clearing up after each killing, and he learned an awful lot, during his trial, about how to commit a murder and get away with it. All too late, though. The judge handed down a sentence of life imprisonment and pronounced no possibility of appeal. He'd killed four women in all, and he still showed no inkling of remorse.

Although four victims wasn't nearly enough to make him legendary, he'd clearly obtained the lower status of *interesting*, because lots of people came to analyse him. They talked about his background, his feelings, his tastes, and weird things like what sort of music he liked, whether he believed in God, his knowledge of politics. They got him to fill in questionnaires.

After about a month of twice-weekly interviews, he noticed that not all the interviewers looked like health professionals. Increasingly, they came to resemble minor politicians, civil servants, even military officials. One actually turned up in an army uniform, and since he had silver hair, perhaps he was important.

At the end of a month, two warders came to get him from his cell at 8am. He dressed, showered and changed into the two-piece suit they gave him. They transferred him to a limousine outside the prison gates, curiously without handcuffing him. He sat in silence between two grim-looking heavies for three hours while the car travelled north at a steady 110 kilometres per hour.

They pulled up in front of a low grey brick building on a completely flat, bare landscape. Inside, he was asked to sit at a desk. The silver-haired officer who'd come to see him in prison sat down opposite him. Two other army officers sat on either side. They reminded him of the seriousness of his crimes, but said that his profile suggested something very unusual: that he wasn't mad, far from it: apart from the 'one little vice' of femicide, he was completely normal. They even hinted that he might some day grow out of it. The upshot was, he deserved another chance, and, as luck would have it, they were in a position to make him an offer.

The premise of the offer was that Russia was at war. Not with overseas powers – although that, too, in a low-key way – but with its own citizens. Not with *all* of its citizens, obviously – most were dedicated, loyal and hard-working – but with dissenters, 'rights seekers' and inveterate critics of the government. A list 'had been compiled' (the passive tense clearly intentional) of recidivous men and women whose activity was seriously damaging the state. Those persons needed to be liquidated, ideally in a messy way, as a warning to others. In short, Pavel Nikolayevich Alikhanov could be very useful to his country, and he need never, ever go back to prison.

Of course, one of the officers pointed out, as a kind of aside, he'd have no reason to do a runner. Firstly, where would he go? He had no assets. But secondly, his country was giving him an opportunity to fulfil what he'd explicitly stated was his vocation: to kill enough people to become 'legendary'. And it was offering him much more than that. He'd so far outstrip the 'greats' that historians would have to invent a new category for him. Because obviously, his new sponsors would make sure he was never caught.

Thus began a long and fruitful relationship between killer and state. Over the next two years, Pavel Nikolayevich Alikhanov killed fourteen people, mostly feminists and radicals, but also a few right-wingers from The Liberal Democratic Party and two bothersome regional journalists. He lived alone in a wood cabin in a forest in Krasnoyarsk Krai, in central Russia. He received assassination orders and finance via the internet, to which he had his own private connection. He never travelled outside Russia.

Over the same time-period, he gradually clarified his ideas about serial killing. When he'd gone to prison, he'd been full of regret that he'd never managed to torture, mutilate or eat anyone, and probably never would. But that changed. Serial killing, he realised, was a sport, closely related to trophy hunting and bullfighting, in which a powerful predator tried to kill a significantly weaker victim in a ritualised setting where risk to the former was low, but never non-existent. In some ways, it was a natural human activity. And that was why his interviewers had adjudged him 'normal'. Because he really *was* normal. Meanwhile, mutilation and torture played no part in sport. Eating the victim, yes, maybe sometimes, though he wasn't personally obliged to try it.

His days passed chopping wood, building fires, cooking, sleeping, reading, surfing the internet, and occasionally travelling to interesting new places to kill people. Then one day, out of the blue, he received a summons to Moscow.

He packed his bags and a car arrived the next morning at 7am. The journey took nearly three days, with two overnight stops.

When he arrived, he was taken straight to meet two civilian officials in a poky office in the Kremlin. How would he like to go abroad, they asked him, just for a few years?

He said he wasn't keen. He knew no foreign languages, and even in Russia his strong regional accent occasionally made it

8

difficult for him to blend in. Often when he'd committed a murder, there were a number of people who probably suspected him. Some of them likely even went to the police. In Russia, that didn't matter. Abroad, however, would be different.

In response, they made it obvious he had no choice. They'd recently been watching a British TV programme called *Killing Eve*, in which a serial killer gets remoulded into an international assassin. And they weren't its only fans. Officials at the very highest level – including, rumours suggested, the President himself – were converts to what they insisted was its central conceit: that transforming a serial killer into a state-controlled murderer, and putting that person to work abroad, was possible in both theory and practice. Why such a great TV show had taken nearly two years to reach Russia, no one knew, but, anyway, it was here now – at least, for selected individuals cleared by the censors - and Pavel Nikolayevich was the lucky beneficiary. He wasn't as good-looking or stylish as Villanelle, but no one would hold that against him! In the meantime, he should mentally adjust himself to a wholly new, much wider field of operations.

He consoled himself with the thought that, since he'd now killed seventeen people in all, his place in history was probably assured. More, he'd written everything down and saved it securely on the internet. If anything happened to him, he'd no longer be able to keep extending the digital countdown, and eventually it would all be released into the public domain. From posterity's point of view, he had nothing to lose. And he was being forced. So he said yes.

But it turned out to be far more grating a matter than he'd bargained for. To begin with, he needed to be trained and, irritatingly, his trainers kept referring to him as a 'hit man' or occasionally an 'international assassin.' They encouraged him to emulate 'Vasily Grigoryevich Zaytsev', a sniper from Stalingrad in World War Two, even though he'd never previously heard of 'Vasily Grigoryevich Zaytsev' and had no interest whatsoever in copying him. *I'm a serial killer!* he wanted to tell them. *I'm just a simple serial killer!*

Yet it was obvious they admired him. They spoke in hushed tones about his recent exploits and, in a moment of unguarded enthusiasm, one of them even declared him, 'wholly symbolic of Putin's Russia' - almost certainly a huge compliment in their world.

What they envisaged for him was nothing like what he'd been doing previously. He would have three 'contacts': one American, one British and one Turkish - known to him only by the definite article and their nationalities - who were collaborating to advance their own countries' interests, but who, to the extent that they were successful, would be helping Russia even more. Of course, their own governments had no idea what they were doing, otherwise they'd put an immediate stop to it.

Pavel Nikolayevich's job was to liaise with the three men and kill anyone they needed killing. The Russian embassy in each country would give him some support in emergencies, but his first port of call when he needed assistance should be one of the three collaborators. They'd give him anything he might need: accommodation, a false passport, food, phones, even weapons. He could expect to do a lot of killing along the way.

On the plane to Istanbul, he finally saw that the whole thing would be very good indeed for his CV. He could add it to his online journal, and it would give him an increased roundedness in the eyes of future readers. No longer exclusively the killer of Russians, now he was going after... well, the world was his oyster, really. Obviously, he had to kill the official targets, but he didn't have to kill *just* them. A German or two would be nice, maybe a Pole, or an Austrian. But he'd have to be careful not to overdo it. There could be no second release from prison. Not abroad.

Although prison did have its attractions. It consolidated your fame, for a start. And you always had a structure to your day. On the negative side, if you were young and good-looking, like he was, you'd be raped on a twice-daily basis, and one night, after lights-out, you might even get beaten to death.

It was while he was in Turkey that he met the woman he quickly came to consider the love of his life. To begin with, he didn't actually know her name. His American contact wanted her frightened – not killed, unfortunately – and the best way of achieving that was probably at close quarters, with a knife. One gloomy Tuesday afternoon, he followed her into Istanbul's Grand Bazaar. He grabbed her hand as she passed a rug seller's stall, and raised the weapon. She screamed. The rug seller yelled and advanced. Pavel Nikolayevich ran away.

He'd been following her since she came out of the CIA substation on the waterfront, but it was only when he saw the terror in her face that she became a powerful object of desire for him. She was about his age, tall, slim, well-dressed, with pale skin and piercing brown eyes. He thought about her constantly after that, and the next time he was asked to 'frighten' her, he managed to grab her bag for long enough to look inside. *Daisy Hallenbeck.* And she had an asthma inhaler in there too, which melted his heart: underneath her steely American exterior, she was clearly fragile and vulnerable.

And then things took a turn for the frantic. A British woman everyone had apparently been looking for suddenly arrived in London. His instructions came with an 'urgent' tag, and they were unambiguous. He had to kill her immediately, precise instructions to be issued after he'd arrived in Folkestone. According to the brief, she had to look as if she'd been shot, but only to the untrained eye.

It didn't feel right to be leaving beautiful Daisy in Istanbul, but then he received a message from the goddess of good fortune. *Don't worry, Pavel Nikolayevich, I'm sending her ahead of you!* For some reason, she was going to England too.

Killing the Englishwoman was no trouble at all, especially with the streets depleted thanks to coronavirus: he followed her into a Soho side alley and inserted a long blade into her chest, then he twisted it and thrust it through her back as she lay on the ground. Tricky, but she probably didn't feel anything. Others – friends of 'The Brit' – were on hand to dispose of the body. He went back to his hotel room, washed his hands for a long time to get rid of the blood, and reduce his chances of contracting the virus, and lay on the bed.

Just as he was dropping to sleep, 'The American' contacted him to disclose that the reason Daisy Hallenbeck had come to Britain was to meet the Englishwoman. Which meant she might be at the funeral. If so, it was just a question of following her afterwards.

And the time for merely frightening her had long passed.

Chapter 2: Not the Retiring Type?

Ruby Parker sat alone at her desk in her small, neat office in Basement One, Thames House, with the Queen's portrait behind her and a variety of house plants against the wall on one side, reading the email about Angela Barnes. A depressing end to something she'd fully understood, and even secretly admired at the time. She deleted it, as per protocol. She'd never personally known the woman, nor even met her; she'd been informed of her death solely as a formality.

It segued – as everything seemed to at the moment – into thoughts of her own mortality, more specifically the now visible road to it that began with her retirement; how for decades now, she'd hardly had a private life, and in her professional capacity, she'd been someone to be reckoned with.

That wasn't just going to change. It was going to do a complete about-turn. In two months, she'd be just another old black woman, living alone, probably, in Brixton.

It didn't have to be that way. She'd already been given to understand, in the peculiarly oblique way British civil servants and cabinet ministers had of intimating confidences, that a damehood awaited her when her contract of employment ran out; that, in fact, honours of all kinds were little more than a formality, including, possibly, an invitation to join the Privy Council. The Queen herself wanted her, so she'd been told. *Dame Ruby Parker, former Head of Red Department MI7*. Oh, that would sustain her someone-ness! There would be literary agents clamouring for her memoirs!

And yet the proximity of retirement had brought a bitterness whose principal symptom was an aggressive bloody-mindedness. She didn't want any of these things. She wanted to be an old woman in Brixton. She wanted to sit at home, reading most days, go to communion every Sunday morning 8am, shop in Iceland, collect her old age pension, get up at six, do the chores, go to bed at ten, get a cat. She wanted a complete break from spies and international subterfuge. Neither social standing nor civic responsibility meant anything. Not really. *Do not store up for yourselves treasures on earth…*

The trouble was, *Dame Ruby Parker, former Head of Red Department MI7* wasn't a detachable element of her identity. It was who she was. And that might mean her little house in Brixton was a no go. She'd be a target for foreign governments and terrorists. She'd need protection. And she'd get it, whether she wanted it or not. Along with reaching the job's end, that was another fixed parameter.

But there was a third option, if one could call it that. Only looked at close to, it seemed to evaporate like it had never been there. She could leave the country for good, and go and live in Havana with Vilma.

About two decades ago, she'd actually believed that might be a practical possibility. But as the years went by, it became less and less conceivable, until now it scarcely registered at all. It raised all the problems of a life of fantastical obscurity in Brixton – predatory personages in the shadows, hence the need for some sort of personal protection (or at the very least, external oversight of her movements) – only more so, and without compensations. She'd be in a foreign country, not even a particularly friendly one, and on the other side of the world. There was undoubtedly some committee in Whitehall with the power to forbid it and, if not, someone would quickly convene one.

Which simply added to her bitterness. Or did until, as soon as she'd begun re-entertaining the idea, she recalled its stupidity independently, without any sense that invisible others were constraining her future choices. Like it or not, she'd be the *former Head of Red Department MI7* until she died. Entirely her doing: it was what she'd chosen when she took the job. In becoming an *x* of any species, you necessarily committed yourself to one day

14

becoming a *former x*. In that regard, the only real question was whether she wanted the add-ons.

The second question, though – by no means minor – was how she was going to tell Vilma that Cuba was out of the question, and that, if she wanted them to spend the rest of their lives together, they'd have to live in Britain. 'Rainy Britain', as Vilma rightly called it. Getting to the House of Lords – if it came to that – would probably mean living in London rather than anywhere provincial. Which, for convenience's sake, would probably mean staying in Brixton.

Problems, problems. And then there was the anger. Did everyone feel angry when they were about to retire, or was it just her? The sense of a job you'd subconsciously considered doable, years ago, being just as challenging now as when you first took it. Fresh threats to national security, unresolved threats, threats returned from the dead, and everyone in governments everywhere getting seemingly less capable and more complacent.

She signed a batch of forms, put the lid on her fountain pen, and looked at the clock. 5.30. The phone rang.

Colin, the receptionist. "Your car's ready, ma'am."

As she put her coat on and switched out the lights, she thought of Angela Barnes again. On the surface, a life worth living, albeit a short one.

But who could really know that? *Call no man happy until he is dead:* that was the ancient wisdom. Of all the enterprises known to humanity, war was the one most susceptible to moral bad luck: chiefly, the people you thought you could have saved, but hadn't. Poor Angela.

Still, brave Angela.

John Mordred looked in the window of another closed bookshop on his way to work that afternoon – coronavirus was beginning to recede now, but lots of businesses had still to emerge from lockdown – and accidentally caught sight of his own reflection. Tall, blond haired, muscular, no one to write home about. He

15

recoiled from the self-ghostliness and carried on walking. Soon he'd be in Millbank and looking at the mysterious 'letter' that had arrived for him at reception.

On reflection, at least he didn't look like a lot of spies his age: older than he was, stressed out and greying at the temples. He was thirty-five now, the prime of his life really, so why did it feel like he was about to fall off a cliff?

Because once Ruby Parker was gone, that would be – well, what? Black's offer still stood, although he'd heard no more about it. No news was supposed to be good news, he wasn't even sure he wanted to work in Basement Ten alongside the likes of Jessie Sekuda and Nolan Carver.

On the other hand, staying in Red was probably a bad idea. Phyllis was on her way to the top job: she'd had the second of three interviews yesterday, and she'd seemed pretty optimistic. She'd want a new set of paints on her palette, one that didn't include her own husband. Alec was on his way out: major promotion, probably. He hadn't said anything for a while, but his body-language perpetually betrayed him. Edna too, so they said, and Annabel.

He remembered Jessie's assessment, last time he'd spoken to her, over coffee in the canteen, about two months ago.

"Alec Cunningham's probably bound for Head of Grey, as you already know. Marciella Hartley-Brown's likely a shoo-in for Head of White - she's been very active in Syria and Yemen in the last three or four years - though she might set her sights on something a little more prestigious, in which case, theoretically, she could give your wife a run for her money. But if she does look that way inclined, Stella will probably offer her Head of Blue. As I'm sure you know better than me, Phyllis is sentimentally attached to Red. If she doesn't get it, I can't see her accepting Blue, and White would be a step down. She'd leave, in other words, and she's got lots of other strings to her bow: she could easily make an excellent career for herself outside MI7. Edna Watson's due a significant promotion, so she may follow suit, or she may get

Assistant Head of White – she's still very young. As for Annabel al-Banna, you'd think she'd deserve Head of Something-stroke-Anything – a new department, in other words: Purple or Indigo - but I doubt that'll happen. Not yet. It'd be a bit like taking Pele, or Johan Cruyff, at the height of their powers, and making them a manager. I think she'll follow you down to Black for the time being. Five or six years down the line: Head of Turquoise, if Stella's still there. Which I'm sure she will be."

He'd not seen Jessie since, and he was left with the impression that this was no idle speculation, rather it was a communique from the top about the rough state of play. Stella's way of keeping him informed.

But that had been eight weeks ago.

Edna was the surprise. The fact that she'd been active in Kenya, Somalia and Uganda almost since joining MI7 three or four years ago, had been completely concealed, even within the department, on the usual worn-out 'need to know' grounds. A shame, in some ways, that she was going places. For him, not her. They shared the sort of sense of humour that Assistant Heads of Things can't usually afford to indulge. *Ho, ho, very droll, John* was what she'd henceforth have to say, and even though she might be laughing inside, she'd never be able to let him know. And that would, in any case, decline with the years, as she gradually grew to resemble her role, and that alone, as everyone always did.

He couldn't believe he was going in to work just to get a letter: this was supposed to be his day off. And he'd be surprised if it hadn't already been opened, though Colin claimed otherwise. They must know what was inside. And it must be important for them not to want to forward it. He wouldn't normally be curious enough to make a special trip. This was a measure of how dispirited he'd become: the whole 'changing of the guard' thing was making him desperate enough to come all the way from Camden to pick up a letter when he could easily have asked Phyllis to get it for him on her way out of the building.

Maybe he'd won something. A cash prize of some sort, or a holiday. Maybe it was a letter from an old foe, one of those although-I'm-in-jail-now missives that never failed to lift his spirits. Because they weren't allowed to send nasty ones, only nice ones. 'I've forgiven you, even though I sold a lot of secrets to the Russians and that was entirely my own fault', that sort of thing. He'd call Phyllis afterwards, and they could go home together. Pointless trying to go for a meal in what was still effectively Virus City.

He crossed Horseferry Road, sped up slightly as he entered Millbank, skipped up the steps to Thames House and crossed the floor to reception. Colin Bale, bald, forty-ish, and remarkably thin after having lost several stone in a particularly nasty bout of the infection, stood with both hands on the desk, and a mask over his face, presumably for others' benefit.

Mordred took his mask out and put it on by way of expressing solidarity. "I believe you've got a letter for me," he said, as he wrote his name in the signing-in book.

Colin retrieved it from beneath the desk. "Nice to see you, John."

Now that they were closer, Mordred could see that Colin's mask had a cartoon elephant on.

"I know what you're going to say, John," Colin said. "What's the significance of the elephant?"

"I wasn't - "

"No significance at all. I bought this mask here, in Thames House. While I was away, Shawna – that's Shawna Seydoux, who filled in for me: I believe you met her once or twice, you must have – made these from scratch, using nothing but a roll of fabric, an old-fashioned sewing-machine, and her own unlimited talent. Five pounds each, and all the profits go to our wonderful NHS. Each one's different. They make wearing masks fun, and they save lives. Would you like one? Astonishingly, there's more than enough for everyone in the building. Shawna's been very busy indeed. Saving lives. Or that's how she likes to see it."

Mordred shrugged. "Okay. Can I see the range?"

"I'm afraid not. You've got to select one at random from a big box, using a litter-picking tool, and you've got to sanitise your hand before operating the tool's handle. That's what makes it fun. The random element, I mean. Not the tool or the hand-sanitisation."

"What if I get one I don't like?"

"You mean, one with an elephant on?"

"Not necessarily. I mean - "

"With the greatest respect, John, what's the chance that someone as nice as Shawna is going to put something unpalatable in there? Just to set your mind at rest, though: if you get a phallus or a swastika, you can have another pick."

"Fair enough." He tore his letter open, while Colin reached beneath the desk to produce the picking-tool and a large bucket, but he didn't get a chance to look at it before Colin advanced the hand sanitiser across the desk with a pen. He cleansed his hands, then dipped in and fished a mask out, wrapped in a brown paper bag.

"Open it then," Colin said.

"I already have."

"I meant the mask, silly, not the letter."

Mordred removed it from its bag. It was identical to Colin's except, instead of an elephant, it had a big yellow smiley face.

"You've won the jackpot!" Colin said. "That's probably the best one in there! Oh my God, put it on!"

"I'll just have a look at my letter."

"Maybe that's good news too. You never know. Perhaps you're on a roll, John!"

Mordred looked at it. A single card with a heavy black border. "It's an invitation to a funeral."

A moment's silence, as this permeated the surrounding air.

Colin took a deep breath. His eyes wobbled, apparently looking for something to fix on. He puckered his lips. "Maybe take another pick."

*

Half an hour later, he sat two metres apart from Alec Cunningham in the canteen, next to the window. Alec was ten years his senior and resembled a latter-day Sexton Blake: tall with receding black hair and a habitual glower like he was eternally displeased with the way 'the investigation' was going. Both men had a coffee and a chocolate éclair.

"Well, that's the last of the Famous Three," Alec said. "Ian, Thelma, now Angela. I actually thought Angela would make it out. I mean, ISIS are finished now. She could have come home."

"That would have been complicated."

"If we can let Shamima Begum back in, I'm pretty sure Angela Barnes wouldn't have been a problem. And she'd have been a hero in most people's eyes."

"I don't really know anything about Angela. I never met her. To my knowledge, I'd never even *seen* her until I went to Ian and Thelma's funeral; that video message she sent."

"And that's what confuses you, yes?"

"Her parents sent me the invitation, at least that's what it says on the card. Maybe they thought we were friends. Don't get me wrong, I'm happy to express my condolences to them in person, but I don't want to be there under false pretences. What if I'm asked to say something about her?"

"Why would you be?"

"That's what happens at funerals nowadays. People are asked to get up and pay personal tributes. Again, I've no problem with the custom. But I can't participate in it if I never met her."

"Under normal circumstances, I'd be tempted to say you're overthinking this. We know Angela used to work for MI7. You're the semi-public face of MI7, especially with Knebworth Jannison – your 'novelised' incarnation, courtesy of Smarmy Steven – running away up the bestseller charts. I'd normally imagine they want some representative of Angela's old workplace at the ceremony, and yours is the only name they know. Hobson's choice."

"But?"

"These aren't normal circumstances," Alec went on. "With the virus still watching our every move, you're only allowed a certain, very limited number of people at most funerals. Of course, one possibility is that Angela didn't know that many people – although given how well she came across in that video message, I'd say that's unlikely. Another possibility is that most of her friends and family are unavailable or uncontactable. Which seems equally improbable. The third possibility is that the parents have something very specific to say to MI7, and yours is the only name they have. They've invited you as our representative, and they have an agenda. If RP gives you the green light, I'd advise you to go in there with both eyes open. I'm sure she'll counsel the same thing."

"Yes, I see your point. I'd forgotten how restricted these things are at the moment."

Alec sipped his coffee. "Do we know how she died?"

"*I* don't. Ruby Parker might know something more."

"Apart from that, how's life?"

"So-so," Mordred said. "Been on any more demonstrations recently?"

"Sadly not."

"'Sadly'? Last time we met, as I remember, you were torturing yourself. *Should I Shouldn't I? What if it -* "

"Well, I'm glad I went. It's about getting, and keeping, your daughters' respect. Doing the right thing. Obviously, I'm totally opposed to pulling Nelson and Churchill down, but I can see there's an issue there. And like you said, why should that affect my job prospects here? We need forward thinkers, not reactionaries. In any case, my duty as a parent is to build a better world for my girls, and if I can show them that's what I truly believe, then so much the better. Yes, I'm a saint now."

"Did Valentina go?"

"Well, that was the lovely thing. She did. And now we're all one big happy family. Me, Valentina, Cecily, Sophie, Estella. I almost couldn't care less about the greasy pole."

Mordred raised his cup. "Cheers."

"To Angela."

"To Angela."

Chapter 3: Not the Best Ever Commemoration

Mordred arrived at the church early so he could speak to Angela's parents before the service, if that's what they wanted. He noticed a loudspeaker above the porch. Presumably, some mourners would be standing outside, so possibly there had never been an artificial cap on invitations. Even so, the fact that he was inside made all the difference.

A man of about his own age greeted him sombrely at the entrance, checked his invitation as if it was a ticket – which, in the present circumstances, it effectively was - fixed him with an earnest expression, and expressed the hope that he would join the family for a brief reception afterwards. He didn't break eye-contact until he'd secured an affirmative. He indicated the reserved pew. Mordred said sorry for your loss, then walked halfway down the nave to where his exact seating position had been marked with masking tape and a name-plate. He said a brief prayer asking God to look after Angela's soul, then read the custom-made service sheet, a gold-embossed card with a paper insert.

His interview with Ruby Parker, two days earlier, had been perfunctory. She saw no objection to him attending, but she agreed with Alec: the present restrictions on numbers at formal gatherings made the invitation ominous. Possibly, someone in the family wanted him to investigate the circumstances of Angela's death, which were currently 'obscure' in the official jargon. "You need to be prepared for that," she'd told him, "and have a tactful way of declining to hand." Unconfirmed reports said she'd been killed somewhere near the Iraqi-Turkish border during a recent skirmish between Turkish troops and Kurdish YPG fighters, but that might just be informed conjecture. Her body had been flown back to Britain and now lay in the closed coffin just in front of the

23

lectern. It would be buried outside in the churchyard immediately after the service.

The building gradually admitted mourners until it was about a quarter full with the deceased's immediate family sitting together at the front, and everyone else socially distanced and looking straight ahead. The equidistance and deliberate avoidance of eye-contact gave it a slightly dystopian aura.

The vicar, an old man with a double chin and woolly grey sideburns, spoke ineffectually about Angela's life, foregrounding her most public achievements – school in Watford, university in Edinburgh, job in London – and skipping over the idiosyncratic details. He referred so obliquely to her time in Syria that probably the only people who grasped his meaning were those who already knew where she'd been for the last four years. Four people – two men, two women – came to the lectern to speak about her. All were former university friends. All had lost contact with her after she'd left Scotland. Singing was prohibited, so the congregation silently read *Nearer, My God, to Thee,* the vicar read from 1 Timothy 6: "We brought nothing into this world…" The pallbearers carried the coffin outside to the sound of a pre-recorded song, a young woman singing what it took Mordred a few moments to recognise as *Ey Reqîb,* the Kurdish national anthem. The congregation, most of whom had remained relatively impassive up to this point, suddenly seemed to break down simultaneously.

Mordred followed at the back of the cortège. It was a sunny summer's day. A big crowd stood outside, roughly two hundred strong, including a lot of the same ethnic group who'd attended Ian and Thelma's funeral in such numbers: members of London's Kurdish community. Mordred's position in the porch made him temporarily higher than them, and he scanned the faces, looking for people he might recognise. He didn't know who, or even why. More habit than curiosity.

He couldn't stop moving forward, so his search wasn't as thorough as he'd have liked, but it didn't draw a complete blank.

Daisy Hallenbeck, CIA. A few years younger than him, long dark hair, cerebral brow, eyes that never seemed to rest, a slightly knobbly chin. About a hundred yards away, on the crowd's periphery.

What was she doing here?

She'd spotted him now. She didn't look pleased, and their eye-contact lasted less than a second. She looked down and began to move unhurriedly away. In other circumstances, he might have deduced that she wanted him to follow her, so uncertain was her mode of departure, but of course even catching up with her here was impossible. She knew she had all the time in the world to get away. If she'd wanted to talk to him, she'd have stayed put.

He watched her go, then descended the two steps from the porch, when the physical reduction in sight-line removed her from view.

Still, she hadn't seemed annoyed to see him.

The man who'd greeted him on the way in took up position beside him and gestured for them to follow the coffin together, as if there was an alternative. Now that Mordred had clocked Daisy Hallenbeck, the whole ceremony had taken on a subtly different flavour, as if it might somehow be riddled with foreign agents. He surreptitiously re-examined the man beside him. Red hair, mid-thirties, about five-ten, strong jaw, slightly flat eyebrows. They walked to the graveside. The vicar read more Bible passages, then the relatives crumbled soil on the coffin and the crowd began to disperse.

Mordred turned to his shadow. "I don't believe we've been properly introduced. I'm John Mordred, but of course, you know that from my invitation."

"Daniel Batsford," the man said. "I'm the family lawyer. Mr and Mrs Barnes are very anxious to meet you. Obviously, they asked me to facilitate that, or I wouldn't be sticking so closely to you. Apologies if my behaviour seems officious."

"I thought they might want to say something," Mordred said. "There was no other reason why I should have been invited. With respect to Angela, it's not like I ever met her."

"Brave woman."

"I don't know anything about her behaviour on the battlefield," Mordred replied, in a tone designed to suggest, 'and neither do you', "but she definitely had the courage of her convictions. How many of us can say that?"

"Exactly right."

"In that regard, I thought it was a poor sermon."

"Yet it may have been what the family wanted," Batsford said. "These things often are. The embarrassing bits – the bits they find difficult to cope with – are downplayed. Okay, so she did go to Syria to fight ISIS, but she must have known the effect that would have on her mother and father. They saw it as a suicide mission. And tragically, they were right."

"Can I ask why they want to meet me?"

Batsford chuckled. "I'm afraid that's more than I'm entitled to divulge. It's their daughter's funeral. Give them their opportunity to speak."

"Fair enough."

"However, I'm sure you've a fairly good idea."

Mordred suppressed a sigh. "Let's get it over with. For their sakes."

Chapter 4: Unanticipated Encounters

Outside the church, Pavel Nikolayevich Alikhanov stood in a flat cap and a long coat too heavy for the weather at the back of a crowd of mourners. The loudspeaker relayed the words of the priest speaking inside the building. A few people cried, some leant on others, yet others looked indifferent. He couldn't see Daisy Hallenbeck anywhere.

Since he'd come to London, he'd killed three people. He was attending the funeral of the first. The other two had been prostitutes, and he'd chosen them mainly as an homage to Jack the Ripper. He was really glad he'd come to England now. He was rapidly becoming the serial killer to end all serial killers. No one had ever achieved what he had, and probably no one would ever best him. True, he'd had help, but in the end, all that mattered were the numbers, and that occasionally you did something ghastly enough to count as creative in the minds of the many, many people who felt drawn to this sort of thing. It cost $30 to go on a Jeffrey Dahmer tour in Milwaukee. The organisers of the Pavel Nikolayevich Alikhanov tour could probably charge considerably more, given that it would take in two continents and far more victims, and it would be worth every cent. You'd never have to go on another serial killer tour in your life. You wouldn't even want to. How could you possibly top the Pavel Nikolayevich Alikhanov tour?

He'd written a lot about beautiful Daisy in his journal. Future generations should recognise that he'd loved her. But obviously that was inconsistent with her knowing nothing about him. Killing her was therefore going to be a complex business. He needed to kidnap her and introduce himself. They might even need to make love, but they'd address that issue when they came to it. After all, she might not even be attracted to him. Girls were like that sometimes.

Of course, it would all be ruined if she remembered him from Istanbul.

But that seemed unlikely. She'd been in such a panic, she probably hadn't seen him properly. She'd likely been totally preoccupied with the knife, and completely missed the wielder.

But it didn't pay to be blasé. By way of radically altering his appearance, he'd grown a moustache and two millimetres of beard. He probably needed to change his hairstyle too, but that could wait.

He suddenly spotted her about twenty metres away, almost in line with him at the back of the crowd. He drew a sharp breath of surprised air, totally consistent with the agonies of love. She looked fabulous. Designer suit, perfectly styled hair, face of a cherub.

He suddenly had the overwhelming sense that he couldn't kill her. It wasn't a moral sense, more as if the universe had erected a barrier around her.

Suddenly, the mood of the crowd seemed to shift slightly. The service was over. The church doors opened and the congregation emerged.

He noticed Daisy start slightly. Nothing that would have been obvious to someone who didn't care for her, especially not from this distance. She made eye-contact with someone in the emerging congregation. A blond haired man, reasonably good looking, in his mid-thirties. He clearly meant something to her, because she turned around and began to walk away, as if she was embarrassed.

A former boyfriend? The look hadn't been friendly enough for a *current* boyfriend. An American colleague? Someone she was afraid of, disliked, or had slighted in some way?

He went after her. He didn't really want to kill her, but he'd brought a knife, and he might as well get it over with, especially as she now looked to be voluntarily separating herself from the flock. He had a hoodie under his coat, just in case such an opportunity should present itself. He pulled the hood up and removed the knife from inside his kangaroo pocket.

She walked straight into a country lane, empty apart from her, almost as if she knew what was coming, and she wanted to get it over with as much as he did. Thirty metres separated them. He began to run. She obviously heard him, because she turned, and seemed to recognise his intention. She turned back and accelerated pathetically.

A car honked its horn. It was loud enough to make both of them jump. It did a better job of speeding up than Daisy ever could, and pulled in between them. A fat middle-aged man leapt from the driver's seat – obviously a mourner: he was all in black - and squared up nervously for a confrontation with the knife-wielder.

Pavel Nikolayevich leapt over a fence into a field and ran for his life.

The reception was a modified repast in the beer garden of a pub half a mile – within walking distance for most people - from the church. On arrival, an usher in a red waistcoat and a face visor directed each guest to the hand sanitiser, then to a table full of identical paper plates with snacks under cling film, and a regiment of sealed bottles of orange juice or water. Everyone stood apart in the open air. Since this was a funeral, casual conversation wasn't exactly at a premium, and it was difficult to speak without being overheard. After five minutes, most people found themselves standing in awkward silence, just eating and looking appropriately sombre. Mordred noticed that everything on his plate – the mini quiche, the vol-au-vent, the strawberry tart – was vegetarian, though he hadn't communicated any preference to anyone. They obviously knew more about him than he'd imagined.

There was no sign of Daisy Hallenbeck. After five minutes, storm clouds began to appear, and the sky darkened. Then, just as quickly, it cleared again and the sun resumed normal service.

Daniel Batsford emerged from within the pub and made a beeline for Mordred. He didn't have any food, so he was able to clasp his hands together like a man asking a favour.

"Mr and Mrs Barnes would like to see you inside whenever it's convenient," he said. "It doesn't have to be now. Finish eating, and I'll lead the way."

It was tempting to put his plate to one side and say 'I'm ready now', but that might be interpreted as an insult, as if he didn't like what he'd been given. He still had half his quiche and the strawberry tart.

On the other hand, if he didn't drop everything, it might look like he lacked any meaningful sense of urgency.

"I'm ready now," he said.

"You don't want to finish your strawberry tart?"

Message received: he had to get a move on if he wasn't to transmit the food-rejecting-insult. Always difficult to do that when someone was standing silently in proximity telling you not necessarily to speed up but there's something very important happening as soon as you've finished. At the last moment, the strawberry tart broke in two and almost dropped on to his tie, but he retrieved it and popped it into his mouth.

"Let's go," he said.

Batsford led the way inside and up a stairway to a corridor with two guest rooms adjoined. He opened the first door and ushered Mordred in.

The occupants were both in their late sixties. They sat side by side on the bed and rose when the two men entered. Mrs Barnes had a blonde pixie cut, scarlet lipstick, and heavy, streaked eyeliner. Her husband was swollen-faced with a bulbous nose, a shallow gathering of white curly hair, wire-rimmed glasses and a goatee.

The room was olde-worlde: dark walls, heavy curtains and antique furnishings. Two chairs faced the bed, obviously meant for the visitors.

"Mr Mordred?" Mrs Barnes said.

Batsford cut in. "Mr and Mrs Barnes, please allow me to introduce Mr John Mordred."

"Tony and Rhiannon," Mr Barnes said. "Please call us Tony and Rhiannon."

"Ree," Rhiannon said. "Call me Ree."

"I'm very sorry for your loss," Mordred said. "I have to confess I didn't know Angela personally. If it's any consolation, I very much admired her willingness to put her life on the line for the sake of a better world."

"I bloody well hope she killed a lot of them," Tony said. "Especially the British contingent. The so-*called* British."

"Let's not talk about that now, Tony," Ree said. "It doesn't help."

"Any of them ever come back to this country," Tony said, "which they will – they'll sneak back in like the cowards they are, and start availing themselves of our welfare system and our rule of law - I swear I'll kill them myself, even if I have to do it with my bare hands."

"Tony," Ree said.

"Mr Barnes," Batsford said. "Tony."

An awkward silence.

"Shall we all sit down?" Batsford said.

Tony and Ree resumed their positions on the bed. Mordred and Batsford sat in the chairs.

"I sympathise with your anger," Mordred said, "but I'm not sure what I can do to help." He felt like reminding Tony that Angela hadn't been forced to go to Syria. She'd done something noble, but she'd also known what the consequences might be.

"Well, Mr Mordred," Ree said.

"John," John said.

"Well, John," Ree said. "We'd like to make you an offer."

Mordred inwardly rolled his eyes. Here it came. Lots of money to go forth and be a detective, and so great was their confidence in his investigative powers, that it wouldn't be payment by results. They'd probably read both Knebworth Jannison books.

"Five hundred thousand pounds," Tony said. "Regardless of results. We just want you to do your best, and we know enough about you – you may not have known Angela, by the way, but she knew you: I mean *about* you: and she deeply admired you – to know you're a man of his word who always gives his best. We want you to find out what really happened to her."

"I can't accept your offer," Mordred said. "And certainly not at this stage. I'm very sorry. Angela was a British citizen. I'm pretty sure that right now, the Foreign Office is doing all it can to discover her exact cause of death. At the moment, the evidence suggests she was killed in an exchange of fire with Turkish troops somewhere near the northernmost Iraqi border, but that may be subject to revision when new information appears. I'm certain you'll get a definitive result sometime soon, and without having to waste your money on me. In any case, I couldn't do anything from Britain. I certainly couldn't hope to compete with the FCO."

Ree and Tony looked at each other and linked hands. They turned back to face Mordred.

"John," Ree said, "if I ask you a question, will you promise to answer truthfully? It's simply a yes or no. The thing is, as Tony just said, we know you're an honest man. If you say 'yes' or 'no' that's fine, but if you say 'I'm sorry, I can't answer that question', we'll know it's the answer you think we least want to hear, in which case, your real answer will be equally obvious. Of course, you can't stop me asking the question anyway, but it's polite to ask for permission."

Mordred shifted uncomfortably in his chair. "Of course. Go ahead."

Ree looked directly into his eyes. "Before you came here today, did your boss, by any chance, call you into his office and tell you that we might make you an offer like this, and that, in such an eventuality, you should decline?"

Mordred almost paused. "Yes," he said.

Tony and Ree turned to each other again.

"They've got there before us," Tony told Ree. "We thought they might."

"Closing all the available doors before we've even reached them," Ree replied. "We're on our own. Again."

They turned back to face Mordred and something about their attitude had completely changed. The interview was over. They stood up.

"Well, thank you for coming," Ree said. "And thank you for your honesty."

"Did your boss say *why* you should decline?" Tony asked. "Just out of interest?"

"Largely because I'm not permitted to do freelance work," John said. "The intelligence services don't work like that. It could lead to a serious conflict of interest."

"Just that?" Tony said. "No more than that?"

"It's a decisive consideration," Mordred said.

Ree smiled. "But I get the impression you're a bit like Angela," she said. "Ultimately, you'll go where your conscience leads you, and protocol be damned."

"Perhaps," Mordred replied, "but with respect, I don't think we're anywhere near that point, and I can't see us reaching it. I'm confident you'll get the answers you want in due course, and you'll have saved yourselves a considerable sum of money."

"Oh, *damn* the money!" Tony burst out. "What does that matter now? What does *anything?*" He put his hand on his face, sat down clumsily on the bed, and wept.

Ree put her arm round him, but turned to John as he was retiring. "Call us when you're ready to reconsider."

"I'm genuinely sorry I couldn't be more helpful," Mordred said. He left the room, descended the stairs, and exited the pub briskly. The whole thing had gone just as disastrously as he'd expected, and he felt as miserable as he'd expected. Time to find a bus into Central London, call in at Thames House, make his report and forget all about it.

The awful thing was, Tony and Ree were a bit like his own mother and father. He suddenly had a mental picture of them with Batsford, just before Batsford's appearance in the beer garden, Ree saying, *Let John finish his strawberry tart, don't rush him,* and Tony adding, *Let the lad come up in his own time. Besides, they're good tarts those. Made specially.*

He'd let them down, but what choice did he have? Sometimes, you've got to be cruel to be kind. Which didn't stop you loathing yourself -

He heard footsteps behind him. Please, God, don't let it be one of them. He turned round.

Batsford. Walking no more or less briskly than him, only about ten yards behind. "John? A word?"

"I can't reconsider," Mordred replied.

"Okay, here's the deal," Batsford said. "Angela wasn't killed in Syria. She was killed in Britain. She had information she wanted to trade for immunity to prosecution for leaving on charges of terrorism. Some very high-up people are covering up her murder. They almost certainly sent some people to her funeral. Did you recognise anyone?"

"Er – what? Back a bit. Why didn't Tony and Ree mention any of that?"

"Because they know you'll have to report it to your boss. *You* may not be in on the conspiracy, but he probably is. He or she, I mean. Once they know that we're on to them, anything's possible. Any bad thing."

"What makes you say she was in Britain?"

"Because I met her."

"You *met* her?" It took a moment to sink in. "And she didn't tell you what her information was?"

"No. Look, John, I know you're not going to believe me. That's of no consequence. We've told you now. That's all that matters. We hoped you'd find out for yourself. After you'd left, Tony said to me: get after him, you might as well tell him the full story. It's up to you what you make of it, but, as you almost said yourself, the truth has a way of coming out. If you don't help us, we might be killed, and then you'll be sorry."

"If you don't mind my saying so, you seem more personally involved in this than any mere lawyer should be."

Batsford shrugged. "Angela Barnes came to see me. She's been murdered. I'm a lawyer, but I'm also a citizen, and I'm like you – allegedly – in that respect. And Angela. I've got a conscience. There are more of us than you might think."

Mordred put his hands on his head. "Is this a way of making me change my mind?"

"Am I lying, do you mean? No, I'm not lying."

"I - "

"But maybe *you* are. Let me ask you again, John. Did you recognise anyone at the funeral? Anyone at all?"

"No, I - "

"Because you very much looked as if you did. When we were coming out of the church, and we were moving through the porch together, I thought I saw you catch sight of someone. A definite glint of recognition in your eyes. No, look, forget I said anything. This conversation never happened, okay? You were right the first time. You should just let sleeping dogs lie. Sorry I pestered you. In my defence, it was Tony's idea, not mine. But as we both saw, Tony's not thinking straight right now. You don't have to get involved. I'll continue to investigate this on my own. I'll contact you again when I've got something more concrete. And hey, don't discount that possibility."

He backed off, turned about and walked away even more quickly than he'd arrived.

Chapter 5: Questions about Daisy

Two days later, Mordred sat in Ruby Parker's office next to his wife. Phyllis was tall with long hair, a wide mouth and discerning eyes that seemed to change colour according to the light and her mood. At the moment, they were grey.

As was her custom, Ruby Parker spent a full minute re-reading selected parts of the report under discussion before speaking.

"You're quite sure it was Daisy Hallenbeck, John?" she asked at last. "You only saw her for a split second. On the other hand, you are trained to make those sorts of identifications."

"She saw me," he replied. "She recognised me in the same way that I recognised her."

"Do you think she intended for you to see her?" Phyllis asked. "I only ask because making herself conspicuous to you would be consistent with some of her behaviour in the past."

"She didn't look frustrated about making eye-contact," John said.

"Is that a 'yes'?" Ruby Parker asked.

"It's an I-think-so," John replied. "It's a long shot, but could we ask the American embassy? They probably wouldn't tell us, but since she knows she's been made, what have we got to lose? It might look suspicious if we *don't* ask them."

"It's very easy to make a false move here," Ruby Parker replied. "Notice that, almost without considering it, we've begun to shift subtly towards Daniel Batsford's apparently wild claims: that Angela Barnes's death was, to say the least, suspicious, and that it's worth investigating. There may be a completely innocent explanation. Angela and Daisy are about the same age. They're on the same side, in global terms. It's not inconceivable that they may have met in the past, in a work-related capacity. They may even have become friends."

"So why did she walk away when she saw me?" John asked.

"Maybe she doesn't actually like you," Phyllis said. "Or she might be smarting after our last case. Remember, she expected to accompany you to its denouement, but it didn't quite work out that way."

"On the other hand, she did rescue me."

"Which was very kind of her," Phyllis replied. "But no more than her professional and moral duty. It doesn't mean she's forgiven you."

"What did the post mortem say?" John asked Ruby Parker, by way of changing the subject.

"The body was flown to Cyprus in the first instance," Ruby Parker replied, "where it was examined by a British pathologist under the supervision of the embassy. His conclusion was that Angela died instantly from a single bullet to the heart which passed straight through her body and came out of the other side. We have a time of death consistent with her being killed in Iraq a day earlier. The body had been washed and wrapped in a shroud, as a mark of respect. As soon as the pathologist reached his verdict, the body was flown to Britain for burial."

"I hate to say this," Phyllis said, "but all of that's perfectly consistent with Batsford's claim. Say she'd been killed in this country a day earlier. I mean, just for the sake of argument."

"It's perfectly consistent with virtually any conspiracy theory at all," Ruby Parker said.

"Ian and Thelma were buried in Syria," John said. "That seems sensible, and respectful, and both families accepted it. A day seems like a disrespectful rush to get the body into British hands. Presumably, the Kurds passed it to British forces in the region who passed it to Cyprus. *Are* there British forces in the region? Sorry, I should know this."

"The army's training the Kurdish and Iraqi Security Forces," Phyllis said. "There's nothing too implausible in the official chain of events."

John nodded. "The question is, can we put names and testimonies to the various elements of the chain? The Kurds who witnessed her death and were her comrades? The British personnel in Iraq who took receipt of the corpse? The officials who arranged for it to be flown to Cyprus?"

"The last two, yes," Ruby Parker said. "The first, no. The YPG isn't on our list of official partners. Turkey's a member of NATO, and it considers the YPG a terrorist organisation. Whether that's accurate is another question. Almost certainly not, but the claim suits President Erdoğan's agenda, and so there's an end to the matter."

Phyllis folded her hands. "In any case, we can't start making enquiries in that area without making it look as if we suspect something is amiss."

"Which means we probably have to sit on our hands," John said. "And people's memories will fade. If anyone *did* take receipt of the body in Iraq, that will gradually become, at best, a distant recollection. In any case, I think we're looking at this from the wrong side. My sole reason for thinking there might be anything at all in Daniel Batsford's claims was that Daisy Hallenbeck was present at the funeral. But as you just pointed out, that could be totally insignificant. What's more likely? That there's some kind of major conspiracy to prevent Angela Barnes releasing information which, although she met Batsford, she couldn't quite bring herself to divulge; or that Daisy Hallenbeck and Angela Barnes knew each other? Answer: the latter. End of conspiracy-theory based mystery."

"I've been looking into Daniel Batsford," Phyllis said. "He's not what you'd normally call a crank, and I've been told he doesn't even fit the profile of your average conspiracy-theorist. He's a high-flyer. Public school, Oxford University, well connected, ambitious."

"Maybe stressed too," Mordred said. "I'm not necessarily arguing with you, just trying to keep a level head. There are lots of reasons a person gets a crazy idea. They don't have to fit any

38

profile. It's a recognised human trait, and it's even admirable, under the right circumstances."

"I think this could be resolvable in principle," Ruby Parker said, "which is why I'm going to assign you to gather a little more information, John. You're not doing anything else at the moment, and I think we need more clarity here, if only for the family's sake. Daniel Batsford may not be doing them much good."

"Fair enough," he replied. "It's easy enough to know where to begin. We've got a few pictures of Daisy Hallenbeck on file, I assume. I could show them to Mr and Mrs Barnes, ask if they recognise her. If they say, 'That's one of Angela's old friends', case solved, though I doubt it'll be that simple. I'll show them to Daniel Batsford too. Do we know anything about Daisy at the moment? I'm assuming she's still based at the US embassy in Nine Elms?"

Ruby Parker took a deep breath. "From the little I can discover, for the last two years, she's specialised in the rather arcane specialism of document authentication, so she's normally sitting in front of a computer screen or a table spread with papers. Interestingly, our records show that she flew in from Turkey a few days before the funeral, but there's no record of her leaving Britain yet, so she's probably still in the country. Her arrival from Turkey seems at odds with the idea that she's currently based in Nine Elms, and it does add to the Angela Barnes connection. She may have been gathering evidence about the killing, which would be interesting. It would suggest that Angela had some value to the Americans."

"That's something we might never be able to discover," Phyllis said. "Unless Daisy tells us." She turned to John. "If she does, it won't be an act of charity, so it won't be any use you being nice to her."

"I'm nice to everyone," John said. "That's my nature."

"Thank you for your time," Ruby Parker said in her 'meeting over' tone of voice. "Keep me informed, John. Phyllis, I'm happy to inform you that you've got another interview with the Head of the Diplomatic Service at eleven. I've already asked Kevin to bring the car round. Good luck."

Chapter 6: The Quest for Batsford

Mordred went straight to his desk, switched on his PC and retrieved five recent pictures of Daisy Hallenbeck from the encrypted counter-intelligence folder in TRACES, none of them ideal: all looked as if they'd been clandestinely shot from a distance, which of course, they had. Even a non-conspiracy-theorist would probably conclude that the subject was someone shady, possibly a little dangerous.

Still, that couldn't be helped. He emailed them to Lily in Graphics for printing on gloss photographic paper. When he went to pick them up from the ground floor an hour later, they came in a plain brown envelope and, just as expected, exuded a sinister 1970s-spy-movie feel.

Time to call Daniel Batsford at his office in Ealing. He went back upstairs to his desk, sat down and keyed in the phone number.

It went straight to voicemail.

He hung up. Too early to be leaving a message. *Hi, this is John Mordred from the funeral* might well give the impression that he'd been nobbled by his 'boss' and briefed to send Batsford on the wildest of goose chases. No, he needed to speak to him in person. He Googled his business address.

Office hours 9am-5pm Monday-Friday. Open.

Okay, he'd go over there now. Face to face was always better than phone, anyway. He put the photographs in his briefcase – important touch: lawyers were men with briefcases, and men with briefcases always felt a subliminal connection to other men with briefcases – and called a taxi.

The one thing he had going for him was that Batsford considered him a good guy. He could open any exchange with, *Look, I know I said I didn't recognise anyone at the funeral but I wasn't quite telling the truth, and I need to show you these.* Batsford would probably want to know why he'd felt the need to lie, but that was easily explicable. And the good thing was, he'd then have told the truth, the whole truth and nothing but the truth. If Batsford still felt the need to strike out on his own, so be it.

He arrived in Spring Bridge Road at 10.30 and ascended eight steps to the heavy front door in one of the brutal Edwardian piles with brick-pillar entrances that lined the thoroughfare opposite the park. He pressed the buzzer beside Batsford's small brass plaque, stated his own name, and waited for a response.

Nothing.

He walked down the steps, found a bench in the park and tried phoning again.

Another instant diversion to voicemail.

Time to lay a card on the table. He called again, and after the beep he said, "Hello, Daniel, this is John Mordred from the funeral. I've been thinking about what you said, and I'd like to show you something. We can meet anywhere you like, as publicly as you like. I'm not out to trick you. This is a genuine offer. I may be able to help you, and vice-versa."

He hung up and congratulated himself on a perfect message. 'I'd like to show you something': masterly. Who the hell could resist that? He'd probably ring back immediately.

But he didn't.

Maybe he wanted to make John sweat. Or perhaps he was genuinely conflicted about whose side John was really on, and whether he could afford to trust him. Either way, this was beginning to turn into a wasted journey.

He walked back across the road, re-ascended the steps and looked at the other names by the entrance. *Robertson's Financial Planning*: that ought to do. He pressed the buzzer.

"Robertson's Financial Planning," a cheery female voice said. "How can I help?"

"I need to book an appointment to get some advice," he said. "Would it be okay to come in and just book a time?"

Whoever it was up there could probably see him on closed circuit TV. She'd register his briefcase and think, 'Well, he's either who he says he is, or a Mormon, or a travelling salesman, and since the last two are very rare nowadays, it's probably the former, and since, in addition to his briefcase, he's reasonably well dressed, he's probably worth admitting.'

There was a buzz and the door opened. "Come right in, sir," the voice said.

As always, he felt bad about lying, but he had no choice. He walked up a flight of creaky stairs to a landing and located another Batsford plaque on a closed door.

He knocked.

No sounds within. He knocked again.

Clearly, the occupants were out.

"We're just in here, sir!" the woman's voice called.

He walked along the corridor to the open door. A woman of about fifty in a pink cardigan and thick-framed glasses sat behind a desk wearing a huge smile, as if Robertson's had never had any custom before, and this was rather like winning the lottery.

"I do apologise," he said. "I meant to push the Batsford buzzer."

"I don't think Mr Batsford's in today," she said, as if this was precisely the bad news she'd learned to expect. "I'd normally have seen him or heard him, or he'd have knocked and asked if I wanted a coffee – we take it in turns here – but I could tell him you called, if you like. What's your name, sir?"

"John Mordred."

"Would you like me to call him, sir? I've got his mobile number too, just in case there's an emergency."

"That would be very helpful. Thank you."

"You just sit yourself down there, sir. Before I do that, could I interest you in a free financial consultation? Robertson's is one of the oldest financial service firms in the UK. We've won The IFGRE Best Small Independent Adviser Award three years in a row now, including last year, and we've been highly commended by *The Guardian, The Times, The Telegraph* and *The Daily Mail*. If desired, one of our advisers can contact you within twenty-four hours of asking, and arrange a consultation at a time and place to suit your convenience. Robertson's is CISI accredited – accredited by the Chartered Institute for Securities and Investment – and all our consultants are trained to the highest degree of professional probity. We will always inform you in advance of any fees, and, if necessary, explain such fees in detail. We can give help with insurances, pensions and retirement investments, general investments, tax planning, mortgages, savings and ISAs and business forecasting and planning."

"Er, no, thank you," Mordred said.

She made a little noise at the back of her throat like a guinea pig being smothered. "Maybe just have a look at some of the leaflets on the chair next to you, sir. You might change your mind."

Mordred picked up a leaflet with the banner, 'Whoa! Look at what *I* saved on my mortgage!' and pretended to read it while the woman sat with the landline receiver to her ear, looking ever more puzzled and pressing different buttons on the handset.

"Well, Mr Mordred," she said eventually, "it looks like he's disappeared off the face of the earth! I'll tell him you called when I see him. Does he have your number?"

"I've been calling his landline, but if you could let him have my mobile number, that would be very helpful."

"Absolutely!"

Mordred read out his number and thanked her for her help. A few seconds later, he was back on the street.

Something about all this running around was beginning to unnerve him. *It looks like he's disappeared off the face of the earth!*

There was nothing for it now, but to head back to base. It seemed wrong to go to Mr and Mrs Barnes with Daisy's photos before contacting Daniel Batsford, but maybe they'd know how to get through to him. He needed to find out how to contact them. He called for a taxi.

His phone rang. He took it out, expecting to see the *Unknown Caller* that would turn out to be Daniel Batsford. But no. *Tracy Island*.

"Have you found Batsford yet?" Ruby Parker said.

"I'm at his office now. He's not here, and he's not answering his phone."

"His wife's just been into Wandsworth police station to report him missing. The police aren't prioritising it yet, as it's only been twenty-four hours, but they don't know what we know. I'm thinking Mr and Mrs Barnes might give us some leads. You need to call them. Don't mention Batsford in the first instance: we don't want to scare them off. Arrange a meeting with both of them on the Daisy Hallenbeck pretext, ideally today. If they were at all serious in their talk with you, that shouldn't be too difficult."

"Send me their number."

Chapter 7: Not Toni and Ray

Mr and Mrs Barnes – 'Tony and Ree' – lived in a 1950s semi- in Enfield. When Mordred's taxi pulled onto the small side-road fronting their row of houses, their front door opened and Tony stood outside, possibly by way of indicating which house. He wore a surgical mask. He didn't smile as Mordred walked towards him, but that might not mean unfriendliness. Mordred was already wearing his mask.

"Please come in," he said softly, and gave Mordred wide berth to pass. "Go ahead into the living room. Door right in front of you."

Ree, also masked, was waiting on the sofa. She stood up, as if he was an important person whom she'd offended once, and didn't want to offend again. He felt bad. She asked him to sit down, and gestured to the armchair facing the French windows. On a coffee table in the middle of the room stood a teapot, a cafetière, a set of cups and saucers, a milk jug and a plate piled with wrapped biscuits. The room itself was spacious with an expensive-looking suite, a landscape painting on each wall, a mantelpiece with a grate, and a group of framed photos of Angela on a Victorian sideboard. The large window gave a view of a small greenhouse. The thick silence, punctuated only by the ticking of a carriage clock, seemed as integral as the physical fixtures and fittings.

Tony entered morosely and sat next to Ree, and it was as if they had gone back in time to the upstairs room in the pub, only minus Daniel Batsford.

"Tea or coffee, John?" Ree said timidly. "It is, er, still all right to call you John, isn't it?"

"It's what I'd prefer," Mordred replied. "Tea, please. Milk, no sugar."

"I'll have tea too," Tony said.

"Call us Tony and Ree, then," Tony said. "I'm Tony, she's Ree."

"He knows that," Ree said in a semi-whisper.

"People sometimes get confused," Tony said, addressing John. "It could be Tony with an 'i', and Ree could be 'Ray'. We've had that before."

Ree began to pour and Tony settled to watching her intensely with his hands clasped. It struck Mordred that there was already something marked about their behaviour, the tiniest indications in their eyes and gestures. For some reason, they felt guilty.

Which might be anything. They were decent enough to feel blameworthy for making apparently impossible requests after the funeral, and the reaction that had provoked in him. He should get down to business.

"Well, John," Tony said suddenly, "you mentioned on the phone that - "

Suddenly, the clock above the fireplace began to chime noon. They sat uncomfortably through a dozen prolonged dings, each considerably louder than the instrument's size might suggest.

"We ought to get that fixed, Tony," Ree said afterwards, as if there was something wrong with it.

"Well, John," Tony said, "you mentioned on the phone that you had something you wanted us to look at."

Mordred reached into his briefcase and passed three of the photos to him and two to Ree.

"Who is she?" Tony said after a few seconds.

"I don't … recall seeing her before," Ree said. "Angela used to bring friends here to stay when she was at university – I mean, during the holidays - but that stopped when she got a job in London. I don't remember this particular woman, but she could have been one of them."

"She was at the funeral the other day," Mordred said, accepting the photos back. "When Daniel followed me out of the pub - "

47

"Yes, we're very sorry about that," Ree broke in. "I said to him, 'Yes, John *may* have recognised someone, but it might just have been a *friend* of his. It mightn't have been anyone *suspicious*.' He wouldn't have it, though."

Tony put his hand on her knee. "Shush, Ree, John's trying to tell us something important."

"He was quite right to challenge me," Mordred said. "The importance of the matter justifies him risking offence. The truth is, I did recognise someone, but I wasn't sure whether I was entitled to say who it was. I mean, professionally speaking. The woman in the picture is an intelligence agent. A spy, if you like. Not a British one, but one from a friendly foreign power. Not one that would have any interest in harming Angela, and not one that supports the Turkish incursion."

"'Operation Olive Branch', Erdoğan calls it," Tony said bitterly. "Invading a country, indiscriminately bombing its civilians, attacking aid convoys, shooting refugees: funny use of the term 'olive branch'. Mind you, that's Erdoğan. Another Robert Mugabe."

"They love power, these people," Ree said, "and they'll go to any lengths to hold on to it."

"What do you think she was doing at Angela's funeral, this woman?" Tony asked.

"I don't know," John replied. "That's the truth. We'd occasionally be inclined to ask the relevant embassy, but that doesn't always help. If they don't want us to know, they simply spin us a yarn they think we'll believe, and that further complicates matters because, if the truth's discovered, they're then in the position of having to defend the lie. The most likely answer is that she was somehow connected to Angela when she was in Syria. Angela may have been feeding her useful information, just as you would any ally. The woman in the photo may simply have been at the funeral to pay her respects, like everyone else."

"Mystery solved," Ree said sadly.

"I wouldn't go that far," Tony said. "We still don't know what happened to Angela."

"Mr Batsford said she was in England," Mordred said; "that she went to see him. Did she come to see you?"

"I think she believed we might be being watched," Ree said. "That's what Daniel told us."

"You do know she was a member of MI5?" Mordred said. "I mean, before she went to Syria? By leaving the country to fight against ISIS, she effectively tendered her resignation of course, but it's what she was doing up until that point."

"We… suspected," Tony said. "When she was younger, and everyone else in her class was reading Harry Potter, she always had a thing about Alex Rider. And she never said anything about what she did in Central London. Only that it was mind-crushingly dull. I think that's partly why she went to Syria."

Ree frowned. "Tony, don't say *that!* She was an idealist!"

"I'm not denying it, sugar," Tony said. "I'm just saying the boredom probably helped."

"To be honest, we thought she was still in MI5," Ree said. "We thought they'd sent her over there under the mere pretence of being just a swashbuckling adventuress."

"MI6," Tony said. "That would be MI6, dear. Not MI5."

"What's the difference?" Ree said. "I mean," she added, before he could reply, "now."

Tony cleared his throat. "Would you like a biscuit, John? They're all factory-wrapped because of the coronavirus. We want you to feel safe here."

An odd thing to say, but the sense that here was a guilty-feeling couple had re-emerged. They were overly anxious to be nice to him. Some sort of confession might well be in the offing, but it would probably be a mistake to attempt to force it.

"Thank you," John said. He picked up a Blue Riband.

Tony took a Penguin, unwrapped it and dipped it in his tea.

"I'll do my best to discover what the woman in the photo was doing at Angela's funeral," John said. "And I'll keep you informed."

"That's very kind of you," Tony said. "I have a feeling she might know something. Did she see you?"

"We made very brief eye-contact," Mordred said. "And that's what I believe prompted her to leave."

"You mean she walked away when she saw you looking at her?" Tony said. "You didn't tell us that, John. That might mean something. It might mean she knows something and she's scared of being grilled about it."

"On the other hand," Mordred replied, "it might mean the opposite. Let's say she knew that Angela had been killed by shady personages in this country. She might well conclude that those persons would attend the funeral in an attempt to make sure nothing went wrong at the last minute. That's how it often works. In which case, she'd know she risked being recognised. She might be prepared to take that risk if it was the only way she could communicate the truth to someone trustworthy. But then, why would she bolt when she saw me? What I'm trying to say is: she probably wouldn't have come to funeral if she'd thought there was anything to be afraid of."

"Maybe there was some third person who saw you both look at each other," Ree said. "It's possible. After all, I think Daniel saw it. He said he saw you recognise someone. He didn't say who."

Tony stood up like he'd been electrocuted, inadvertently firing his Penguin across the room. "You *must* find this woman, John! For all you know she could be about to go the same way as *Angela!*"

Ree had buried her face in her hands, apparently for the same reason. "Oh, my word, yes," she said. "Oh, my *word, yes!*" She started deep breathing like she was about to have a panic attack.

Tony got down on his knees next to her, trembling. He put his arms round her. "Just give us a moment, John," he said.

"We need to tell him," Ree said, in the same half-whisper she'd used earlier.

Tony laughed. "I think he can hear us," he said acrimoniously.

"I don't care," she said.

Mordred held his hands up. "'Tell him' what?" he said gently. "I'm on your side."

"Nothing," Tony said. "Don't mind us. Nothing worth…" He closed his eyes slowly, clearly as an alternative to completing the sentence.

John finished his Blue Riband: they wouldn't tell him if he tried to force their hand. He needed to give them time and space. "Okay, well… the other reason I asked to see you was to ask about Mr Batsford."

The couple flinched violently again.

"What about him?" Tony said weakly.

"He's not answering his phone," Mordred said. "Mobile or office landline. But it's more serious than that. His wife contacted the police to report him missing a few hours ago."

Ree and Tony looked at him without moving.

"He's dead, then?" Ree said.

"If he is," Mordred said, "we've no evidence of it. We've no evidence of anything at all. He's presumably been under a lot of stress recently. He may think people are after him. He may be running away from what he imagines to be an imminent threat. He may have gone into temporary hiding. In other words, he may have had some sort of breakdown. That's the most likely scenario."

"You really don't believe that Angela went to see him, do you, John?" Tony said.

"I'm keeping an open mind," Mordred said. "The truth is, Mr Batsford may have his own agenda, of which we know nothing at present. It just strikes me as strange that Angela arrived in this country with some sort of 'information' to impart, after four or five years away, and made no attempt to see her parents, but did see the family lawyer, yet didn't give him the information. And then she was killed. How did anyone – not least the alleged killer – know where she was? If they knew where she was, why didn't they kill Mr Batsford too? She may *not* have given him the information, but it would be reasonable for any third party to *think* she had. And what *was* the information? She's been in Syria with the YPG for four years, so what could it possibly be? And how would anyone know she'd got it?"

"So in conclusion," Tony said languidly. "You think Daniel's delusional."

"Did he give you any concrete evidence that Angela had visited him?" Mordred persisted. "A letter, say, or a memento?"

"Okay, okay," Tony said. "It's time."

He stood up and left the room.

"Would you like another biscuit, John?" Ree said softly. "Sorry about Tony shooting his Penguin across the room just then. I'm glad it didn't hit you. I mean, even apart from the coronavirus."

Tony came back in, brandishing a smartphone in a small sandwich bag. "There," he said. "I've sanitised it and self-isolated it so you don't get infected." He opened the bag and turned away so Mordred could reach in without getting close.

"Whose is it?" Mordred asked.

"Mine," Tony replied.

"What's the pin?"

"Four-nine-seven-zero-six-six-nine-four-three-two-five-eight-six," Tony said. "I wanted it to be secure. Would you like me to repeat that?"

"Please," Mordred said.

Tony obliged.

"Success," Mordred said. "What do you want me to look at?"

"Go to my Hotmail app. If you tap it, it should just open: no need to enter the email address or the password. Go to my inbox if it doesn't take you there straight away. Don't worry, there's nothing personal in there."

Mordred did as instructed and found himself confronted by a list of messages beginning with *Moss Bros. Big Brand Offer* and ending with *AutoInsuranceForLess $19/Month*. He scrolled down and came to a block of five emails from Daniel Batsford, despatched one after the other just after 8pm yesterday. Each had an attachment.

"Found what I'm trying to show you?" Tony said. "Good man. Tap the lowest one. That's the earliest. Then open the attachment. It's a video file. The volume control's on the phone's left-hand side if you need to turn it up. Ree and I will just sit here. We won't interrupt. I'll just get my Penguin."

"Put it in the bin and get a fresh one," Ree said. "It'll have fluff on now."

"I might get a Club," Tony said absently.

Mordred opened the first video file. A street scene, obviously taken with a hand-held device: a phone or a body cam. It showed two men from a distance, both middle-eastern-looking, both alone, attempting to look casual, although their body-language betrayed them. They looked to be in their mid-thirties, and wore track suits. It lasted five seconds.

In the next video, the camera was moving. Nothing much in view, and Mordred didn't recognise the location; somewhere urban.

"Those were the guys who have been following me all day," Batsford said. "They were waiting outside my office this afternoon. I'm more or less certain they're after me because of - " It cut out.

The third showed one of the same two men in a different location to the original video. He glanced in the direction of the camera, then hastily turned his head and walked away. Presumably, he noticed that Batsford had been looking at him.

The fourth showed the London Underground, bottom of an escalator, obviously taken from around a corner. The two men were descending the steps, walking slowly, one several yards behind the other, looking at the ground.

The fifth was taken on the tube. Batsford's voice again, shaky. "I'm on my way home now. Keep these, in case anything happens to me. I'm sure it won't. Take care, Tony."

Mordred took a deep breath. Okay, so this altered things. Maybe not a lot – perhaps instead of going home, Batsford had ducked into a B&B somewhere in hope of avoiding a beating or worse – but it definitely added credence to his claims.

Especially since right now, he wasn't answering his phone.

"You're probably wondering why we didn't give those to the police," Tony said.

"Because no one believes us," Ree said.

Tony nodded. "We didn't know he'd disappeared. And he didn't tell us to take them to the police. He just told us to keep them."

"I'm going to have to send them to my own phone," Mordred said. "Is that okay?"

"If it helps," Tony said. "While you do that, can I just ask a question? Has this put you any closer to accepting what Daniel told you after the funeral?"

"I'm not one hundred per cent convinced," Mordred said. "There are lots of different elements to what he claimed, and they're not all interdependent. But I'm certainly closer. This is something we can investigate. There's CCTV all over London. Once we've worked out where Daniel was when he took these, we should be closer to finding out what's happened to him. And in finding that out, we might even be able to identify the two men."

"Poor, poor Daniel," Ree said. "I really hope he's all right. I couldn't bear for anything to happen to him, not after Angela."

"There's a bigger, practical consideration," Tony said. "Sorry to sound brutal, but let's say that Daniel has been killed. The bad guys might have accessed his phone, looked at his 'sent' folder, and thought, 'We need to deal with this *Tony gringo* before he sees those emails and shares them on Facebook.' Ree and I could be in real danger. I mean, I don't know how much information Daniel kept about us in his contacts list, but he *could* have our address."

"That's actually a good point," Mordred said. "Let's get you out of here for now, and put you in a hotel somewhere. Better safe than sorry."

Tony and Ree looked at him with horror.

"Oh, my God, it's serious," Ree said.

Tony swallowed. "I expected you to poo-poo me, John."

"We'd better get packing," Ree said. "Oh my God. Oh my God. Oh my God, Tony."

Chapter 8: Epic Interview Pressure

John sent the video files to his own phone while Ree and Tony went upstairs to pack. Then he sent them to Ruby Parker. Then he called Ruby Parker.

"I've told them we'll put them up in a hotel for a while," he said. "I know that's going out on a limb a bit, and you might say no but - "

"You're an experienced officer," she cut in, "and I trust your judgement. If the worst comes to the worst, I'd rather I had to explain why we went over budget than why we didn't seek protection when it was obviously necessary and why two people are now dead, or in hospital, or seriously traumatised. Is that all you wanted?"

"I suppose so, yes."

"I'll get Mildred to arrange a hotel. I'll also send someone round to where you are to keep watch while they're getting ready. Give me a call and I'll despatch Kevin when you're all ready. Then take the rest of the day off. We need to analyse those video files before we know what our next steps should be, and that's not your department. You've done enough for today."

"Get anything you want from the fridge!" Ree shouted from upstairs.

"We don't want things going to waste!" Tony added. *"There's some ratatouille in the Tupperware!"*

"The hand-sanitiser's on the unit next to the hob!" Ree called. *"You can't miss it!"*

"I'd better be going," he told Ruby Parker.

"Pour yourself another cup of tea!" Tony called.

It took them two hours to get ready. Mildred Pierce, Ruby Parker's chief assistant, had booked them a room in The Jonson Herald Hotel in Barnet. Mordred went in with them, checked everything was okay, assured them they'd be safe here and that their house would be monitored for possible intruders, then he left them to settle. He arrived outside his flat at 5pm, went straight up the external steps and let himself in. He was dead beat. Maybe he and Phyllis should eat out tonight. But that was often as tiring as cooking: all the getting ready, then the walking or bussing or taxiing, then the being-on-public-display. Maybe something microwaveable instead. Or a pizza delivery.

He went into the living room. The first thing he noticed was Phyllis's bag on the sofa. Then a depleted bottle of Prosecco on the table with an empty glass next to it.

She must be home. If so, she was very quiet.

Something must be wrong.

He checked the kitchen, then went into the bedroom. She lay on the bed in her Edmund Burke T-shirt and Donnington FC shorts. She looked at the ceiling. "Hi," she said. "I heard you come in."

He sat on the bed and picked up her hand. "Are you okay?"

"I'm not ill, if that's what you mean."

"Something's wrong. What's going on?" Then it hit him. "Of course, your interview. I mean, it's just one of several. If that's what it is."

She smiled. "That *is* what it is, actually. It's nothing to do with you, in the sense that you haven't done anything wrong, and I'm not feeling miserable. What I'd like you to do now, sweetheart, is get me that bottle of wine, and some thermal socks from the drawer. My feet are cold."

"Why don't you get under the covers then?"

She scoffed. "In the daytime? What sort of a slob do you take me for? Come on, get moving: socks and Prosecco, please."

She hauled herself up so she was propped up against the headboard. He went into the living room and grabbed the bottle.

"And bring two glasses!" she called.

He returned with the Prosecco and two glasses, and put them on the bedside table. She poured the remaining wine while he rummaged in the drawer and found the socks.

"We need another bottle," she said.

"I'm not sure whether it's a good idea to drink on an empty stomach when you're feeling low," he said. "Sorry, I know that sounds preachy. Maybe we should talk about what happened."

"Sit up next to me on the bed, then. Here you are." She gave him a full glass. "Cheers."

"Cheers."

"Okay, here goes," she said. "I went for an interview this morning, as you know, with Fergus Kaluuya, Head of the Diplomatic Service. Obviously, the panel was a surprise; it was *meant* to be a surprise, of course, and I still don't know who they were. Three men, including Fergie K, and two women. We talked about Russia and China and the EU, as expected, and I gave frank answers in which I veered on the safe side – as you do, in these sorts of things – and they asked questions about my private life – they seemed very interested in you, but certainly not in a negative way: being married to The Ultimate Londoner seemed to work entirely in my favour – and then they said, 'Thank you for your time, Mrs Mordred', and I thanked them in return, and no, I didn't trip and fall on my arse as I was leaving the room, and no, I didn't accidentally slam the door on my way into the corridor, and no, I didn't realise I'd left my bag behind, and have to knock gingerly on the door and ask to be re-admitted so I could retrieve it. None of those things happened. It was a one hundred percent, absolute, out of this world success with golden bells on. And I got out, and I stood in the summer breeze on the pavement in Whitehall, and I thought, *I've actually done it!* I mean, I haven't, not yet, but we're three-fifths of the way through, and so far it's been a triple-century in every innings. And I really, really wanted to celebrate. And there was no one to celebrate with, of course, because you were otherwise engaged, and I'm not allowed to go round talking about it, not even to my closest colleagues. But *man,*

I was buzzing as the hippies used to say. *Buzzing!* Anyway, I thought, 'Why don't I celebrate on my *own*? I could buy a bottle of bubbly – not Champagne, because I might be captured on CCTV, and Fergus Kaluuya might be watching, and he might say, 'Who does Phyllis think she is, taking the result for granted like that? I'll teach *her* a lesson!' But a bottle of something similar: Chardonnay, maybe, or Schwarzriesling? Anyway, I settled on this shit – actually, scratch that: it's not shit, just a bit bitter, but what can you expect for five ninety-nine? – and I came in, showered, changed into my favourite clothes, as modelled here, then put Wagner on, and poured myself a big glass of substitute bubbly."

"Well, that's hardly - "

"Not the end of the story."

"Oh, fine. Sorry. Go on then."

"Cheers."

He clinked her glass. "Cheers."

"I don't think we've got another bottle of anything drinkable in the cupboard. Could you go to the shop and get some more once we've finished this? I know I've already asked that. Not Champagne."

"We've got beer."

"Real ale? Dear God, not one of those four percent ones?"

"I think it's about eight. Black Rats Army, it's called."

She chuckled. "I should probably give up drinking now. Anyway, to get back to the story. I got in, put Wagner on – I know: ominous, eh? – and donned my superhero costume. And for about ten minutes, I was elated. Buzzing. Then I started to de-buzz. And then I began to re-buzz, but in the wrong way."

"Some kind of panic attack?"

"You could call it that. Similar to what psychologists call 'impostor syndrome', but where you actually *are* an impostor."

"You mean, where you're convinced you are," he said. "I'm fairly sure that's one of the symptoms."

"It had suddenly dawned on me: there's an actual *job* at the end of this. *Ruby Parker's* job. And, my God, I'm not fit to hold a candle to her! And that's so obvious, I can't understand why it hasn't occurred to me before! Well, yes, I do. I *do* know, actually. It's because, so far, I've been totally focussed on the interviews. It's been all about hitting a succession of sixes and coming off the field with my bat raised and a big smile on my face. All about me, and how bloody clever I am. Me, me, me. The truth is, I'm a nonentity, with ideas way above my station. I should concentrate on being a good officer, because it isn't even as if I'm *that* good at *that*. I'm not cut out to be Ruby Parker Version Two, not remotely. And it's only going to be a few weeks before people start noticing. *Oh dear, Ms Parker wouldn't have done it that way.* I'll have responsibility for other people's lives, John! *A very bad blunder by Mrs Mordred, there goes another of our best officers.* And another thing: what about children? I'd like children."

"They must have asked about that in the interviews?"

"Only in an innocuous way. You know how it is nowadays. It wouldn't be possible to cite 'she wanted children' as a reason for passing a woman over for a job. What would The BBC and *The Guardian* say? Not to mention, they'd be right; the BBC and *The Guardian*, I mean, not the sexists."

"I meant, what did you tell them?"

"I told them I *did* want children, yes. Which may not have been sensible, but at least it was honest."

"They must have probed you about that?"

"They did. I told them you'd be happy to house-husband for a while or indefinitely. As we discussed, at the start, remember? I hope to God you haven't changed your mind." She shrugged. "Or *do* I hope that?"

He smiled. "Maybe you should have told them I'm quite looking forward to it. I mean, I'm not somehow *grudgingly* willing. I need a break from shooting people and being shot at. I can't be lucky all my life."

"I'm scared, John. Scared I'll hate myself if I don't get the job, and scared I'll crash spectacularly if I do."

"Do you want to know what I think?"

"I might as well hear it, but a big pile of empty reassurances isn't going to reassure me."

"Ruby Parker's been Head of Red Department for decades. She'd been fairly senior in MI7 since the nineteen-eighties. How could any new appointee hope to emulate that on arrival? No, you should go for a job only if you think you'd be better than all the other appropriately qualified candidates, not because you think you'll be as good as the present or previous incumbent. Not right away, in any case. As far as I know, there are only two other people who could conceivably give you a run for your money. Alec's going for Head of Grey, and he's not as good as you, anyway: he doesn't have the people skills. Annabel's far more a field-officer than a desk-bound commander, and she's too much of a perfectionist to be a department head. She knows that. Now, ask yourself: who *else* do you want to have the job? You can't say 'Ruby Parker', because that's not an option. It could be someone neither of us knows, of course, from Grey, say, or Blue. But even so, the likelihood is they won't be as good as you. And since you certainly don't *know* they'd be better than you – how could you? - it would be irrational for you to bow out in their favour. Maybe cowardly as well. And perhaps detrimental to the national interest.

"One other possibility is that your rivals might be a clutch of chinless wonders from academia or the civil service, men and women with silver spoons in their mouths and rhino-thick skins, so that their response to, *Oh, Dear Ruby Parker wouldn't have done it that way* or, *A very bad blunder, there goes another of our best officers* would simply be to take two aspirin and carry on as if nothing happened. If you've got any faith at all in the selection process, then just do your best, and let it do its work. You'll grow into the job – assuming you get it - and you won't be left to fend for yourself in the early stages: that's not in anyone's interest."

"How was your day?"

"Well, it was - "

"I love you, by the way." She slowly kissed him. "I think I might put Wagner on. Do you think I can go out to the shop like this? I'll put a coat over the top. But I want another bottle of plonk and something microwaveable, and then I think we should watch a bit of catch up – whatever you like: something from BBC4, if you want – and just chill. You go in the shower and get that Black Rats Army out. When I get back, I want you to tell me all about your day, and I'll shut up."

Chapter 9: More Angela-Related Mysteries

John and Phyllis reached Thames House at 8.55, signed in, and went straight to Ruby Parker's office, as arranged. Phyllis was scheduled to attend the meeting in an observational capacity. For the last two weeks, she and Ruby Parker had been spending significant parts of the day together. The idea was that, whatever the prospects for Phyllis's present job application, she was likely to move up in the organisation sooner rather than later anyway, and there weren't many people in a meaningful enough profession position, right now, to benefit from a course of mentoring by Ruby Parker herself. This wasn't Ruby Parker's own idea. It had been imposed on her, presumably by someone who thought the organisation should squeeze every last drop of value out of her before she left. Stella Mackintosh, the Head of Black, was John's bet.

They sat next to each other in the same seats they'd occupied yesterday. As usual, there were no polite preliminaries.

"I'd like you to brace yourself for some bad news, John," Ruby Parker said. "It turns out that Daniel Batsford has been murdered. The police recovered his body from the Thames last night, after some witnesses reported the killing. His wife has been informed."

"I was half-expecting something of the sort," John replied. "The two men in the bodycam, I assume."

"In fact, no. Let me explain the bigger picture first. Armed with Batsford's five videos, we identified the various sections of London where they were taken, then we used CCTV, as per the conventional methodology, to piece together the movements of the three people in the films: Batsford and his two shadows. Sometime after he got on the tube, Batsford was persuaded to get off. We don't know whether that was the result of menaces, or blackmail, or what. He's next seen at Albert Bridge, apparently having a tense conversation with the two men. They all part, apparently to go their separate ways, then a third individual – white, early twenties, dressed in a leather jacket and black trousers – appears from nowhere and stabs Batsford and throws him over the parapet into the river. The two men on the bodycam witness the killing, but it either happens too fast for them to do anything, or they're in cahoots with the assassin. Either way, they run. They enter the Underground, and we lose track of them. Luckily, by that time, we've got enough imagery to identify them: they're members of the *Millî İstihbarat Teşkilatı*, the Turkish National Intelligence Organisation – TONI, for short - Ahmet Yalabik and Naz Kurtitz by name. Both men made straight for the airport after the killing. They're now presumably back in Turkey. The murderer, we think, may be British. He seems to have known how and where to avoid the CCTV, and it clearly occurred to him to conceal his face in such a way as to make him unrecognisable to the cameras. If the Turkish agents had been expecting a killing, they'd probably have taken similar precautions. We therefore don't think they had anything to do with it. At least, that's the hypothesis we're currently working on.

"The second thing is that, at around the same time Daniel Batsford was being murdered on Albert Bridge, two men were also breaking into Mr and Mrs Barnes's house in Enfield. Because you'd anticipated something of the sort, John – well done: you made exactly the right call – we were watching it, and we were able to catch the burglars red-handed. Would it surprise you to find we now have two more Turkish agents to contend with?"

"Named?" he asked.

"I could give you their names, but they're low-level."

"Where are they now?"

"The police station on the embankment by Waterloo Bridge. We've interrogated both separately. They're saying nothing, of course. Since the attempted coup in Turkey, in 2016, all positions like theirs have been vetted for loyalty to Erdoğan, so no one's expecting their cooperation. However, we are able to use them as bargaining chips."

"Yes, I can see that. Have we asked for Yalabik and Kurtitz to be extradited?"

"We have, but the Turkish are humming and hawing. They've probably calculated we can't charge the two with anything, but they may not be sure: they haven't seen our CCTV footage. But they know we've got the two burglars. I was on the phone to the Turkish ambassador early this morning, and I hinted that we may have to release our footage of the killing to the BBC, plus the little information we've got, if they don't take the extradition seriously. We are, after all, talking about the murder of a British citizen here. It's a very serious matter."

Phyllis raised her eyebrows. "That would be the nuclear option, I assume."

"Since I'm about to retire," Ruby Parker said, "I'm not exactly feeling timorous. True, the idea that a pair of Turkish agents might be implicated in the murder of a British citizen in Central London would probably spell the end of Turkey's already precarious membership of NATO, and spell the, possibly long overdue, beginning of its reclassification as a rogue state, but that's why I'm confident of getting the results I'm looking for. They've got so much more to lose than I have. And they know it."

"So a lot's happened since I clocked off yesterday afternoon," John said. "I'm not sure where it leaves us. The reference point for all this has to be the claims Batsford made after Angela's funeral. I'm just trying to work out how all this fits with that. He said she was killed in this country. Okay, that fits with the white guy, possibly British, who stabbed Batsford on Albert Bridge. But how are the Turks involved?"

"Angela was killed by the Turkish military," Phyllis said. "Allegedly. But you're right, John: why that would merit a series of follow-up actions by Turkish intelligence agents is a complete mystery."

John turned to Ruby Parker. "When you say the two burglars are 'low level' agents, what do you mean? How 'low level' are we talking?"

"'Low level' enough to know nothing of the bigger picture," she replied. "They were probably given a specific set of instructions and told to follow them without hesitation or deviation."

He frowned. "Shame."

"I can see what you're thinking," Ruby Parker told him. "I had the same idea, but it might backfire." She turned to Phyllis. "What would you advise? Can you see what John's driving at here? It doesn't matter if you can't. I've had a relatively long time to think about it, and John's directly involved."

Phyllis sat up slightly. "I'm guessing John's considering the possibility of interrogating the burglars himself. As an expert in body-language, he'd be able to tell whether they were lying or being evasive, and that, in itself, might yield clues."

Ruby Parker smiled. "Very good. And the drawback of that is?"

"John asks them a long series of questions," Phyllis said, "to which they don't know any of the answers. So we end up with nothing. What they get, meanwhile, is a sense of the avenues we're currently probing. Which could be very useful to the Turkish Intelligence Service when they're eventually debriefed. We'll have inadvertently given them lots of information. Even if they go to prison for burglary – which is unlikely – it's not as if they won't be allowed contact with outsiders. The information we've given them will get out."

"Good," Ruby Parker said.

"However, I can see how we could use that to our advantage," Phyllis said.

John looked at her and nodded.

"I see what you mean," Ruby Parker said. "We could supply John with a set of questions whose sole purpose is to transmit disinformation."

"We could get the Turks looking in all sorts of nooks and crannies," she said. "And, of course, we'd always be waiting for them. It would eventually dawn on them why we were always one step ahead, of course, but by that time, they'd almost certainly have blundered into creating a variety of new avenues of enquiry."

"It's definitely worth a try," John said. "It'll require a bit of preparation. We need a firm idea of what it is we want to communicate, and we need it to be consistent."

"Not necessarily," Phyllis replied. "If we transmit one, big false idea, and we're successful, they'll direct all their resources at it. If we give them lots of different inconsistent ideas, they'll scratch their heads and possibly scatter their powers. Which is a recipe for internal dissension."

"Do we want them to be at loggerheads?" John said.

"It wouldn't be our prime objective," Ruby Parker said. "But it might throw up more leads."

"If they become desperate," John said, "they'll probably resort to 'educated' guesswork, and that might well generate false leads. They'll be thrashing about, and then so will we."

The desktop phone rang. Ruby Parker looked at it as if it had no right to do that, then picked up. In fact, the only person who could get through during a meeting nowadays was Mildred Pierce, and she had orders only to call for emergencies.

"Could you put me on the phone to him now?" Ruby Parker said, after listening for several seconds.

"When?" she said, after a few more seconds.

She listened again and emitted a frustrated sigh. She blinked slowly and put the handset down.

"The Turkish embassy has lodged a formal complaint about the treatment of its agents," she said: "the two we have in custody. Diplomatic immunity. It came with an offer to 'explain'. Well, the 'explaining' has now been done, and we've got a junior minister from the Foreign Office on his way over here with six or seven civil service minions to explain the explanation, plus why the suspects are now on their way to Heathrow airport, plus why we were in the wrong, plus why we now need to move on."

"If he's bringing a posse," Phyllis said, "he must know he's in for a pretty rough ride."

"I bet it's to do with 'an understandable reluctance to jeopardise important trade partnerships'," John said.

"I'll round up the rest of the department," Phyllis said. "Two can play the numbers game, and we're on home turf."

Ruby Parker sighed again. "Yes, all things considered, that was probably a tactical error on his part."

Chapter 10: Doyle Injects Some Plausibility

Lecture Room One was empty when John entered with Ruby Parker. They sat on the same row, at the recommended distance apart from each other. Before leaving her office, Ruby Parker had loaded a briefcase with documents from her inbox and, when she sat down, she retrieved a wad of these. She donned her glasses, took a pen from the inside pocket of her skirt-suit jacket, and began methodically marking each in turn, frowning occasionally, and even shaking her head.

John considered taking his phone out, but he felt self-conscious enough to know it might look juvenile, even though everyone did it nowadays, it needn't mean anything crass, and Ruby Parker had apparently forgotten his existence. He found himself watching her through the corner of his eye; not because he wanted to, but because she always made him slightly nervous. He realised for the millionth time how much he was going to miss her when she'd gone. They might never see each other again. If Phyllis took over, that would be the best that could happen, but even that couldn't be as good as RP staying on another decade or two.

Time was always passing, of course, but you probably only noticed it at times like this, when you pulled into a siding for a change of engines, and there was a lot of jolting and noise and no one quite knew where to look or what to do or how long it would last, and then suddenly you were moving again, and it took you a long while to discard the intense consciousness of moving, but you knew things had definitely changed now; an adjustment had been made, and you were supposed to be better for it, but you couldn't see why, and in the meantime, all the nice scenery had disappeared, and you were increasingly going past tall embankments and uniform rows of houses and even patches of wasteland.

The doors opened. Phyllis entered with Alec, Annabel, Edna, Suki, Ian and Victor. Presumably, she'd briefed them, because they all looked up for a fight. Which might be counterproductive, since no one knew what this junior minister was going to say yet, or even who he was. Since most politicians had booming voices and they were skilled in the art of rhetoric, he'd probably carry the day. Even aside from that, he was part of the government, and the government - however muddle-headed and dissipated - was always the ultimate arbiter.

The newcomers silently sat down. Edna, Alec and Ian took their phones out. Suki put on a face mask and took a book from her bag. Annabel also had her face covered: her mask had floral patterns and looked like it had been designed by a high-end fashion-house. She sat rigidly up and looked straight ahead. As a rule, she was even more in awe of Ruby Parker than he was, and he guessed she wasn't looking at her phone for the same reason. Victor leaned back, as if he'd had busy morning, and he could do with a rest.

Suddenly, there were voices outside the room, and one voice in particular above the others: the voice of a House of Commons performer. The door opened. Five people in suits entered, led by a small man of about fifty with thinning red hair, a broad face, and narrow eyes above a pair of rosy cheeks.

"Oh, *there* you all are!" he exclaimed in a tone midway between amusement and mockery. "I must admit, I wasn't expecting to find something *this* formal. My God, I thought we could just talk about it person-to-person over a few biscuits and a pot of *tea!*" Before anyone could reply, he shook his head and continued, "So be it, so be it! I expect you want me to address you from the *podium*, do you? So be it! Who's in charge here?"

John already felt irked at the barely concealed contempt. He had already raised his hand to ask something else, so he received the full force of the man's attention.

"I'm not in charge here," he said. "But with respect, who are you?"

The man looked as if he'd been shoved, but it was no less than he deserved, and he could more than absorb it. He took a mock step backwards, grinned, and held up his palms, "Oof! My apologies. You're quite right, my apologies. *Oof!* Busy morning, and I'm *very excited to be here!* Sorry for barging in like a bull in a china shop. You're entirely correct: very discourteous. Yes, my name's Walter Doyle, I'm the Parliamentary Under Secretary of State for the European Neighbourhood and the Americas. And you are?"

"John Mordred."

"The famous *John Mordred!* Well, this *is* a treat. First time in Thames House, and a meeting with *John Mordred*. Something for the memoirs, to say the least. Pleased to meet you, John. Sorry, could I just ask again, which of you nice people here is in charge?"

"That would be me," Ruby Parker said irritably. "This is a matter of considerable importance, Mr Doyle. I got the impression from my private secretary that the 'explanation' you supposedly dangled, concerning why two foreign agents have been released from police custody, is far more complex than the mere words 'diplomatic immunity' might suggest. It's likely therefore, to take some time. And after it's complete, we'll probably have more than a few questions. The whole business is sufficiently serious to warrant formal treatment, and that is why we are here, and why, yes, I *would* like you to take the podium. And I'd like you to do that as quickly as possible, please, because I *also* have a busy morning, and so do my colleagues."

He cleared his throat. "Right, of course." He strode to the back of the stage, and when he appeared behind the lectern a moment later, he looked like a different man. Someone less frivolous, more self-assured.

"A few days ago," he said, "we received 'news' that a former MI5 officer called Angela Barnes, who left this country in 2015 to join the Kurdish resistance to ISIS, was killed in a skirmish between YPG militiapersons and Turkish troops, somewhere south of the Iraqi-Turkish border.

"The truth is - as I think you may have been on the verge of discovering - that that is not an accurate record of events. I can go further. There's no truth in it at all. It's a cover story partly for the benefit of Ms Barnes's parents, and partly designed to smooth potentially disharmonious relations between two long-standing allies. As I hope you'll appreciate in a moment, we're benefiting far more from the PR compromise than the Turks are.

"The fact is, at the time of her death, Angela Barnes was part of a Kurdish cabal, called, in English, 'Justice by Lightning' – JBL, for short - dedicated to the assassination of the Turkish president, Recep Tayyip Erdoğan. She was killed in Turkey, not in Syria. She wasn't the only conspirator to be dispatched in the particular Turkish Special Forces raid in which she lost her life. After as many as possible of the 'terrorist' corpses were identified, they were buried in unmarked graves... all apart from Angela's, which was flown to Cyprus, then back to Britain. Obviously, it's a favour to this country. I'll leave aside the obvious possibility that Turkey needs all the friends it can get at the moment...

"In the last twenty-four hours, however, events have moved on dramatically. Following Angela's death in Ankara, other members of Justice by Lightning were rounded up across the country, and Turkey looked for assistance, from its precarious ally in Syria – Russia - in tracing the 'infection', as they called it, to its source. With Moscow's help, they located a significant clique of Western European Kurdish collaborators – Swedish, French, British, Germans, plus three or four Americans - devoted solely to the assassination of President Erdoğan. After a prolonged battle near Hass village in southern Idlib, involving air strikes, thirty-five JBL militants were captured. Since then, the Russians claim to have discovered evidence that JBL is being sponsored by MI7 and the CIA.

"Erdoğan of course, is furious. He was prepared to overlook Angela Barnes, but now he feels we've double-crossed him. And we all know how ruthless he can be when his nose is out of kilter. From our side, there's not the slightest reason to think MI7 *was* bankrolling JBL, and the Americans have made similar noises concerning the CIA's alleged contribution… or lack of it. But Turkish Security now wants to know who, in Britain, might be persuaded to join Angela Barnes *in future*. Because obviously, one way of interpreting the phrase, 'the source of the infection' might be: *potential* members of JBL: men and women presently in this country, who could feel tempted to follow in Angela's footsteps. Hence the two Turkish officers who followed Daniel Batsford; hence the attempted burglary; hence our willingness to release the suspects. Remember, none of the men I've just mentioned can possibly be suspected of Daniel Batsford's murder. We know who killed Daniel Batsford, in the sense that it wasn't any one of them: it was some fifth person we've yet to identify. Who? Well, yes, it could have been a Turk, but that seems unlikely given that there were two perfectly well-qualified potential Turkish assassins already *in situ,* who certainly didn't look like they were expecting a killing. Other than that, it's guesswork. It could have been a Russian, out to stir up mischief, as the Russians always seem to be, or it could have been a Kurd, or it could have been a British citizen, perhaps someone with mental health issues. In any case, it's a matter for the police, not the FCO or MI7.

"Questions."

John looked around to see whether there were any hands up. He had to credit Doyle: he'd done a pretty good job, and there was nothing particularly contemptible in there. Even the bit about 'smoothing potentially disharmonious relations between two allies' hadn't been cringeworthy: in context, it had sounded like common sense.

Which didn't mean there were no questions to be asked. He raised his hand.

"John?" Doyle said sweetly.

"Daniel Batsford told me that Angela Barnes came to see him here, in this country," he said. "How are we to account for that?"

"We now think he was telling the truth," Doyle said. "She had 'information' which she hoped to exchange for immunity to prosecution for the going-to-Syria charges she thought the Director of Public Prosecutions would bring against her. The 'information' was almost certainly that an attempt was going to be made on President Erdoğan's life. In other words, she was toying with the idea of betraying her collaborators. But she seems to have overcome her jitters without divulging anything to Batsford at all. She returned to Turkey that same night, and was killed by police marksmen in Ankara. So Batsford was right to query the official account. From his point of view, why *would* she leave this country to go back to the Levant – which is where everyone was told she was at the time of her death - when she'd clearly told him she wanted to stay? And the small amount of time between her being at his house and the announcement of her death probably cemented his conviction that she was still here."

"I've heard nothing about any of this on the news," Annabel said. "From what we know of Erdoğan, he's always keen to flaunt his victories, show everyone what a 'strong leader' he is, etcetera. This is a therefore significant deviation from form, isn't it?"

"And presumably, if he's hopping mad," Alec put in, "he'd want to rub Western Europe's nose in the inadequacy of its representatives. He hates Merkel and Macron and just about anyone from abroad who stands up to him. Why hasn't he said anything?"

"I think he's probably preparing to," Doyle said. "It's important to stage-manage these things properly if you want to derive maximum benefit."

"They're going to have to get moving," Ruby Parker said. "Too much delay, and it'll look *too* stage-managed. In this day and age, that signals 'fake'. You mentioned thirty-five POW's. Where are they now? Do we know?"

"We're trying to avoid the term 'POW's'," Doyle said. "But to answer your question, they're apparently being moved to central Anatolia. One possibility is that the Turkish security forces will try to extract 'confessions' from them, in return for relative leniency. It's also possible – some would say likely – that when they've 'confessed', they'll be traded with their countries of origin for concessions of some sort. Erdoğan has a large number of supposed 'enemies' abroad - all Turkish nationals, many associated with the Gülen movement - whom he might feel tempted to ask for, in exchange for individual members of JBL. He might even feel inclined to ask for Muhammed Fethullah Gülen himself, depending on how many captured US citizens he can dangle. Three or four is what we've heard, but it may be more. And he might decide to make that easier for western governments by keeping the whole thing out of the polarising spotlight of the headline-makers."

"With respect," John said, "some of this seems unlikely."

Doyle looked like this was the second time Mordred had shoved him. This time, he didn't look so forgiving. "Oh?"

"Between fifteen and twenty per cent of the population of Turkey is Kurdish," John continued. "Yet the YPG appoints a group of French, Swedish and British mercenaries to the task of killing Erdoğan? Let's take Angela as a representative example. By all accounts, when she left for Syria in 2015, it was on the spur of the moment, so she probably didn't know the language. The YPG are mainly Kurmanji speakers. In 2020, her command of that language probably wasn't perfect, and, although it is one of the official languages of Turkey, she probably still spoke with a heavy, identifiable accent. To blend in in Ankara, she'd probably have to have known some Turkish. And all the YPG's European and American mercenaries would have been in the same boat. They'd have stuck out like a sore thumb in Ankara, and just about anywhere in that part of Turkey. And yet, they were supposedly based in Syria where their *bona fide* Kurdish comrades would have been able to see that, and would probably have warned them off. After all, there's nothing like a botched assassination attempt for setting your cause back a decade or two."

Silence.

"I – I don't – I can't answer that," Doyle said, at last. "You're asking me to speculate. I can't really say what the YPG in Syria would have preferred. I don't have access to that sort of knowledge. No one does."

"If you put that together with what two of my other officers just said," Ruby Parker put in, "about the complete absence of any mention of any of this in the news, then I think we're entitled to *ask* you to speculate, minister. After all, *we* will."

Doyle took a deep breath. "Very well. Yes, I'll speculate. Give me a moment. Okay, here it comes. My speculative theory is that JBL has long harboured the aim of killing Erdoğan. Until now, the indigenous members of the YPG discouraged them. But after Operation Olive Branch, they changed their minds. The YPG's facing an existential threat. It may think it's got nothing to lose any more. And so it releases the hopeless Hell hounds of the JBL. Put it another way. There are reports that the YPG is using child soldiers. I'm not saying those reports are true, but I wouldn't be surprised: not because I have a particularly low opinion of the YPG, but because I believe people will have recourse to anything when their entire future as a people is under threat. I know I would. I'd arm my nine-year-old son and eight-year-old daughter with rifles if I thought it was the only way I could stop them being bombed or gassed or raped to death."

John nodded. Doyle was an intelligent guy. He'd been asked to speculate from a position of weakness, and yet again he'd brought everyone back on board. Not the sort of person to underestimate; very different from the amiable buffoon he'd looked when he first came through the door.

Probably best to stop asking him questions then. There were other, better ways of getting to the truth.

Although given how plausible he was, he might well be telling it.

Doyle smiled. "If there are no further questions, this is something you'll have to start working on right away – in conjunction with multiple other agencies, of course. From the FCO's point of view, the principal questions are: who *are* those thirty-five individuals, how many of them are British, and how

76

should we coordinate our response? That said, I'll leave you to get started, ladies and gentlemen. Good day, and thank you for your time."

After he left the lecture room, Ruby Parker took her phone from her bag and switched it on. Only someone who'd known her for a long time would have noticed her wince as the screen lit up. She turned to Phyllis.

"Get everyone together upstairs in one of the seminar rooms," she said. "They can drop whatever else they're supposed to be doing. Inform Tariq. Bring everyone up to speed. Field questions. I've got an 'extraordinary' meeting in Whitehall. I'll speak to you as soon as I get back, and probably update you. John, follow Phyllis, see what everyone has to say, and then I'd like you to prioritise Daisy Hallenbeck. I'll call the US embassy about her in a moment. She's probably not involved, but right now, she's a loose end, and we urgently need to speak to her."

Chapter 11: Disgruntlement at the After-Party

Under normal circumstances, everyone in a meeting would sit. However, Doyle's address had created hidden tensions which became visible when, instead of taking a chair, every one of the eight people in the room stood with their backs to the wall: Phyllis, Alec, Edna and Suki along one side; Ian, Annabel, Victor and John on the other. Even apart from that, it was another surreal socially-distanced event in which ninety-five percent of the floor-space was all too obviously empty.

"I think most of that was self-explanatory," Phyllis said. "John, this is your case. You probably need to fill in the gaps. Tell us what happened at Angela's funeral, and how matters developed from there."

John recounted the funeral, the meeting with Daniel Batsford, his meeting with Mr and Mrs Barnes. Phyllis asked if there were any questions. Alec raised his hand.

"Annabel and John made some good points down there in the lecture hall," he said. "I think if there was any assassinating to be doing, the YPG wouldn't leave it to a bunch of foreigners who'd obviously have difficulty getting anywhere near El Supremo."

Edna nodded. "I can't imagine how it can have worked. I mean, you're either a soldier or you're an assassin. If you're the latter, you've got to train as such, and have dummy runs. In this case, you'd need at least a few trips to Ankara beforehand, just to familiarise yourself with the territory. But let's leave that aside for the moment. Doyle just told us that when Angela was killed, she was in company with other members of JBL. Fair enough. It makes sense that they'd travel to Ankara together in a group, offer each other mutual support. But then, Angela must have disappeared for a *long time* if she came to England and had a chat with Batsford. What did they all think she was doing? Where did they think she'd gone? They were supposedly on the verge of a major operation, and one of them just goes AWOL? And *stays* AWOL? Sorry, that doesn't make sense. And why would she then go back to Turkey? What sort of explanation could she have given them? It must have occurred to her they'd be furious, and possibly suspicious enough to kill her. But then, why were they even still *in* Ankara at that point? Why didn't they think, 'Hang on, Angela's split; we'd better either accelerate the mission, or call it off'? That would be the natural reaction."

There was a general hum of agreement. Everyone, without exception, was nodding.

"I can't get past the fact that there's been nothing on the news about any of this," Annabel said. "When an assassination attempt fails, the putative target usually issues a, 'you've had your chance, it went badly wrong, and now we're coming for you with all guns blazing' announcement, designed to strike the fear of God into everyone involved. He doesn't sit on the story in the hope that its PR value will accumulate over time."

"And, of course, assassination is supposedly *all* JBL did," Alec said. "It was devoted to a single calling. So Erdoğan orders everyone to find it, and even gets the Russians on board. How does he describe it? Well, the most obvious description would be, 'An organisation devoted to the killing of Yours Truly'. And how to explain the urgency of tracking it down? The most obvious explanation would be, 'Because it's just almost topped Yours Truly'. In other words, an awful lot of people would get to know what happened. Now, I know there's no press freedom in Turkey any more – the country's more or less gone back to the dark ages, for the time being – and there never really has been any in Russia, but surely someone in the media would get to know. And they'd tell someone outside the country."

John nodded. "True, but it's still early days."

"Even so," Alec replied. "Nothing? And news doesn't work like that any more, by the way. It begins on Facebook and Twitter. Reuters just gets with the program."

"MI7 must have a record of British individuals who left the country to go to Syria," Ian said. "If we could get names of the POW's-stroke-hostages from the Turkish authorities, we might be able to achieve a match. If the Turks are bluffing, we might not get names."

"But the Turks might just have captured a bunch of Western Europeans and Americans," Edna said. "It doesn't mean they belong to JBL, or even that there *is* a JBL."

"Or the POW's-stroke-hostages might not reveal their names," Victor said.

Suki pulled her mask down. "Sorry to play devil's advocate here, but at least Doyle's account gives us *some* explanation for Batsford's claim that he met Angela in Britain shortly before her murder. Without it, we've *no* explanation. And it *can* be reconciled with her going AWOL then changing her mind. Say if she went back to Ankara, her comrades killed her, then the Turkish authorities killed the comrades, and either *thought* they'd killed Angela in the same operation, or took the credit for killing her when they knew they hadn't. I don't think that's implausible."

"It still doesn't explain why Angela was stupid enough to go back," Victor said.

"Guilt," Suki said. "She felt guilty."

"It's a good theory," Alec said, "but if that was the case, she'd stay in Britain and keep schtum about JBL and take her chances with the police. Most judges would be fairly lenient. The YPG aren't ISIS. If she handed herself in over here, she'd probably get some sort of suspended sentence, and she could bring out her war memoirs, and she'd probably be a hero in most people's eyes. The woman who fought ISIS, a well-known genocidal freak show."

Victor shook his head. "And then she hears all her compatriots have been killed in Ankara, after a botched attempt to zap Erdoğan. After four or five years in a war-zone, she probably already had a degree of PTSD. Knowing she'd abandoned her friends to a grisly death wouldn't help."

"So she's got PTSD," Edna said. "She's not quite mentally there. Which might explain why she comes to Britain, talks to Batsford, then changes her mind and flies back to Ankara."

"Batsford didn't mention her seeming mentally fragile," John said. "Although, to be fair, she did turn up with 'information' which she didn't disclose."

"Batsford wouldn't necessarily have recognised PTSD," Alec said. "He was a lawyer, not a trained psychologist."

"We're beginning to go round in circles," Phyllis said. "The bigger question now is, does anyone have any practical suggestions? I'm sure Ruby Parker will have a substantial to-do list when she gets back, but I mean, in the meantime? Taking into account everything we've just said?"

"We need to find Daisy Hallenbeck," Alec said. "She may or may not have anything to impart, but John's good at detecting fibs. If she says she knows nothing, but she's lying, he'll know. That *might* give us a lead, but it's clutching at straws, I admit."

"Ruby Parker's calling the US embassy as we speak," John said. "I might have a word with Mr and Mrs Barnes. There were a lot of mourners outside that church. But I'm sure a lot of potential mourners were at home, self-isolating. A video of the event might be something they'd asked for, and their friends were happy to supply. Mr and Mrs Barnes could probably issue an appeal, through Angela's Facebook page, for video footage and photos. That would enable us to see who else was at that funeral besides Daisy. I mean, who of a suspicious nature."

"Another long shot," Alec said, "but, again, not to be sniffed at."

"Aren't we missing something obvious here?" Annabel said. "If Angela Barnes went to see Batsford, it ought to be on CCTV somewhere."

"She was a trained MI5 operative," Alec said. "And she knew she was wanted by the police. If she entered this country at all, she'd have had to use a false passport, and she'd have been heavily disguised, and she almost certainly wasn't naïve about CCTV - "

John held up his hand. "Hang on."

"What?" Alec said.

"You're right, Annabel," he continued. "She'd have needed a false British passport. Where on earth would she get one of those at short notice in Ankara?"

Everyone gave a quiet, 'Ah'.

"I see your point," Alec said.

"If she was ever in this country at all," John continued, "she must have come in either by sea, or by lorry like a migrant. And the passport-problem would also mean she was never on a plane *at any point*. She must have hitch-hiked across Europe, or stowed away on a ship, or maybe stolen a car, or perhaps even walked."

"Which opens a relatively huge gap between her departure from the middle-east and her arrival in Britain," Phyllis said. "She can't have left the JBL in the lurch in Ankara at the eleventh hour, then gone straight back. Doyle's account must be wrong."

"Which in turn raises the possibility that there *is* no 'JBL'," Alec said.

"It also makes Batsford's claim exponentially more likely," John said. "He insisted that Angela was killed in this country. If she really *did* come to see him when he suggested, then in fact, her being killed in Britain's the only possibility."

"So who killed her?" Annabel said. "We need to take a much closer look at the man who killed Batsford on Albert Bridge."

There was a knock on the door. Mildred Pierce, a thin woman with grey hair and spectacles on a chain, put her head round. "Mrs Mordred, I've a confidential message to deliver, but only if it's convenient."

"I think we're done," Phyllis said, "unless anyone's got anything they need to add?"

No one had.

"John, you go and see Mr and Mrs Barnes," she said. "Annabel, have a word with Tariq, see if he can pull up any

82

footage of the environs of Batsford's house on the night of Angela's supposed visit. Edna and Suki, see what you can discover about the JBL on the web. Ian and Victor, keep an eye on Turkish social media, see if anything's emerging. Alec, have a look at the footage of Batsford's murder, see what you think. Obviously, all this is only provisional till Ruby Parker gets back, but that could be some time."

Chapter 12: Planned Re-jigs

"What is it?" Phyllis asked Mildred Pierce, when the others had dispersed. The two women were walking along the corridor to the lift.

Mildred Pierce had her phone out and was dialling. "You've been scheduled a meeting," she replied airily. "Yes, ma'am," she said to whoever she was calling. "She's just come out. I'm bringing her now."

"Who - ?" Phyllis said, but Mildred Pierce stopped, opened the door to Seminar Room H11, and stood aside to allow Phyllis to enter. Phyllis obliged, and Mildred Pierce gently closed herself out.

The room was occupied by two men and a woman, all familiar. Steven Mancroft and Danesh Sohna were civil servants from the Home Office and the Foreign Office respectively; both in their fifties, slim, with expensive cuff-links and delicate, office-habituated hands. Stella Mackintosh was the Head of Black Department, a tall, black, glamorous woman with close-cropped hair. Her knee-length yellow dress and matching heels made the men's suits look dowdy: either she or they had come inappropriately dressed, and since she never made that kind of mistake, it must be them. All three stood up when Phyllis entered the room, but without obvious enthusiasm. Phyllis heard herself swallow.

"Please sit down, Phyllis," Stella said. "I won't beat about the bush. Congratulations. Your job application to become the next Head of Red Department has been successful. We're about to call off the last two interviews, because you're so far ahead of the rest of the field, we didn't think it was worth wasting any more of anyone's valuable time. Before we do that, however, we need to be sure of your acceptance."

"Congratulations, Phyllis," the two men said cheerily, before she could speak. Stella Mackintosh beamed her approval – there could be no handshakes in the current climate - and they all sat down in a wide circle.

"That may sound odd," Stella Mackintosh continued: "'your acceptance', as if you might have come all this way, just to decline!"

The men chuckled.

"I accept," Phyllis said.

Stella Mackintosh smiled indulgently, then her attitude became more sombre. "I appreciate your positivity, but now you need to hear me out. MI7 is about to change. We're using Ruby Parker's departure as an opportunity to introduce a significant raft of reforms. I say 'reforms': it's something akin to a revolution. You need to make sure you'd be happy working in the new setup before you commit yourself."

"Don't worry if you eventually have to say no," Steven Mancroft said, as if it was a real possibility.

"A bit of history first," Danesh Sohna said. "As you probably know, the current MI7 dates from the year 2000. It was designed to replace the old MI5 and MI6, partly on the grounds that a variety of governmental and administrative bodies decided it was no longer possible to divide the world into 'domestic' and 'foreign', not in the days of the internet; even though, in those days, the internet was still fairly rudimentary.

"The idea was that the new organisation would comprise five more or less independent 'levels', each designated by a particular colour - White, Red, Blue, Grey, Black – each succeeding level with a unique remit, an increased level of clearance in terms of knowing what the levels 'above' it were up to, and even powers to disrupt that level if it considered such disruption necessary to the interests of 'the realm'.

"The whole edifice was originally designed, in the words of the slogan, to bring intelligence – in the cybernetic sense of the word – into intelligence."

"It worked for a while," Steven Mancroft said, "but then Red Department began to be far more successful than the others, and with that increased accomplishment, its purview unavoidably got wider. Ruby Parker turned out to be not only an inspirational head of department, but also a deeply perceptive interpreter of world affairs, and an incredibly gifted talent-spotter."

"Very good at bringing out hidden talents too," Stella Mackintosh put in. "You, Alec Cunningham, Annabel Gould and your husband, John, all worked for Grey before Ruby Parker 'inherited' you. Please don't take this the wrong way, but as Grey agents, you were merely ordinary. Somehow, Red made you blossom.

"Of course, Red's ascent didn't go unnoticed by the other departments," she continued. "Blue and Grey in particular have had a history of resentment, and even active opposition, dating back to at least 2010."

"We believe that's when things started to go wrong," Danesh Sohna said. "Although, in retrospect, it was a miracle it took that long."

Steven Mancroft chuckled. "And there's a very specific reason for that. It's only recently that we discovered the entire thing was an elaborate confidence-trick played by the politicians."

"For fairly laudable reasons," Stella Mackintosh said. "Back in the nineties, they saw the security services as a threat to democracy. A secret organisation, staffed largely by ex-public schoolboys and Oxbridge graduates with little connection to the real world: *of course* it would want to take over! Such a thing had almost happened already in the 1960s, when Harold Wilson was PM."

"It's probably 'almost happened' on several other occasions," Steven Mancroft said. "Only of course, that hasn't come out... yet."

"In short, the *real* reason the politicians reorganised MI5 and MI6 into MI7 was to foster infighting," Danesh Sohna said. "The different departments would be too busy scrapping with each other to worry about undermining the wider society. And yet they'd still be independent enough to do useful work."

"MI5 and MI6 had always been wary of each other," Stella Mackintosh said, "but their era witnessed nothing like the internecine wars we've seen in recent years. The tragedy is that the body politic didn't need the secret services to undermine it. We now live in a fairly crass era in which foreign powers regularly intervene in our democratic elections, our politicians are bankrolled by tax-avoiders, crooks and oligarchs, and people's beliefs and values are governed by whatever happens to be trending on Twitter. Don't get me wrong: I'm opposed to that – as I believe every sensible person ought to be – but I don't see it as my job to rectify it. I *do*, however, see it as my job to 'defend the realm'. I hope you do too."

"I'm not sure the two things can be separated," Phyllis said. "But you mentioned 'changes'?"

"We're going to continue with our five departments," Stella Mackintosh said, "but *as* genuine departments, under one ultimate head: myself. If that sounds like an ego-trip, it isn't. We'll have a written constitution and an internal democracy, something like 'rule by cabinet' used to be in government. We'll all count for one, and no one for more than one. But once we've made a decision, we all get behind it. And one of our departments will be devoted to scrutiny of the whole, and will report primarily – on an annual basis - to the government of the day. There will be no more internal wars."

"So my being Head of Red department will mean … what?" Phyllis asked.

"You'll be head of a department with a large degree of autonomy," Stella Mackintosh replied, "but within an organisation that behaves consistently because it cooperates internally."

"We realise it's a far from perfect solution to the present configuration," Danesh Sohna said. "Stella could, for example, do a Putin or an Erdoğan: surround herself with obsequious nonentities eager to grant her increased powers."

"And there may well be competition amongst the heads of department to impress Stella," Steven Mancroft said, "in hope of stepping into her shoes when she retires."

"I will have the power to choose my successor," Stella Mackintosh said. "But only because the post requires someone with substance. It's easy to pull the wool over politicians' eyes with a string of glittering 'results', where the actual quality of those results leaves much to be desired. And I'm not the type to indulge toadies."

"Hopefully, the new organisation will be a lot more proactive," Danesh Sohna said. "The Russians have been pretty aggressively interfering in our system of late. They'll soon find that two can play at that game, and since their system's a lot more fragile than ours, I imagine they'll eventually be laughing on the other side of their faces. The Americans are already on board with that, of course."

"There's going to be a complete reshuffle," Stella Mackintosh said, "designed to give all the department heads a new start. We'll be offering a generous, but not obligatory package of early retirement to our oldest members, and we'll be going on a major recruitment drive, designed partly to increase our diversity. You're still quite young, Phyllis. You may benefit from having a rather younger department. People you can mould."

"How is it all looking so far?" Steven Mancroft asked.

"I certainly see nothing to object to," Phyllis replied.

"We're utterly determined to make a break with the present system," Danesh Sohna said. "So there will be an element of re-branding. From 2021, MI7 will become something else. We're toying with 'MI8', but we may go for an entirely different moniker. After all, we haven't really been '*military* intelligence' for a long time."

"I do *prefer* MI8," Stella Mackintosh said. "Call me a traditionalist, but I think we've got to have *some* continuity with the past. And I'm worried that when the government finds out we're re-branding, it'll farm the task out to some ghastly PR firm, and we'll end up paying two and a half million for a name like 'inspire' or 'equate' or 'global solutions'. And we'll be stuck with it."

"I'd be happy with MI8," Danesh Sohna said.

Stella Mackintosh turned back to Phyllis. "I'm hoping John – your husband – will join me in Black Department. I spoke to him about the prospect a few months ago. He seemed receptive, although he didn't commit himself at that point. I'm pretty sure he recognises that his continued presence in Red might 'cramp your style', at least initially."

"He didn't mention it," Phyllis said.

"I asked him not to," she said. "Does that bother you?"

Phyllis smiled. "No, it doesn't. Not at all."

"Why not?" Steven Mancroft asked. "I mean, just out of interest."

"John and I work in the same organisation," she replied, "one whose chief purpose is the keeping and exposing of secrets. We realised long before we got married that, if we were to both carry on working here, *and* have a successful marriage, we couldn't share everything. Frequently, one of us would probably learn, or be told, something, and be unable to share it with the other. We agreed to live with that. The only exception would be in matters of imminent life and death. This isn't that. Had our situations been reversed, I wouldn't have told John, and I'd have expected him to accept that. So yes, it's no problem. None whatsoever."

"And, assuming that John ultimately says yes to my offer," Stella Mackintosh said, "you're happy to 'lose' him."

"I want what he wants," she said.

"I'm very glad you said that," Stella Mackintosh replied, "because we need you to keep a secret from *him*. Now you know something about the new conditions under which you'll be working, we'll re-submit our offer to you: would you accept the post of Head of Red Department? But whether you say yes or no, you are to keep it *completely under wraps* until further notice. Even from John. If word gets out that there's about to be a major restructuring, people will naturally become jumpy, and we can't permit that. It's bad for morale, and bad for the country. As far as anyone else is concerned, your selection process is still ongoing."

"You might think you could tell them without divulging anything about the changes," Danesh Sohna said, "but that wouldn't work. When the restructuring process begins, people will know that you couldn't have accepted the job without knowing something about it. No, we intend to make a general announcement about it first - by which time, a significant number of individuals, including nearly all your closest colleagues, will have been notified and consulted privately - and then your appointment afterwards, so that you can't possibly be implicated."

"... In the eyes of those who, for whatever reason," Steven Mancroft said, "might feel they need a shoulder to cry on. Which would be normal in any restructuring."

"That sounds reasonable," Phyllis said.

Silence. Danesh Sohna looked at Stella Mackintosh, who looked at Steven Mancroft, who nodded and looked at Danesh Sohna. They all turned to Phyllis with what felt, even from her position, like a collective sigh of relief.

"In that case," Stella Mackintosh said warmly. "I'll ask you for your final answer."

"I accept," Phyllis said.

Everyone was grinning. Steven Mancroft said a quiet 'hooray'. Stella Mackintosh gave a little handclap. Danesh Sohna nodded appreciatively, then picked up his briefcase.

"I look forward *very* much to working with you," Stella Mackintosh said.

Chapter 13: Conference in Victoria Tower Gardens

Mordred switched on his phone as soon as he got out of The Jonson Herald Hotel in Barnet, but there had been no new messages. He got off the tube at Westminster at 3pm. Overhead, on a background of deep blue, a few isolated clouds threatened to dim the sun for thirty seconds or so at a time. His phone pinged.

An email from Tony Barnes with an attachment. He opened it, just to confirm it was what he hoped. Another arrived, while he was looking at it.

After two minutes, he'd received five such messages, all from Tony, all containing forwarded footage of Angela's funeral, shot outside the church by a variety of different former acquaintances of Angela. He'd never imagined so many people would want to film this sort of event, but, well, that was the contemporary world: everything was fair game. He sent them to Tariq, and asked him to check them for unfriendly faces from abroad.

He bought a cheese and cress sandwich in Tesco Express and ate it walking along Abingdon Street. His phone rang as he turned left to walk through Victoria Tower Gardens. He half expected Mr and Mrs Barnes, but it was Ruby Parker. He sat down on a bench facing Emmeline Pankhurst's statue and took another bite of his sandwich.

"John, where are you?"

"Three minutes from base. The park off Abingdon Road."

"Before I get to my principal purpose in calling, how were Mr and Mrs Barnes?"

"Still very upset about Batsford, of course. In some ways, I found it quite difficult not to tell them what was going on. In other ways, it was easy, because I don't actually know myself. It was a very interesting discussion in H7, by the way. I wish you'd been there."

"Phyllis told me all about it. I agree there are grounds for scepticism, but given that the next twenty-four hours should determine the issue one way or another, I think we should allow ourselves to be dragged in the direction of the official interpretation, for the time being, as summarised by Doyle. It's not just the FCO that's dragging us, either. In any case, I really called - "

"Before we change the subject, I've given the Barneses a bit of an extension in the hotel. It's probably safe for them to go home now – I doubt the Turks will bother them a second time: once bitten, twice shy - but I don't think we can be a hundred percent sure."

"As you like. We're still having the house watched, and we can continue that during the initial period of their return. I really called to talk about Daisy Hallenbeck."

"Did you get to see her?" he asked.

"I'm afraid not. And the worrying thing is, no one seems to know exactly where she is. We shouldn't necessarily read anything sinister into that. As we surmised, she's not working at America's London embassy any more. She's been in Istanbul, attached to the CIA substation on the Bosphorus. Apparently, they required her services, so she was transferred. Not her choice."

"By 'her services', you mean - "

"I assume, document authentication, since that's supposedly her specialism nowadays. But the Americans weren't terribly forthcoming. She's allowed a large degree of independence, which is why they didn't know she'd gone missing. In fact, they're not even sure she *has* 'gone missing'. As we all know, spies aren't necessarily required to phone home every night before bedtime. However, it was obviously news to them that she'd been spotted at Angela Barnes's funeral. Whatever they think she's up to, I got the impression that wasn't part of the agenda. But of course, Angela could have been a friend. They couldn't rule that out."

"How concerned do you think they were, on a scale of one to ten?"

"I don't know how to answer that. More concerned than they were before I spoke to them, that's all."

"We can find out whether she's left the country, can't we? I mean, left by official means: via an airport or a harbour."

"I've already done that. She hasn't."

"Okay. That's good." He suddenly became aware of someone on a bench about ten metres away, watching him. Swarthy, thirty-ish, casually dressed, hands in pockets, making no attempt to disguise his interest. "I'm being watched," he told Ruby Parker. "A Turkish-looking guy. Doesn't look unfriendly, but I suppose you never know. I'm going to investigate."

"John - "

He hung up. She wouldn't call back. Staying on the phone could achieve very little, and she'd know that. Getting off meant she could call for reinforcements, which she almost certainly would. In her eyes, he was a boffin-type with emaciated muscles and a penchant for trying to subdue bullies by being nice. He wondered who she'd choose to come and rescue him.

Alec or Annabel. Probably not both.

He looked at the Turkish guy. The Turkish guy looked back and smiled. A bit like a gay encounter circa 1955, probably. Plus it had overtones of Cold War meetings in Hyde Park. All in all, a heady combination.

The Turkish guy got up and sauntered over, with his hands still in his pockets. John moved to the end of the bench. The Turkish guy sat down at the opposite arm-rest. Mordred realised the man had his hands in his pockets for a reason: he wanted to show he meant no harm. To augment the impression, he suddenly stretched out his feet and crossed his ankles.

Of course, that might mean nothing. A third party might be crouching in the bushes, ready to pounce with a crowbar. But Mordred didn't think so.

The Turkish guy – it'd be really weird now if he turned out to be, say, Australian – reached into his pocket and took out a packet of cigarettes. He offered Mordred one.

"I don't smoke," Mordred said, "but thanks, anyway."

The man took out a lighter, picked out a cigarette, took three puffs, inhaled deeply, then blew out a long flute of smoke. He looked at the object between his fingers as if he was trying to identify its precise vintage, though he already knew it was a top quality one. "You're the world-famous John Mordred, eh?" he said, apparently to the cigarette.

"Yup," Mordred said. "Nice smoke?"

The man grinned. "Oh, yes. My first of the day."

"Turkish tobacco?"

"Naturally. Allow me to introduce myself, Mr Mordred. I'm Hulusi Erkekli. I probably won't be giving anything away if I tell you I'm a spy, like yourself, only not as legendary. And yes, I do work for the Turkish secret service."

"What happened to Daniel Batsford the other day?"

"I don't know. We didn't kill him, I do know that. We simply wanted him to tell us about Angela Barnes. We didn't think – nor do we know - that he'd have information of a quality worth killing for. If he had, we'd have tried to access it. We wouldn't have stabbed him to death. Do you honestly think we did?"

"No. Not really. Why are you here?"

"Two reasons. One official, the other unofficial. Which would you like first?"

"I'll take the official one, please," Mordred said.

"It's come to our attention that there's an American agent in this country called *Daisy Hallenbeck*. Have you met her?"

"Being a spy, I'm probably not going to answer that question."

"Understood. We happen to know you were in North Africa together a few months ago, so you obviously do know her."

Mordred shrugged. "Why ask then?"

"It's likely she'll try to find you sometime in the near future. She's in Britain somewhere. In hiding, we believe. But you're her friend, and she probably thinks you'll believe her when no one else will."

"She's probably right. I quite like her. Bit bossy, but kind-hearted."

"You may have heard that she's working as a document authenticator. That's a very misleading job-description, to say the least. What she really is, is a professional *counterfeiter*. The CIA have assigned her the task of fabricating documents designed to prove that Turkey is selling NATO secrets to Russia. We believe she's putting a fake dossier together. She's been targeted many times in Istanbul, so I believe, but she's always managed to escape."

Mordred frowned. "That doesn't sound like the Daisy Hallenbeck I know. What's her aim?"

"To get NATO to oust us, of course. Persuade the United States Congress and its Senate, and the great Commander-in-Chief himself, that Turkey's a 'loose cannon', as they say."

Mordred laughed. "With respect, I think your president's doing a pretty good job of that all on his own. He certainly doesn't need help from Daisy Hallenbeck."

"Excuse me, if you make fun of my president, I'll make fun of your Prime Minister."

Mordred laughed. "Please, no."

"Or your Queen."

"I'd imagine she's past caring nowadays. Once you've been on *Spitting Image* and *The Windsors*, you're probably immune to jibes from the likes of Hulusi Erkekli. Of course, Mr Erdoğan's far too exalted to tolerate anything in the way of satire."

"Please, John, let's not fight."

"You're right. It's not your fault you've got a crap President, and not mine I've got a crap Prime Minister. I quite like the Queen, though, but she's more than capable of looking after herself. She does it by ignoring morons." He wondered why he was getting so agitated. There was probably an element of Ruby Parker and his mum in there somewhere, as there always was in his conception of the Queen.

"We're wasting time," Erkekli said. "We're talking about irrelevancies."

"You're right. Okay, so stay away from Daisy Hallenbeck. Got it. What was the unofficial message you mentioned?"

"'Angela Barnes was killed in Ankara after an abortive attempt to murder the Turkish President.' Yes or no?"

"What do you mean, 'yes or no'?"

"I mean, do you believe it?"

"No, I'm afraid not. Don't ask me why. I keep my reasons close to my chest at this point in an investigation. I take it you're unofficially going to warn me against being sceptical of the official version?"

"I don't believe it either. I'd never even heard of 'JBL' before yesterday."

"That needn't mean anything. I assume it was a secret organisation. There's always a first hearing for everything you've heard of."

"But I don't think she was killed in Turkey," Erkekli said. "I'm talking 'off the record' here, remember? No one seems able to tell me where *precisely* she was killed. It's all very, very secret. And I don't know why. Unless it didn't happen."

"Maybe you're right, but what does it matter? I mean, from your point of view."

"I'm not sure I follow."

"Don't take this the wrong way, but Turkey's no longer a free country. What 'happened' is whatever it suits Erdoğan to say happened. The truth doesn't matter. You're not going to get a medal for unmasking the 'official' version, is what I'm trying to point out. More likely, you'll end up with a prison sentence."

"There are various ways the truth can cut. We're assuming it's a plot *by* President Erdoğan, but what if it's a plot *against* him?

96

"Why would it be?"

"Think, John: what does he get out of all this? A group of Kurdish sympathisers trying to kill him? It's plausible, but how does it play to his interests? The 2016 failed coup, yes: I admit, he may have manufactured that, at least partly. It allowed him to consolidate his grip on power. But what does *this* do for him? Whatever it is, it's got to be worth going to a lot of trouble for."

"You mean, you think someone may be plotting to bring him down? Well, it's about time."

"My point is, the truth is the truth, whether it works for or against him. At the moment, I think we've got a falsehood, and it's certainly playing against Angela Barnes in a way I think the truth probably wouldn't. But either way, let me repeat: the truth is the truth. It's valuable for its own sake."

Mordred nodded. The sort of thing *he* usually said. Maybe Hulusi Erkekli had researched him, and he'd worked out that 'the truth is the truth' was the sort of thing likely to elicit a favourable response. But he didn't think so. Erkekli wasn't coming across as a confidence-trickster, not even an unusually sophisticated one.

"So what do you want to do now?" he asked. "An exchange of phone numbers so that you can track me across London?"

Erkekli scoffed. "That would work both ways."

"But given that I'm apparently Daisy Hallenbeck's best friend, it'd be more useful to you."

"You would think that, though, because you don't know how important I am. Anyway, stop being difficult. I must say, I expected better from the great John Mordred. I didn't even *suggest* exchanging phone numbers. That was your idea. And on the basis of it, you get indignant and start accusing me of trying to track you across London!"

Mordred took a deep breath. "You're right. I'm sorry."

"Apology accepted. Your colleague's over by the railings, by the way, if you want to call for help."

Alec. Looking out towards the river. He hadn't even noticed him.

"I'm leaving now," Erkekli said. He gave Mordred a scrap of paper with a string of numbers on. "If you get an insight into the actual truth that you'd like to share with someone sympathetic from my side of the fence, call me."

"Thank you," Mordred said.

Erkekli chortled. "Are you sure you won't take a cigarette? It might help you calm down."

Mordred laughed as the Turk walked away. Alec somehow noticed and came casually over.

Chapter 14: The George V Restaurant

As soon as John hung up on her, Ruby Parker called Alec. A few seconds later, her car pulled up at Thames House. As she walked across the entrance hall, she saw him leave at speed.

In reality, no one was likely to attack John in broad daylight in Central London, but a few precautions in that sort of situation never went amiss. She said good afternoon to Colin, signed in, and went to her office. She dealt with a long series of urgent requests, messages and updates. Then she rang Tariq.

"We need a CCTV search to locate an American agent called Daisy Hallenbeck," she said. "We've got several photos of her on file. She was last seen at the church outside Angela Barnes's funeral. I can't remember the name and location of the church off hand, but you can locate it in the 'recent events' section of the database. John's asked Angela's parents to oversee the collation of a number of photos and video files relating to the event. If you have a word with him when he gets back, he'll probably have some files to send you."

"I've already got five. He sent them about an hour ago. It appears Daisy Hallenbeck wasn't the only anomalous visitor to that funeral. Believe it or not, we've actually got a Turkish army colonel called Tuncel Alasya. I've sent you the pictures. Whether he doubles as an intelligence agent, I don't know. I suppose he must do. He's looking at Daisy Hallenbeck. Maybe that's why she left in such a hurry."

"That would be truly disturbing. Thank you, Tariq. Good work."

She retrieved Vilma's latest letter from her bag and re-read it. Her phone rang.

"Stella Mackintosh here," the voice said. "Have you had lunch?"

"Not yet."

"In that case, I'm buying. George V Restaurant, on the top floor. I'm on my way back from Downing Street right now. It's been a very busy morning, and I imagine you haven't exactly had a ball. In any case, the brewing crisis can do without us for an hour. There are things we need to discuss."

"I'll make my way up there in about five minutes. Thank you."

"Ciao."

Ciao: it sounded so breezy, but that was probably intentional. And that 'there are things we need to discuss', the sort of thing that sounded like an ultimatum, but which had come across like a question: is it okay with you if we have a discussion?

Old habits die hard. Stella had been part of her department, back in the late eighties and early nineties, when it had still been 'SIS'. Ruby had actually headhunted her from university. They'd been all over West Africa together on missions neither could remember very much any more. Then she'd left to have children and, naturally, MI6 being what it was, they'd lost touch. Until very recently, when, dumbfoundingly, she'd materialised from the ether as Head of Black Department. Up until that point, 'Head of Black Department' had been a placeholder, a label for an individual so clouded in secrecy that some people actually considered him/her fictional.

So Stella was now the boss of the boss. But she clearly didn't relish it, which was why she was always so subtly deferential: is it okay with you if we have a discussion? And it was why – apart from her own obvious merits – Phyllis would almost certainly inherit the Headship of Red. And why lunch. All because Stella wanted to be nice to her.

Ruby Parker shut down her PC, left her office and took the lift to the restaurant.

A waiter stood by the door like he'd been expecting her. Maybe Stella had rung ahead. He showed her to her seat at one of five widely separated tables in a room that looked like it belonged in a gentleman's club - wainscoting, heavy lampshades and framed portraits of long-dead politicians – with a window overlooking the Thames. When she'd first arrived in Thames House in 2001, it had been used much more frequently than now: for visits of top civil servants or cabinet ministers, for example or when adverse circumstances compelled departmental heads to have a quiet *tête-à-tête*. The last time she'd been here was about eight years ago, when she'd been misinformed about the death of one of her best agents. It had possessed bad associations ever since.

And it had always been fraudulent. Everything on the menu was brought up from the canteen on the floor below.

But it allowed a degree of privacy, and of course, it chimed with certain British notions of social class: us up here, them down there. Unfashionable notions, nowadays, and getting more so, yet still surprisingly resilient.

She picked up the menu. Mostly roasts, braised meats and pies. A bit like going back in time, and therefore probably comforting for some people.

She was allowing herself to become bitter again. Angry, more than bitter, but even so, she needed to stop it. Be positive.

The door opened and Stella entered wearing a yellow dress that contrasted so violently with the surrounds that Ruby Parker almost emitted a laugh of surprise.

"Gosh, it's dark in here!" Stella exclaimed, making the waiter jump slightly.

"We can sit by the window," Ruby said.

"Let's."

The waiter preceded them and pulled out Ruby's chair for her. Possibly, he was deferring to age, although there was only five years difference.

Stella scanned the menu. "I'll have the roast chicken, please," she said. "Ruby?"

"The same."

"Can I get you anything to drink?" the waiter said.

"A cup of tea," Ruby said.

"Bring a pot, please," Stella said.

The waiter put his heels together but mercifully without clicking them, bowed from the neck and withdrew.

"I know you're not keen on small talk," Stella said, "so I'll come straight to the point. We've appointed your successor. Phyllis Mordred. You're only the second person to know, and I've told her to keep it quiet."

Ruby smiled. "I'm very pleased. I haven't seen the other candidates, but I have seen other similar posts within this organisation filled by time-serving mediocrities. That was my greatest fear. Thank you for helping me avoid it."

Stella hooted. "*I* didn't do anything."

"I'm not taking anything away from Phyllis, but I know she had your support."

"Because she had yours. I'm damn sure you know what's best for Red Department. But like you just said, she triumphed on her own merits. Just while we're on the subject, Alec Cunningham prospects are also looking increasingly good."

"I think he imagined recent developments in his personal life might have hampered his chances."

"You mean his marriage to Valentina Morozova? Far from it. She's completely beyond suspicion now, and she's persuaded him to learn Russian. Ten or fifteen years ago, that would have made him a throwback. Not any more. And did you know he went on a Black Lives Matter march the weekend before last? That's exactly what we need. Someone who's not 'above' new ideas. And of course, in a peculiarly modern way, he's a 'family man'. I like that. I mean, being a 'family woman' myself. It keeps you grounded."

Ruby Parker took a deep breath, then chuckled slightly

"What's so funny?" Stella said politely.

"The way I took a deep breath just then. As if it was a comment on what you've just said. It wasn't. At least, it wasn't meant to be."

"That's partly what I asked you here to talk about: what happens when you retire. In any normal job, it would be no one else's business, but of course, this isn't any normal job. Last time we spoke, you mentioned a 'Vilma Cuesta'. I've looked her up, obviously, so there's no need to describe her to me. Genuine question: how do think that's going to work?"

Ruby took a deeper breath this time, and hardly noticed it. "It isn't."

"From what I remember of your plan, you intended to move in together. Obviously, you couldn't go to Cuba – I mean, technically, you *could,* but there would be an almighty stink, and you'd probably be putting yourself in danger - "

"I know that."

"Yes, of course. Of course you do."

Their tea arrived, then their meals. The food never took very long in here, because it wasn't a case of cooking it from scratch, but only of sending down, and possibly pressing a few buttons on a microwave.

"I've been a fool," Ruby said, when the waiter had gone. "I really don't know what I was thinking, why I didn't consider it in more detail. I can't go to Cuba, and, with all the restrictions on immigration nowadays, Vilma can't come here. And please don't tell me someone can 'arrange' it, because I wouldn't want that. And in any case, she's not keen on coming here. She's lived in Cuba all her life, and she loves it. The re-adjustment would probably kill her. The truth is, we're both the sorts of old dogs who can't learn new tricks. We're not exactly happy as we are, but we're not actively *un*happy. And that's probably as good as it's going to get."

"So you're going to live alone for the rest of your life?"

"Life is life. It has a beginning and an end. When you're young, you travel, you have sex, you go to parties, you try to keep up with the latest fashions, you endeavour to get on in the proverbial office. As you get older, you slow down. If you're sensible, you eventually come to terms with your own mortality.

103

I'm unusual nowadays in that I believe there's an afterlife. Everyone else seems to want to avoid thinking and talking about death altogether. Or they want to pretend it's not important. Old people are expected to wear purple and clatter their walking sticks along park railings. Sorry, but that's how children behave, and pointing that out doesn't make me a Grinch. God, I sometimes wish I lived in one of those middle-eastern countries where old people are actually expected to be old people, not ersatz youngsters."

Stella laughed. "That's quite a speech!"

"It's how I feel. I was born out of my time."

"It is possible to wear purple *and* believe in the eternal soul. If that's what we're talking about."

"I don't even like purple. But I take your point. I'm not sure what bearing it has."

"Let's get back to next year," Stella said. "Let's stop talking so generally. I don't wish to sound brutal, but Vilma Cuesta's your only friend, yes?"

"I like to think *we're* friends, you and I."

Stella put her hand over Ruby's. "I'm honoured, and it's mutual. Although I'm not sure how you'd feel about me coming to live with you."

They laughed.

"She's my oldest friend," Ruby Parker said. "And there's the continuity. I never lost contact with her. Even in the years before the Berlin Wall fell, we were still very much in touch. And if I'm honest with myself, I don't find making new friends easy. I'm not sure whether the job made me that way and I just went along with it, or whether I slotted so well into the job because I was that way to begin with."

"Probably a combination," Stella said. "What about the second chamber? From what I hear, about six or seven people are falling over themselves to recommend you. And it wouldn't be like you to decline a challenge. You'd certainly keep the government on its toes. And you'd have friends in there."

"I'll accept if I'm offered. Look, Stella, I understand your concern, and I'm touched. But there's nothing to worry about, really. For a while, I thought I'd made a mistake – maybe I should have asked to stay on till I was seventy – but that would have been selfish."

"Hardly!"

"True, Vilma isn't coming to *live* with me, nor I with her, but that doesn't mean she can't come to *stay* with me for long periods, nor I with her, up to a point. And maybe she'll change her mind after a few years, who knows? In the meantime, I'll go to the shops, and cook meals, and watch TV, and read, and make the odd speech in the House of Lords, and maybe sit on a select committee or two. And maybe, ultimately, I'll go back to being something like I was when I was eighteen or nineteen. I won't wear silly colours or behave like a toddler, but I'll try to do good things, the sort of things eighteen-year-old idealists do: work with disadvantaged children, maybe, or refugees, or the terminally ill. Like I said a moment ago, life is life. I know I can't expect the future to be anything like the past, but it's open, and it's for me to make it as good – morally good – as possible. And yes, I may be in a sort of decline now, and I may have just one long-standing friend, but I can still please God and His angels. That's really all that matters."

Stella finished her meal. She put her knife and fork together. "Above all," she said emotionally, "we mustn't lose contact. I really mean it."

They held hands for a second over the table. "We won't," Ruby said.

They stood up. There was an international crisis to deal with, though it would probably turn out to be another storm in a teacup.

As she rode the lift down to her office, Ruby Parker realised she no longer felt angry.

Not at present, anyway.

Chapter 15: Keep the False Flag Flying

"So who was he?" Alec said when he sat down. Despite the sunshine, Victoria Tower Gardens was almost empty, a result of the falloff in tourism everywhere, perhaps.

"A JBL sceptic, believe it or not," Mordred replied. "Name of Hulusi Erkekli. I don't know how seriously to take him."

He took his phone out. He emailed Ruby Parker to let her know he was safe. There were four new messages from Tony Barnes and one from Ree. He forwarded them to Tariq.

"What was Erkekli's angle then?" Alec asked.

"He'd never heard of JBL before yesterday, and he can't see how Mr Erdoğan can really benefit from a false flag operation."

"Well, if the Head Honcho can't benefit, that would suggest it's genuine, unless the whole thing's some sort of massively disguised coup attempt in the making. I don't see how, though. Come on, let's get back to base. I've work to be doing."

They stood up and walked.

"Did Ruby Parker tell you to come and get me?" Mordred said.

"Of course. Otherwise, I'd be at my desk. Like I just said, I'm busy. Or was."

"It seems odd that all of us should express scepticism after Doyle's briefing, and then, a Turkish agent turns up and also expresses scepticism."

"Bit *too much* of a coincidence, you mean? I very much doubt we're either bugged or that we've got a mole. He was probably just sounding you out. The Turks know the whole JBL thing's a setup, designed somehow to trick the evil West. They want to know whether we know."

"That's an interesting theory, but it's too early for them to be running those sorts of tests. If they think they've got a workable hustle, they'll stick with it, at least till it looks shaky. 'Sounding me out' at this stage would introduce the possibility of doubt in my mind where there had previously been certainty. From their point of view, it could only be counter-productive."

"I take your point. So we think he's genuine. What else did you talk about? Anything?"

"He offered me a cigarette. I said I didn't smoke."

"Good boy."

"I had a go at Erdoğan. He had a go at Boris Johnson. I had a *bit* of a go at Boris Johnson, but only to show how hard I am; that nothing scares me."

"Did he have a bit of a go at Erdoğan?"

"Nope."

"Wimp."

"Then he had a bit of a go at the Queen. But I could tell his heart wasn't in it."

Alec laughed. "She's ninety-four, for God's sake."

"And that was about it. The funny thing is, I feel bad about having a go at Boris Johnson now. I mean, I can see he's weak – he's got no control over his cabinet or his advisers - and I can see he's not a particularly good person. But I just feel... I don't know: if I met him in the pub, over a pint of Apoplectic Crow or something, we'd probably get on."

"A lot of people think the same thing," Alec replied breezily. "It's why he's in power. Homer Simpson syndrome. Your modern voter doesn't believe politics has much to do with real life, so he'll always prefer an entertainer to an expert. Someone to moan about for five years. Ideally, someone to look down on. It makes him feel better about himself. Which is why you'd like to join Johnno in the pub for a pint. Because everyone would."

"I'm not sure my sisters would."

"Yes, but they're left-wing fundamentalists, John. I mean, don't get me wrong, they're nice enough people, but they're the sort who think that if you hold the right opinions, that's sufficient to make you a good person; if you hold incorrect opinions, you're definitely bad. That's partly what's wrong with Britain: one big category mistake."

They'd reached Thames House. They mounted the steps to the front door, two at a time.

"Well, at least we've solved the problems of the nation and insulted my family," Mordred said.

"Hey, don't thank me. It's all in a day's work."

"Even so: thanks again."

"I *like* your sisters. I mean, I've only really met Hannah. And Julia, briefly. I don't know the other two at all. But I'm sure we could all have a pint together."

"I'll let them know, when they're next in town."

"Just one pint, though, that's all."

They put their face masks on for Shawna's benefit, although she was nowhere to be seen. Alec had been in such a hurry as he left that he had to both sign out and sign in, just to satisfy Colin. They walked upstairs to the first floor and removed their masks as they separated to go to their desks.

It occurred to Mordred that he hadn't heard back from Ruby Parker. Normally, she'd want a brief run-down on any unexpected encounter with a foreign agent. He knew better than to attempt a follow-up email. She was probably out at another meeting. He spent the next hour and five minutes writing a report, and sent it to her, copying the rest of the department in. Then he went to the canteen for a cup of tea and a Twix.

He was about to go and see Tariq when his phone rang. *Ruby Parker.*

"Thank you for your report," she said. "I would have called earlier, but I've just arrived back from a working lunch. I've already had the opportunity to speak to Tariq. You'll be pleased to know he's managed to put the CCTV together in a way that enabled him to locate Daisy Hallenbeck."

"Bloody hell, that was quick."

"He's getting better and better at it. We're reasonably sure she's actually hiding, in an officially vacant tenth-floor flat in

Tower Hamlets. *Why* she's hiding, we don't know. We won't be telling the Americans until we know roughly what's going on. Right now, we're keeping a discreet eye on her, to discover her next move, if any. We need you to speak to her, because she trusts you as she trusts no one else here."

"I'll get over there now. What's the address?"

"It's not as simple as that, John. From what I've just read in your report, even the Turks know you've got a special relationship with her."

"I'd hardly call it that."

"The Americans even more so. They may be expecting her to try and find you. Or vice-versa. My point is, they'll follow you. They've almost certainly got eyes on Thames House right now, and we can't rule out them knowing something about the supposedly secret exits. You could end up leading them straight to her."

"Okay, so what would you like me to do?"

"I'm going to give you her address, and I'd like you to make your way over there by as roundabout a route as possible. I want you to devise the first five miles of that route so that a selection of agents can meet you at specific points, all roughly disguised as you, and where you can do a quick change. Obviously, your hair's the main problem, so we need a variety of strategies to deal with that, whilst convincingly mimicking it in your imitators. Put a detailed plan together and come and see me in a few hours. It's much more important that we get this right than that we do it quickly. As I say, we've got Daisy Hallenbeck under close surveillance. Nothing's going to happen to her."

"Right ho."

"Take the photos of the Albert Bridge assassin. You never know, she might be able to give us a lead."

"Okay."

She hung up.

He saw himself dimly reflected in the window pane. *Your hair's the main problem*.

Fair enough.

Chapter 16: Chocolates and Smelly Clothes

Six different destinations along a five-mile journey, each a node at which he attempted to swap personal-space-places with an agent he'd never met before. 'Desmond' at the entrance to Hyde Park, by the Wellington Arch, 'Richard' at the first level down on the underground at Oxford Circus, 'Wayne' at the circumambulation of Russell Square, 'Manfred' at the Royal Courts of Justice, and 'Gerard' at Mansion House. He homed in on each new destination as if he was drunk: one step forward, two back, six to the side, fourteen back, northwest, southeast, until, on two occasions, even *he* didn't know precisely where he was. Times like this, you got a feel for how gargantuan London really was.

It took him three hours to reach the intersection of Cannon Street and Queen Victoria Street, where Gerard was. 9pm. He did a circuit of the building, accepted the wig Gerard handed him, slipped it on, and descended the steps to the Underground. He ran five hundred yards along the pedestrian tunnel towards Monument Station, then abruptly double-backed and exited via Bank, his original point of entry.

No, he wasn't being followed. He couldn't afford to relax, though. He flagged down a taxi and told the driver to make for Camberwell. The south side of the river: another dummy move. He'd have supper there, then get another taxi to Tower Hamlets.

He ate an omelette in a greasy spoon café called Regal Al's, then decided that it might help ease his introduction if he called on her with a gift. She had a tendency to start telling him off for no reason at all, and that might kick in even if he was actually rescuing her. He'd saved her life a few years ago in Park Lane, and she'd thanked him with an ear-bashing. He went into a 24-hour newsagent. The only suitable thing they had was a box of *Milk*

Tray. He paid and flagged a second taxi down. He was finally on his way.

He was on his own now. He didn't have his phone, because it just might be trackable. All these precautions. Mind you, the way Colonel Tuncel Alasya and his three henchmen had looked at her in the video footage of the funeral, she probably had good reasons to be concerned. What those reasons could be, well, hopefully, he was about to find out.

Of course, there was the possibility that she was dead. This part of Tower Hamlets was an odd place to flee to, unless you'd arranged a meeting with someone there. And while the CCTV had picked her up entering the building, and Tariq had a good idea of where, within it, she'd gone, no one could be sure she hadn't been killed on arrival. If she had, any time since Tariq's breakthrough would have been far too late to do anything about it. According to the footage, she'd been there for several days now. But – assuming she wasn't dead - how long was she planning on staying there? And why hadn't she come out? She couldn't lie low for ever.

It suddenly struck him that his 'assuming she wasn't dead' was very optimistic: she probably *was*. He couldn't see why the overwhelming likelihood had evaded him before. It probably hadn't evaded Ruby Parker. She hadn't broached the possibility with him, but that was likely because she considered it obvious. So all this wig-swapping and to-ing and fro-ing on the streets of Central London was really predicated on the worst kind of wishful thinking. It made very little sense on any other basis.

He wanted to tell the driver to hurry up.

Twenty minutes later, he stepped out onto a sickly yellow-lit street bounded on one side by low railings with a hard-pruned hedge behind, and on the other by a tarmac pavement and a wide grass verge. Recessed from the road at a distance of about twenty metres, Davidson Heights rose into the chocolate red sky like a huge monolith.

Mordred had the security code to the front gate. He crossed the grass at a brisk walk, entered the compound and ascended the stairs at a steady pace. He traversed a landing until he came to the door of the flat where Daisy was supposed to be holed up. Number 109.

No light on inside, as far as he could tell.

Before he knocked, a new possibility presented itself. She'd teamed up with some sort of bad guy criminal, who'd open the door with a gun or a knuckleduster. He'd step out onto the landing with a snarl and he'd also have reinforcements. He'd be two inches taller than Mordred and –

He knocked. "It's me. It's John. Is anyone home?"

His ears were on high alert, but he couldn't hear anything. Even so, He got the definite sense of someone or something inside. Sixth sense, maybe.

He knocked again. "John, your best Limey friend. Real ale drinking John. John from the Western Sahara."

There was an audible click from behind the door. It opened three centimetres with a chain across it. An eye suddenly appeared from the darkness within. Daisy Hallenbeck.

"Oh, my God," she said. She sounded simultaneously terrified and relieved.

"I've bought you a box of *Milk Tray*," he said, trying to pass it through the gap.

She snatched it and it disappeared. "Oh, my God. Thank you. Thank you."

"They were only four pounds fifteen. It was all I could get. And they didn't seem to sell wrapping paper, otherwise - "

"Oh, my God. Are you alone?"

"Yep. Can I come in?"

But she was already undoing the chain. Even from out here, he could see her hands shaking. The door opened and he stepped aside, then she closed it hurriedly behind him and replaced the chain. They were in complete darkness. There was a strong smell of body odour, emanating, he realised, from her.

112

"Are you alone in here?" he asked. "Are there any lights?"

"No. And there are no matches or candles. If you come into the living room, it's lighter with the curtains open. Mind you, I probably wouldn't even use the lights if there were any. Oh, bloody *hell,* John! I'm so *scared!* And starving! Help me get these chocolates open. *Bloody cellophane!* Sorry. Not very grateful. Oh my God. Oh my God. Thank you *so* much for coming! Bloody, *bloody CELLOPHANE!"*

"What's going on?"

"I'm trying to get into the *Milk Tray!* Oh mercy, I've done it! Oh my God! Thank *God!"*

In the one-eighth-light of what was probably the living room, he vaguely saw her sit down on what looked like a sofa and begin to scoop chocolates into her mouth like she was in a mini-pork pie eating contest. She was crying.

"We probably need to get out of here," he said.

"You *think?* I'm living like a bloody *animal!"*

"Right. I don't want to sound like I'm prying, but why are you here at all?"

She stifled a sob. "It's a long story. I'll tell you if you take me out and buy me some food. I'll tell you *everything.* You're British, after all. We're on the same side. It's not like I'd be betraying my country. And we're friends. Oh God, thank you *so much* for coming. I'll never forget this, John!"

"Where would you like to go? I mean, to eat?"

She laughed bitterly. "Oh, *I* don't know! The Ritz? The Savoy? Burger King? McDonald's? Pets at Home? A wheelie bin? I don't *care!"*

"When was the last time you ate? Go easy on those chocolates, by the way. You'll give yourself a stomach ache."

"Too late. They've all gone. They were delicious, by the way. What time is it? I mean, I know it's night, obviously."

"I can't see my watch. About eleven o'clock, I think."

"Will anywhere be open at this time?"

"It's London. There's always somewhere open."

"I don't want to go into Central London. Too scary. They'll find me. Oh my God, thank you *so much* for coming! I *have* washed, honestly. There's been water – cold water: freezing water - but the soap ran out. They only had a tiny *sliver*, would you believe it?"

"Well, I - "

"How did you get here?" she said. "Were you followed?"

"I saw you at the funeral. Ruby Parker found out today that you'd 'disappeared'. One of our tech guys put together a whole heap of CCTV. No one else has got that. Not the Turks nor - "

"You *know* about the Turks?"

"Something. I don't know why you're running away from them, but I'm pretty sure that's what's going on."

"Were you followed?" she said. "Have I asked that already?"

"Yep. And nope. Yes, you have asked that, and no, I wasn't followed. It'll speed things up if you just take my word for it."

"Okay. Good."

"Are you okay to leave?" he asked.

"My clothes smell. Not me. I've washed. Kind of. But I couldn't wash my clothes. Actually, *I* smell too. Oh God, I don't care if they *do* kill me! I can't go on living like this!"

"Good news. You don't have to. Shall we go?"

"Where to?"

"I'll flag a taxi down," he said. "I'm getting quite good at it. I know a place in Shoreditch."

"No driver will take me, smelling like this."

"Forget dining for a moment."

She laughed hollowly. "I can't."

"We probably need to get you to some sort of safe house. Although that might cause problems. An American agent in a British safe house without the Americans' knowledge. At the very least, it'd probably be bad for your career. Look, I've an idea. You said there's water here, right?"

"Cold water. Like ice. But no soap."

"What about washing up liquid?"

"I haven't checked that. I suppose I should have done, only you can't eat it."

"There must be something in the kitchen. You'll just have to grin and bear the cold water. You can get a wash and we'll share my clothes. We can improvise you a skirt out of my T-shirt. People of all ages wear anything nowadays. You can have my jacket – button it up - and you've already got shoes. Leave everything else behind. I'll get someone to clear it out tomorrow morning. No one will ever know you were here, including your bosses. And when you're washed and dressed, we'll go somewhere and eat, yes?"

He saw her nod in the darkness. "I'll need to take my bag. It's got my inhaler in. Apart from that, thank you, okay, done."

Chapter 17: American Fugitive

Two hours later, they sat in a small recess behind the takeaway section of an all-night noodle bar in Shoreditch. Imitation Chinese lanterns hung from the ceiling, and a wall hung with Song dynasty ink washes hid them from the street. Even before the coronavirus outbreak, this part of the shop was only busy before the clubs opened. For the last five months, it had been virtually sealed off. For a hefty surcharge, the manager agreed to re-open it, just for them. Daisy ate egg foo young, and, to keep her company, Mordred had a tofu chow mein. They drank orangeade. They'd have preferred water, but they wanted to add to the bill, to keep the owner sweet.

"I feel a bit ill now," Daisy said, when she'd finished. "I'd still like another, though. Do you think we can get another? How much money have you got? I can probably pay you back. God, I feel so much *better!* And yet, surprisingly miserable, when I remember what's going on. Still, *you're* here now. Everything will be okay! Famous last words. Maybe I shouldn't have another omelette. Can I have a bit of your tofu?"

"As much as you like. I'm pretty full."

"Okay, so maybe I should tell you what's going on."

"Whose flat was that?"

"Oh, that doesn't take much explaining. And it's got no links to anything. My mum and dad got it through Airbnb three years ago. For a variety of reasons, they decided they'd been scammed. No one actually lived there – at least, as far as we could see – and nothing much worked. And the neighbours played trance till four in the morning, every night. *Lots of bladdy unpleasantness*, as you Brits would say. Okay, I'm still working on that accent. Anyway, at the end of our stay, I secretly got the front door key copied. I told myself it'd be a good place to hide if I ever got into Jason Bourne-type trouble: you know, where everyone in the world's after you with a machete and a machine gun? Payback, because the owners had lumbered us with such a horrible dive. I'm glad I did, in most ways. Although obviously, staying there this time was a total nightmare, and I'd have had to break cover sooner or later. Or had a break*down*, ho, ho. I definitely won't have another omelette, thank you. I probably shouldn't have eaten the rice. Or the omelette."

"Or the chocolates."

"The chocolates were lovely. Seriously, the best meal I've ever had."

"Let's go back to what's going on, shall we?"

"Right. Well, it's a long story. For the last few months, since before we last met, actually, I've been working in *document authentication*. It's more interesting than it sounds, and I've got quite good at it. I've got a background in History, you see. When I was at NYU, I actually considered being a History teacher for a while, but then I realised I hate children. What DA involves is looking at physical documents – pieces of printer or letter paper, usually – and trying to work out whether they are what they say they are. There's an awful lot of 'fake news' floating about at the moment - A's trying to frame B, who's trying to frame C - so we're kept busy. It's to do with things like handwriting analysis, house style, consistency with known instances of the genuine article, vocabulary repetitions, word frequency, hyphenation, even things like size and weight of the paper and the chemical composition of the ink. That may sound dull, but it can spark or avert an international crisis."

"So what specifically happened?"

"Okay, so you know Turkey's part of NATO, yes? But it's like the *bad boy* of NATO. Its ships have clashed with the French. It's continually trespassing in Greek territorial waters. It's decided it's entitled to a naval garrison in Misrata, and an air force base in Al-Watiya, so it's chosen to intervene unilaterally in Libya, against NATO policy. It's attacked the Kurds in Syria. It went ahead and bought Russia's S-400 air defence missiles, which apparently won't work in conjunction with NATO weapons systems."

"I'd heard."

"Anyway, there I was, quietly enjoying life in London, when a call came through: would I like to go to the US substation in Istanbul and do a little serious work? Oh boy, you bet I would! It sounded great for my CV. But when I arrived, there were mounds of documents, and no one else to work with, and it was totally overwhelming. Obviously, someone else – some other document authenticator – was going to re-examine everything I looked at after me, but I never met them, and I was exclusively responsible for the initial sift. Just one person because, you see, it was all so *highly sensitive*.

"And what was the gist of all these documents, I hear you ask? It was that Turkey was clandestinely passing NATO secrets to the Russians in return for military hardware."

"I take it they were genuine?"

She laughed. "No, that's just it! They *weren't* genuine – any of them! They were very, very good fakes, but they were fakes all the same, every last one of them."

It took him a moment to re-adjust. Not what Hulusi Erkekli had told him in Victoria Tower Gardens, but leave that for a moment. "All's well that ends well," he said.

"Er, no. I got the impression that some of my colleagues weren't best pleased with that particular verdict. Which, to be fair, I understood. Erdoğan's a thug and a nut job: it would be just like him to do something slimy. But the truth's the truth. Sometimes it's not totally what you want to hear, but you've got to go with it."

"So what happened?"

"Well, I found it very difficult to make friends after that. I mean, where I worked. The other Americans. Anyway, one day I was out and about in the Grand Bazaar, when out of the blue, a man tried to kill me with a knife. I just dodged in time, and one of the shopkeepers stopped him having a second go. I was pretty shaken, I can tell you. I reported it to base immediately. I'm not sure whether the police were ever told. But do you know what everyone's reaction was? It was: *never mind being so selfish, what it shows is that those documents must be genuine, so you must have missed something, otherwise why would the Turks want you dead?* Sympathy? *Nada.* And then more documents arrived; same gist, same quality: all fakes. And then, another attempt to murder me. Same sequel. Minimal sympathy, more *maybe you'll get it right next time*, another big pile of documents."

"Bloody hell."

"I was pretty scared by now, and I wanted to go home, but I was scared of that too. What I thought must have happened was that the guys in Istanbul - maybe CIA guys everywhere, actually, but I doubt it: I can't imagine Uncle Frank being involved in anything like this – had chosen me because I was new to the job. I'd cave in to a little bit of pressure, and I'd rubber-stamp the documents as genuine. At that point, the documents would go up another level, for a second examination. But of course, the guys at the second level are probably subconsciously steered by the fact that someone's already passed judgement. If they're hard-pressed for time, they maybe cut corners and stick with the original result. And guess who has to carry the can if it later comes out that there's been a major error? That's right: the first in the chain. Me."

"So what did you do?"

"Played along with my bosses. Played more scared than I was. Told them I was going to really get to the bottom of it, said I realised I must have been missing *something*, otherwise why were the Turks trying to kill me, etcetera. I kept an eye on them. Now, you've heard of computer hacking? Stupid question, but it's part of the story, so bear with me. Everyone's on the lookout for computer hacking all the time, right? All that *change your password every six weeks, have a different password for every activity, make it a combination of numbers, letters and Egyptian hieroglyphs.* But have you ever heard of document hacking? No, of course you haven't. But let's say someone comes in to your office with a big pile of papers to be examined and, when your back's turned, she filches a few documents from your outbox, then, later, she puts them back when you're not looking, and you never even knew they'd gone, and if you did, the hacker would just be like, 'they're in with the stuff you gave me, I don't know how the hell that happened', and, occasionally, just to cover her tracks, she'd actually *own up* to a document she'd filched, one you never even knew was missing, and probably wouldn't ever have missed, just to establish a precedent, i.e., to show you how easy it was for your documents to get mixed up in her great big shit-pile?"

"Er... yes?"

"So I got to know a fair bit about what was going on in that place. They were all so paranoid about computer hacking, they'd completely forgotten about the real world. Don't get me wrong: once a month or so, we'd have a big document-shredding fest. Every CIA station does, obviously. But even that worked in my favour, because it gave everyone a false sense of security. And sometimes – even better – as a relative junior, and a pretty useless one at that, I'd be assigned the menial task of feeding the shredder for three hours. Not that I needed it. I knew enough about what was going on in that place. Occasionally, I'd pull an all-nighter – *I really must get to the bottom of these documents: I'm sure their genuineness is in there somewhere: I just need an extended run at them* – and I'd access virtually all physical areas. Oh, I'm so glad I never became a History teacher. I'm a born crook."

"And I take it you discovered something?"

"Would I be in this mess if I hadn't? You saw me in that flat! I was on the verge of eating the upholstery!"

"Fair enough."

"About eight months before I arrived in Istanbul, this British woman called Angela Barnes had left Syria or Iraq – one or the other - to go to Britain. She'd joined the YPG about five years earlier, and she'd recently been involved in an ambush on a Russian military installation, where she'd discovered a cache of documents of considerable importance. She wanted to go home, and she saw the documents as her ticket to some sort of plea-bargain in Britain – this was the theory, in the papers I read – and so she'd set off on foot, with the blessing of her Kurdish comrades, for London. No one knew exactly where she was, but they were quietly looking for her. I got the distinct impression that some people in Istanbul – I mean, my people: CIA operatives – saw her as a deadly threat. Anyway, about three weeks ago, we got a highly excitable wire from the UK to say she'd been seen *by someone* in London. I don't know who saw her, or who sent the communication. The whole thing was very evasive, but it looked as if someone in this country – I mean, in Britain - had been anxiously seeking sign of her for some time. Now I don't know why, but I got the impression that her case and mine were related. Maybe that's not such a leap in the dark. I mean, how likely is it that there would be *two* shady things going on in exactly the same place? To cut a long story short, I decided I'd had enough of being despised and almost murdered, and I went AWOL. I got a taxi to Istanbul Airport and came to Britain. And then Angela was killed, someone tried to murder me again, and I went into hiding. Then you arrived with a box of *Milk Tray*, gave me a T-shirt to make into a skirt, and took me out for an egg foo young, like the knight in shining armour you are."

"But you don't know who sent the message? I mean, the one saying Angela had been spotted in Britain?"

"Someone in the UK is all I can say. Someone very cautious, because they didn't give a name."

"And why were you at Angela's funeral?"

"Two reasons. Firstly, to see if there was anyone else around who might know what Angela had wanted to say, or where she'd put the documents. Maybe her parents, for example. Someone like you, maybe. I just wanted a brief talk, that's all. Secondly, I thought all the psychos were in Istanbul. I never dreamed they'd follow me here. The reason I left in such a hurry was because I recognised the man from the Grand Bazaar."

"Why didn't you go to your Uncle Frank?"

"He's on holiday in the Everglades. And obviously, I thought someone would try to track my phone. I've had it switched off since arriving in Heathrow. It's probably well out of charge now."

"I haven't got a phone either. And for the same reason. I was worried about being tracked. There are a lot of people out looking for you." He took the four photos of the Albert Bridge assassin from his pocket, and passed them across the table. "Do you recognise this guy?"

"Oh, my God."

"I take it that's a yes."

She looked accusingly at him. "Who is he?"

"I don't know. He recently killed a lawyer on Albert Bridge in circumstances linked to the case. How do *you* know him?"

"It's – it's the guy who attacked me in Istanbul, and I'm more or less certain it's the same guy who came for me after the funeral. Are these CCTV stills? They look like them. If I could see him move, I'd be surer. But I'm ninety per cent sure even without that."

He put the photos back in his pocket. "So on the plus side, we now know we're dealing with some sort of international assassin."

"What's our next move?"

"I ask the proprietor if he's got a phone on the premises. He says no. I say, you must have. We strike a deal. We call Ruby Parker. We get you to safety."

"And we need to call the US embassy. I'm not keen on being protected by HM Government. It looks like I don't trust my own. Remember my career, John."

"What if your US friends are actually in cahoots with your assassins?"

"Even if they are, they can't all be. The Istanbul crowd might be. The London crowd? I doubt it. And they're not going to put me through to the Istanbul crowd."

"Don't take this the wrong way, but why didn't you go direct to the US embassy when you ran away from Angela's funeral?"

"Because it was my word against CIA Istanbul. No one would have believed me about the Angela Barnes thing, and I'd gone AWOL, so I was already in deep shit. CIA Istanbul would simply have said I was a dud, and it'd look like I was making stuff up to get back at them."

"Whereas now?"

Her expression changed.

"What's changed?" he said.

"Oh, shit, yes, I see. Nothing at all." She finished her orangeade and slumped in her chair. "I suppose I thought that, because you'd come for me, that changed everything. I don't even know how. I must have been delirious. It just seemed like a happy ending, that's all. But I can appreciate now: you're right, I'm back to where I started."

"Yesterday, I met a Turkish intelligence officer in Central London. He advised me to stay away from you on the grounds that you were forging documents."

She sat up again. *"What? But that's the opposite of what I'm doing!"*

"He said the CIA had assigned you the task of fabricating documents designed to prove that Turkey's selling NATO secrets to Russia, and that you're putting a fake dossier together."

Her expression changed a second time. This time, her features seemed to drop a millimetre and she wiped her eyes. "The slimy *bastard!* That's so *unfair!*"

He smiled. "Wish you'd been a History teacher now?"

"It's not *funny!*" She leaned forward. "You – *you* don't believe that, do you?"

"Absolutely not. If you'd been lying in any shape or form, I'd have twigged way back. I've got a talent for that, and it rarely lets me down. But the interesting thing is, he believed it too."

"I literally don't know what that means. I've reached the end of my sanity and energy now. You'll have to spell it out. Incidentally, did he tell you they'd tried to kill me?"

"He said you'd 'been targeted many times in Istanbul, but always managed to escape.'"

"Well, at least he's not denying it. Good for him. I love him now. What a lovely man. The piece of *shit*."

"I think you'll have to stop saying 'shit', or you'll get us thrown out. Noodle bar owners sometimes interpret a loud 'shit' as a symptom of drunken aggression."

She scoffed. "'Drunken aggression'? Oh, for a neat *Jack Daniels!*" She trembled again, and her eyes shot two more tears. "Tell me what we're going to do, John. I feel wretched saying that. I'm a feminist. I don't like relying on men. But I'm a tired, let down, traumatised feminist who's on the run from a bunch of assassins – not even *one*, but a whole *bunch* – and I don't actually *care* what Femina, the god of difficult women, thinks of me any more. I just want to be told what to do. Preferably by a woman, but you're all I've got, and you're *like* a woman, a bit."

"Okay, you just sit and listen, and I'll try not to mansplain."

"I can live with that." She rested her head on her fist.

"CIA Istanbul wants you to interpret a set of documents in such a way as to show that Turkey's behaving badly. The Turkish secret service genuinely thinks you're forging those documents, and it's trying to kill you in order to stop you. CIA Istanbul also has an interest in getting you killed, because then you'd have to be replaced, and they could pick some other newbie, someone who'd hopefully be a bit more biddable. The question is, who's producing the non-incriminating documents in such quantities? Well, it can't be the Turkish. It would have to be someone inside CIA Istanbul. Almost certainly not the whole substation, but someone with influence. Possibly the boss him or herself. And the other likelihood is that the same person is 'leaking' information to the Turks to the effect that you're actually forging the documents. So there we are. Case solved. Who's your boss in Istanbul?"

He suddenly realised she'd fallen asleep. He gently moved her arm. She awoke with a jump and looked about herself confusedly.

"Welcome to heaven," he said.

"What were you saying?"

"Who's your boss in Istanbul?"

"Nedrick. Nedrick Sullivan."

"There's our man then."

She sat up, "What? Nedrick? He's *here?*"

"If only. What we need to do now is find a phone and get out of here."

Chapter 18: Mike Declares His Love

Mordred had brought a large billfold with him, and although some shops were wary of taking cash these days - it could be a virus-carrier - no one in *Ultimate Noodlation* seemed fussy. The meal itself came to thirty pounds; the drinks, ten; exclusive use of the seating area, sixty; service charge, ten; borrow of a phone, five.

Pricey, on some interpretations – although probably not for Shoreditch - but the phone alone was worth it. Daisy went to the Ladies' to douse her face in cold water. Mordred stayed outside in the empty corridor, so he could talk confidentially and keep her safe. Another successful mission.

"I'm in *Ultimate Noodlation* in Shoreditch," he told Ruby Parker. "I've got Daisy with me, but we probably need to get out of here as soon as possible."

"I'll send Kevin right away. Have you managed to get anything out of her?"

"She told me everything in exchange for an egg foo young and a glass of orangeade. She's actually been *debunking* forged documents that implicate Turkey in wrongdoing, not creating them. Someone in the CIA in Istanbul is trying to frame her."

"Are you absolutely sure she's telling the truth? I'm not saying I accept Hulusi Erkekli's version, but she does specialise in document verification, and that would be a good qualification for project-managing a counterfeiting operation."

"I'm as sure as I can be. She exhibited none of the symptoms of duplicity. And skill in document authentication would no more qualify her to forge credible documents than being able to spot a genuine da Vinci would make her capable of painting a convincing *Mona Lisa*. No, at the very least, she'd have to be part of a team. But the Turks think she's the sole culprit. Someone's framed her, then 'hung her out to dry', as they probably say in Nine Elms."

"Is she planning on contacting the US embassy tonight?"

"I believe so. I wasn't sure whether it was a good idea, but she pointed out that the bad apples are in Istanbul, not London. With us behind her, she might be able to eject them."

"I don't see how," she said. "Unless she's got hard evidence."

He took a deep breath. "I know. It's still her word against theirs. But if she stays with us - "

"Things have moved on since this afternoon, John. I mean, in terms of those thirty-five supposed 'JBL' fighters. Just as we anticipated, they've been taken to a detention centre in central Turkey. Some officials in Washington and London are already discussing the possibility of a joint rescue operation."

Mordred hooted. "That would be madness. It would be almost an open declaration of war."

"On the other hand, a lot of people have reached a similar conclusion to the one you did, in your meeting in H7 this morning: the whole thing is a plot by Turkey to show that the West is aligned with a group of Erdoğan would-be assassins. '*They* know that *we* know that *they* know,' as Walter Doyle put it. In short, it's a deliberate attempt to humiliate us, possibly Moscow-driven. It can't be allowed to stand. That's the feeling, not necessarily shared by me, you understand."

"I take it Doyle's one of the principal hawks?"

"He's ambitious. Sabre-rattling can be a way to get on in politics, but if this gets rubber-stamped, and it fails, it's his head on the chopping block. I'm sure he knows that too."

"It sounds suspiciously like a trap to me. The Turks may be trying to lure us in. I don't know why."

"I agree. But these things have their own momentum sometimes. People in high places get enraged for specious reasons, then they do something rash, then they lose their jobs, and the rest of us end up having to pay. Listen, John, I've an idea, but it involves you and Daisy Hallenbeck taking a serious risk."

"I'd be up for that. She's probably still in danger anyway, so she's probably got nothing to lose. I'm sure I can persuade her."

"Get her to call the US embassy. Get her to tell them where she is, and that she's alone. She can make whatever excuse she likes for having left her overseas post, the less plausible the better. My feeling is that the 'bad apple' in Istanbul won't still be sitting in Turkey. He or she will have come after her. He – let's assume it is a 'he' for a moment – will have found out that she boarded a plane to Heathrow and he'll probably be panicking. She knows people in London. I mean, American officials, who'll probably be sympathetic to her complaints. And she might well have discovered something incriminating. What else could explain her sudden desertion? The bad apple will be here in London."

Mordred chuckled. "I didn't tell you earlier, but the main reason she left Turkey was to see if she could rendezvous with Angela Barnes. According to Daisy, Angela left Syria eight months ago."

"Eight months ago? My God."

"Mind you, we guessed something of the sort in H7, yesterday."

"So from our 'bad apple's' point of view, Daisy Hallenbeck could have actually *met* Angela. In that case, he probably *is* panicking. If we can flush him or her out, we might be able to get to the bottom of the whole thing."

"You're assuming it's all connected."

"It's as good a working hypothesis as any. Okay, listen, John, I want you to get off the phone now. Get Daisy to call the US embassy. Then leave. I'll send some of our team over to monitor the noodle bar. If a brigade of Turkish agents turns up, we've got our evidence. It's no longer Daisy's word against theirs."

"Do you think Bad Apple will fall for it?"

"He might not want to risk leaving it to the Turkish. After all, they haven't been very effective killers so far. He might turn up to get her himself. In which case, you need to be prepared."

"Could you brief Kevin? We may need a fast getaway."

"Consider it done. Alec will bring your phone. Keep in touch."

She hung up. Mordred knocked on the toilet door. "Daisy, you can come out now!"

She emerged yawning. "Pass me the phone," she said. "We might as well get it over with."

"Put it on speaker," Mordred told her.

She dialled and put the phone in front of her. An automated voice told her that the US embassy was working with unavoidable restrictions in these difficult times, so her call might take a while, but an operator would be with her as soon as possible. It gave her a number of options. There wasn't one for 'left CIA job in Istanbul, been in hiding ever since', so she pressed 6, 'Other'. After five minutes of Gershwin, punctuated at forty-second intervals with, 'One of our operators will be with you very soon, thank you for holding', the dialling tone broke in. "Hello, United States of America, British embassy in London," a woman's voice said, "How can I help you today?"

"Hi, my name's Daisy Hallenbeck. I'm a CIA agent, and until last week, I was based in Istanbul. I left my post without giving any notice, and I came to England. I don't have any money, so I need someone to come and pick me up."

Pause.

"I'm sorry," the voice said, "would you mind repeating that? Let's begin with your name. What was your name?"

"Daisy Hallenbeck. H-A-L-L-E-N-B-E-C-K. Hallenbeck."

There was a long pause then a click, then a male voice. "Daisy, where the hell are you? This is Mike here. We've been worried sick about you. Let me come and get you. Where are you?"

"Ultimate Noodlation in Shoreditch."

"In London, right? Sorry, I'm not big on London. You're in London."

"I'm in London, yes."

"Ultimate *what?*"

"Noodlation. It's a noodle bar."

"What the hell are you doing in a noodle bar?"

"I was hungry. I've just had a Chinese omelette."

"Oh, good for you," he said sardonically. "*Good for you*. Are you alone?"

"Yes, I am. Why do you ask?"

"Because London's not safe at this time of night, you must know that. The whole place is full of thugs with knives. And the Turks have already made several attempts to kill you, *so you say*."

"What do you *mean*, 'so you say'? What does that mean?"

"Forget it, I - "

"You're saying you don't *believe* me now? You believed me at the *time!*"

"We *said* we did. Look, Daisy, I really don't want to talk about this now. You're in a very vulnerable position, and you're an incredibly attractive woman, on her own in a goddamn awful city, and - "

"Oh, *bullshit*. What are you saying that for?"

"You're in trouble. Just stay there. I'm coming to get you. I, er, love you."

"*What?*"

He hung up. She looked at the phone like it had just burned her hand.

On the other side of the city, in a small bedsit with a cooker, a toilet and bathroom, and whose sole window gave a view of a brick wall close enough to reach out and touch, Pavel Nikolayevich Alikhanov sat in his underwear looking at his bare feet. Daisy's miraculous escape at the Englishwoman's funeral had left him feeling alone and depressed. Alone, because he couldn't help wondering whether his backers might abandon him, and depressed because he'd heard nothing from them. Both things were connected, of course. The possibility that they might recruit a new killer wasn't lost on him. In which case, what would be more natural than for that whoever-it-was to begin by killing the old killer? They knew where he was, after all. He was at their mercy.

A freak piece of bad luck, that's all it had been. He'd almost been within touching distance of her! That fat guy must have left the funeral early. And – another piece of bad luck – he'd looked exactly like the kind of blubber pot into whom you could thrust a knife to the hilt without hitting a vital organ. Weight meant a lot of different things in that sort of encounter, nearly all of them bad. So he'd been right to run away.

Yet he couldn't help fantasising about *what if*. What if he'd somehow managed to overpower her, and bring her back here? She tried to run, she tripped and knocked her head on something, he flagged down a taxi, *my girlfriend's fainted, I need to get her home,* and then up here, tied to the bed maybe, or just to a chair, no torture or anything, just him undressing, not even undressing her, just so he could later say she knew him. He'd have to kill her, obviously, but he'd make it quick. He –

His phone rang. He jumped and picked it up. *The American*.

"I've located Daisy Hallenbeck," came the heavy foreign accent. "You need to go over to the American embassy and wait outside. I've organised a team of shooters to take care of her, but I'm not completely confident they'll turn up. We may need you there as backup, with your trusty knife. If we do require your services, I'll make sure you get away afterwards. Then we'll get you out of the country. Into France."

"Okay."

"You need to sound *enthusiastic!* This is your big chance to recover your reputation after that fiasco at the funeral!"

"Yes."

'The American' hung up.

Pavel Nikolayevich got dressed slowly, and put his knife in his bag. Weirdly, now that he'd been given a concrete second chance, he wasn't even sure he *wanted* to kill Daisy any more.

Perhaps that was just a new-born suspicion that fate preferred her to him, that no matter how good his preparations,

131

she'd get away again. More: that she'd *always* get away, unto the end of time.

On one interpretation, she'd evaded him on three separate occasions now, because the twice-delivered instruction to merely 'frighten' her in Istanbul could have been fate intervening *in advance* to preserve her. Why *hadn't* he been told to kill her then? He didn't know. He didn't know anything at all about this rotten business. He just did what he was told.

Her skin probably felt nice. Really nice.

He wished he could kill the American!

"I take it you weren't aware of Mike's feelings," Mordred said, by way of testing the waters.

"Er, too *right* I wasn't! He hasn't *got* any feelings! This is *Mike Rasmussen* we're talking about. Forty-five years old, Deputy Section Leader, total jerk. He said that because he thinks he's God's gift to women, and I'll melt so completely I won't be able to move. It's a way of keeping me here, that's all. He doesn't *love* me. He doesn't even like me!"

"At the risk of disappointing you, his voice was fully consistent with that interpretation. But I think you're overlooking the more serious point."

"Which was?"

"The words, 'So you say.'"

Her face changed. "My God, yes. They're going to make out I'm delusional."

"It's a very good pretext for throwing you to the lions."

"You mean, the Turks? Yes, or putting me away on mental health grounds. We've got to get out of here."

"What will that achieve? It'll just make you look even more delusional. You ring up and apparently hand yourself in, then you disappear again. Where are you going to go?"

She sighed. "You're right." She shuddered. "Anything's better than going back where I was two hours ago."

A car pulled up outside. Kevin got out, a medium-sized man with a macho walk, a macho build and a macho face. He was dressed respectably in jeans and an Aran jumper, but he still looked like he should be wearing a stained vest and carrying a machine gun. "Ready to go, John?" he said.

"Hi, Kevin," John said. He came a bit closer so the guys at the counter wouldn't overhear him, which was difficult since one metre was the recommended maximum. "This is Daisy from the CIA; Daisy, this is Kevin, our best driver."

They exchanged awkward hellos, looking as if they didn't know why they'd been introduced.

"Listen, Kevin," Mordred went on, lowering his voice even more, "I need you to stay here for a while. We're not coming with you. A guy from the US embassy's coming to pick Daisy up, probably in about five minutes. I'm going to insist on accompanying her. He won't be very pleased, but he won't have any choice. If he gets violent, I'll try to bring the rumpus outside – I'm sure the owners will be happy to help – and I'd like you to intervene. I shouldn't think it'll come to that. Once we get in the car, I'd like you to follow him at a distance. If he takes us straight to the US embassy, keep a close watch as we go inside – ideally, do a bit of a recce - then you can go straight back to Thames House. If he looks like taking a detour, be prepared to intervene again. Things may get nasty."

Kevin nodded grimly. "I've got a peashooter in the glove compartment."

"Daisy, give Kevin your bag."

She did a double-take. "What? But it's got my phone in, and my inhaler, and the key to the, um, flat."

"I'll keep the inhaler in my pocket," John said. "Your phone's got a flat battery anyway, but if Mike gets hold of it, he might be able to use it to frame you. This way, we can use it to show that you never had any contact with the bad guys."

"But what if MI7 accesses my CIA contacts?"

"Kevin will give it to me when I get back to Thames House. I promise I won't hack it, or let it be hacked. The question is, who would you rather have it: me or Mike?"

"Okay, yes, you, every time." She took her inhaler out, passed it to him, and gave the bag to Kevin. "Thank you, Kevin."

"My pleasure, ma'am," he said. "I'll go and get in the car, John. I'll drive a short way down the road and park where I can't be seen. Don't worry, I won't let you down."

"Are you two intending to order anything else?" the manager, a short man with a close-cropped beard, asked, from behind the counter. He wiped his hands on his apron.

"Two more orangeades," Mordred said. "To drink in."

"This is a takeaway, really," the man said, only half-apologetically.

"We'll be gone in a minute," Mordred said. "We're just waiting for a friend to pick us up."

"Okay, it's just I thought I heard you just then … mention … *violence?* I mean, I may have misheard."

"It won't come to that," Mordred said. "We were just erring on the side of caution."

"Two orangeades coming up!" the man said.

An official-looking black car drew up leisurely outside. Here it came.

Two men in suits got out. He actually heard Daisy swallow. Both men outside buttoned up their jackets for no obvious reason and came in. One was muscular-looking with a wrestler's face and hairy hands: Mike, presumably, since he looked the right age. The other looked about thirty, slimmer, but exuding the same aura of conceit and physical fitness.

"Come on, Daisy," Mike said, beckoning her with his hand. "Let's go, girl."

"Stay here," Mordred told her.

"Who the hell are *you?*" the younger one said, although he only got the question in first by a millisecond.

"I'm the one who found her," Mordred said.

"Yeah, well she belongs to us," Mike said. "So hands off, wise guy."

"This is John," Daisy said, "and you can take a running jump if you think I'm going anywhere without him."

The two men looked at each other.

"John's your boyfriend, right?" the younger man said sarcastically. "Oh, baby, *that's* why you came to England! Look, Mike, she's in *lurve!*"

Mike grinned. "Come on then, John. Let's get you and Daisy in the car. Let's go, big man. Come on."

They were humouring him of course. Mike would get onto the back seat first, then Daisy would get in next to him, leaving John and No Name on the pavement. No Name would then throw a punch, or a kick, then hop in the car, and they'd accelerate away, laughing their fat heads off. Or John would get onto the back seat and Mike would have a gun. They probably both had guns. They didn't look like they were carrying them, though, so they were probably in the car. He might be able to get to one of them first.

He wished he'd had a conference with Daisy now. He should have foreseen all this, but he'd still been working on the assumption that Mike would at least pretend to be a nice guy.

"I'll drive," Mike announced. "You keep the happy couple company on the back seat, Steve."

When they reached the car, Steve opened the back door and got in. For some reason, he closed if after him. Mike pulled a gun on Mordred.

"I don't know whether you've ever seen one of these before, lover boy. We use them a lot where I come from. Now, I'm going to count - "

The back door of the car re-opened to the sound of a little yelp. The distraction was enough for Daisy to grab Mike's gun. Mordred completed the intended rout by forcing him to pull the trigger. The front window of *Ultimate Noodlation* exploded while Mike screamed for Steve to help.

135

But Steve wasn't coming. Kevin calmly got out of the opposite rear door and walked away with his head down. Mike didn't even register him, probably because, in the shop, an alarm sounded and men yelled.

Mordred had the gun now.

"Give it to me," Daisy said, trying to take it from him. "You're British."

"I know how a gun works," he said, "and I don't want you getting into trouble for shooting a US citizen."

"Oh, she's already in *trouble*," Mike said, "believe me, *she's already in trouble!* You're both in *almighty shit!*"

"Well, we'll see who's in trouble when I point out that you drew a gun on me," Mordred said.

Mike scoffed. "I've got diplomatic immunity, dumbass,"

Mordred fired the front tyre through. The car lurched. "So have I," he said. "Give me the car keys and your phone."

"What? Or you're going to shoot me?" Mike said.

The minute you prevaricated with a question like that, you lost authority. Mordred hit him hard in the face with the pistol. Mike's nose bled. He handed his phone and the keys over. Mordred flicked the boot open.

Mordred looked onto the back seat. As expected, Steve lay unconscious. "The police will be here in a moment," he said. "Mike, you're going to drive us to the US embassy."

"My pleasure," Mike said miserably. "As it happens, that's exactly where I want to go, so you won't find me even a bit uncooperative. Let's get this over with, shall we?"

"Daisy, you get Steve's phone and then Mike's going to put him in the boot."

"How did you even do that to Steve?" Mike said as his pulled his colleague out of the car and put him gently in the boot.

"It's a secret," Mordred said. He handed Mike the keys back. "Get in the driver's seat and drive."

He and Daisy installed themselves on the back seat. Mike started the car and pulled out slowly. With a flat tyre, they weren't going anywhere at speed.

Mordred gave Daisy the gun. "Mike, what's the pin for your phone?"

"Up yours, asshole. I ain't telling."

Daisy put a huge shard of glass against his neck. "You didn't know I'd picked this up, did you, Michael? Don't try and grab it, because it's very sharp, and I've got the gun anyway. I know you're trying to frame me, so I don't think I've got anything to lose, do you? I'll probably kill you if I have to. I might as well go to prison for something worth doing."

"Three-two-six-seven," Mike said.

Mordred called Ruby Parker. "John? Where are you?" she said.

"I'm with Daisy Hallenbeck on the back seat of a car belonging to the US embassy, with one CIA officer driving us at gunpoint to Nine Elms, and another unconscious in the boot."

She paused, possibly to access more air. "Well, thank God I'm about to retire. What happened?"

"Two CIA officers turned up. They tried to muscle me out of the way, and threatened me with a gun. I think they're looking to get Daisy killed. I need you to contact the officers who were on their way to meet me at the noodle bar. Tell them I think there are Turkish gunmen in hiding around Nine Elms. The plan, I think, was to take Daisy there and have her topped between leaving the car and entering the building. They'll be well hidden."

"I hope for all our sakes you know what you're doing," Ruby Parker said. She hung up.

Even from his position in the back of the car, Mordred sensed Mike's fury. He put his foot down, presumably on the grounds that if they arrived a bit sooner, the British officers wouldn't have time to flush out the gunmen.

"Slow down," Daisy told him.

He obeyed. He was doomed now, anyway. He couldn't take a detour. With a flat tyre, he'd find speeding difficult, and those Turkish agents would be waiting. And there was only one person who could have told them Daisy was coming. Or two, assuming Steve was also in on the plot.

Mike laughed. "Don't think you're going to get away with this. It may not look that way right now, but I've got you two over a barrel."

Mordred frowned. Mike sounded a little too confident, given his predicament. So what - ?

Then it hit him.

He switched Mike's phone off – trackable - and turned to Daisy. "Make him stop the car. We've got to get out."

Chapter 19: The Quality of Mike's Nightmares

Daisy turned an incredulous look on Mordred. "What do you *mean*, 'tell him to stop'? Did you just say, *tell him to stop?* Who? *Mike?*"

Mike braked. "Always happy to oblige a customer."

"I only hope your name's in those documents Angela Barnes handed over," Mordred told him. "If so, it's only a matter of time."

He nudged Daisy hard to stop her interjecting. Mike looked like someone had just pulled his plug out, draining his smugness. "I don't know what you're talking about," he said.

Mordred told Daisy to get out of the car and he exited from the same side. Police sirens, somewhere nearby. Kevin drew up next to them, apparently from nowhere. They scrambled onto the back seat, and the car pulled away at speed.

"Where to?" Kevin said. "It'll have to be somewhere nearby. The police are about thirty seconds behind us, max. Mind you, they'll probably stop for the other guy before they start thinking about chasing us. By which time, we'll be well gone."

"Charing Cross Station gives us lots of options," Mordred said. "It'll look like we're heading for a train. We can go round the corner there and hire a taxi."

"I'll get the boss to leave you a car in Stoke Newington," Kevin replied. "Look for the Rose and Crown. It'll be in Hawksley Road, just south of that. We'll leave the key on the front tyre. Do you need cash?"

"Thank you, I've enough cash," Mordred said. "Could I borrow your phone, please?"

"Glove compartment," Kevin said.

"Bloody *hell,* John!" Daisy burst out. "What's going *on?"*

"I'll tell you in a minute," he said. "Really, I promise. This isn't me taking charge and ignoring you. We're in an emergency situation."

He removed Kevin's phone from the glove compartment, keyed in the MI7 number – 1317 - and dialled. God help him, please let his memory be accurate.

"Hello?" a sleepy woman's voice said.

"Hello, Ree, John here. John Mordred. I'm still investigating Angela's death, but it's turned out to be much more complicated than I imagined. I'll cut to the chase: I'm in a bit of a pickle, and I'm in company with the woman in the photos I showed you the other day. She's in serious danger. By that, I mean some people want her dead. I wondered if she could come and stay at your house for a while? Obviously, she'd shield for seventy-two hours. But if you could leave The Jonson Herald as soon as possible, and look after her, that would be wonderful. I know it's a big ask, but if we're going to get to the bottom of this - "

"We're on our way now," Ree said. "We'll do whatever it takes to get justice for Angela; to the very ends of the Earth, you know that. There's a back door key under the third flowerpot along behind the shed. Let yourselves in and – I don't know, sit down on the armchairs. Tony, get up! … *Tony, wake up! … TONY!* Don't switch the lights on when you get in, in case the bad guys are still around. When Tony and I arrive, we'll close all the curtains and we'll show her round the house. What's ours is hers, as they say. We'll isolate her for a while and look after her for as long as it takes. I'll go now. We'll be on our way as soon as we've packed, John. Hurrah! Over and out." She hung up.

"When did you show her photos of me?" Daisy said. "And who is she? Add those to my earlier question about Mike."

Kevin's car was about to pull up in front of Charing Cross Station.

"John?" Daisy said. She waved her hand sarcastically in front of his eyes. "Are you still in there?"

They drew to a stop. Mordred handed Kevin Mike's phone. "Give that to Ruby Parker," he said. "The pin is three-two-six-seven, which may save time. It belongs to Mike Rasmussen, the CIA agent who was driving the car when you picked us up just then. Ask her to check the latest call. If the Americans find out Ruby Parker's got it, there'll be hell to pay, so officially, it's still in my keeping. Get her to clear the flat in Tower Hamlets where Daisy was staying. I may be going into hiding for a while. You didn't hear the phone conversation I just had with Ree, by the way. And there's nothing going on between Daisy and I."

"None of my business," Kevin said, "but I believe you anyhow. Good luck."

They got out. Kevin drove away. John and Daisy went into the railway station, left by one of the minor exits and entered a CCTV black spot, opposite a pub and a nail bar.

"We can talk here," John said.

"What's going on?" she asked for the third time.

"I'm sure I'm correct in thinking there are Turkish agents hiding outside the US embassy, waiting to kill you somehow, but, although Mike almost certainly tipped them off, their presence won't necessarily incriminate him. He knows that. He can say they've probably been there since you went missing in Istanbul. And unfortunately, that would make sense. You come to London, a city you used to work in: it'd be natural for your enemies to assume you'd make straight for your former contacts, especially if you've a tale to tell. But if Mike didn't put the gunmen up to it – and his superiors will probably have to give him the benefit of the doubt – then we've got nothing on him. He was a bit brutal when he came to pick you up, but that's not a sackable offence, especially since it looks like he's already been taught a lesson in that regard. No, I think *you'll* be the one in trouble for threatening to shoot him and holding a shard of glass to his jugular. And then of course, no one would ever believe you were being set up for something in Istanbul."

"So what now? I can't keep running for ever!"

"The great thing is, we're both in trouble now, so at least we've got each other's company. And I've got a great record of getting out of trouble, once I'm in it."

"Oh, hooray. Let's hope you're right."

"And the other thing is, Mike's now much more certain than he was that you came to London to meet Angela. If what I told him works like I hope it will, he'll also think you were successful in rendezvousing with her and that she gave you something. He's unlikely to be acting alone: he didn't strike me as intelligent enough to churn out a whole raft of well-crafted forgeries. Until now, he and his collaborators weren't sure you and Angela were connected. Now they'll probably panic, especially since they still don't have the foggiest idea where you've been for the last however many days, or how I found you. They'll throw everything but the kitchen sink at you, and in the process, they'll almost certainly make a mistake. But there's also a bonus prize. If Mike *does* swallow the bait, there's a chance he may not go back to the US embassy. Nor Istanbul. He might conclude it's only a matter of time before he's exposed, and he'll cut and run, thus saving us the effort of incriminating him."

"If I was Mike, I'd probably take the risk of acting normal. Even if there *were* documents, and even if they *did* name him, they might not be backed by proof."

"Whether he takes that approach depends on how vivid his imagination is. And the quality of his nightmares."

"In all other respects though, I'm essentially back to square one."

"Let's get a taxi. Wait till you meet Ree and Tony before you give in to despair."

"'Ree and Tony' being?"

"Angela's parents. And we recovered some video footage of you outside the funeral. I'm pretty sure your assassin's not in there, though. Anyway, I showed your picture to them, because I wanted to know why you were there. They had no idea who you were. Hopefully, that's all about to change for the better."

They found the back door key where Ree said it was and let themselves into the house. They closed the door quietly. When their eyes adjusted to the deeper darkness, Mordred showed Daisy into the living room. They sat on the armchairs.

"How safe are we here?" she asked.

"Totally, I think. It's the one place no one will think of looking for you. For us to have come here, I'd have to have established some personal connection with the owners. Mr and Mrs Barnes would have to like and trust me, and vice-versa. There's no reason in the world for anyone to think that's the case. At one point, the Turks probably thought Angela deposited her secret documents here, but they were caught in the act of burglary and the burglars have gone home to Turkey. There's been no second attempt, nor even a sniff of one. And now, of course, after my little chat with Mike, the supposed 'documents' can't be here, because you've got them. And there's even *less* reason to think *you've* got a connection to Ree and Tony. As far as anyone with a hostile interest knows, Ree and Tony belong entirely to the past in this affair: so completely that their existence has probably been forgotten."

"How much are we going to tell them?"

"We're going to tell them everything. They've got to know we're not using them, and that's the only way. So you tell them everything you told me in that noodle bar, and I'll add as much context as they ask for. We'll omit names, but that's all."

"What about Mike? Are we going to tell them about him?"

"Obviously we won't call him Mike. We'll call him Donald or something."

She sighed. "I'm going to make a great impression, looking like this. A T-shirt for a skirt, totally naked except for that and your jacket."

"They won't realise, unless they've got X-ray specs. Besides, everyone's naked underneath their clothes."

"Some people more obviously than others."

"We'll just have to tell them the truth about that too. They already know you're a spy."

"I see what you mean, yes. So it's not too much of a leap to imagine I've been living in absolute squalor for the last five days, to the point where my real clothes were so filthy, I had to throw them away."

"Try to look on the bright side."

She sniffed, and lifted both hands then let them flop. "I'm sorry. You've been fantastic. You've literally saved my life at least twice in the past six hours. I don't know why God made me such a miserable cow. I'm just tired, I think. I *am* sorry, John, I swear. I can never make this up - "

They heard the front door open and they both froze. Mordred held his hands up in the gloom. *Stay calm.* If it was someone hostile, they had the advantage of surprise, and there were two of them. But for reasons he'd just enunciated, he didn't think it would be.

A person it took him a split second to recognise as Tony strode across the room and closed the curtains to the garden. By the doorway, Ree switched the lights on and beamed. Daisy and John stood up.

John made the introductions. Ree made them sit down, and she and Tony sat side by side on the sofa. John explained about Daisy's mode of dress, then he and Daisy explained everything else, up to, and including Mike, whom John called Donald.

"I'll put the kettle on," Tony said, when the tale was complete.

"I'll have to be getting away before sunrise," Mordred said. "If the bad guys are going to slip up, they need someone to run after."

Ree shivered. "I've done a lot of thinking on the way over here, and I've done a bit of arranging. Tomorrow, my sister's coming to stay with us. Sandra, she's called. She's got a daughter called Madeleine – 'Maddie' – who's about your age, Daisy. As luck would have it, Maddie's stranded in Australia now, thanks to coronavirus. Can't get home. Not that it matters too much. Keith and Audrey are looking after her, who you don't need to know about. They're simply 'putting another shrimp on the barbie' so to speak, a third shrimp, just for Maddie. In return for which, she's helping them out in their shop: *Coulson's General Goods*, in case you're ever in the Melbourne suburbs. The north eastern part, I think. Anyway, as from tomorrow, Daisy, you're going to *become* Maddie. I'll show you her photos – 'selfies', as they're called - later, tomorrow, when you get up. Short blonde hair, Alice band usually, and Sandra's bringing her clothes. I'll get you some hair dye. No one will *ever* suspect. You can stay here as long as you like. You must be shattered. I'll show you your bedroom in a minute. You can sleep in as long as you like, and tomorrow morning, it'll be bacon and eggs, or waffles with maple syrup, or cereal, or whatever you like. And given the horrible time you've been having recently, I won't expect you to get out of bed before midday. And if anyone comes to get you, they'll have to *cross my dead body!*"

Daisy and Ree burst into tears at precisely the same moment. Despite coronavirus, and the fact that neither of them were masked, they hugged.

Tony and John were big, strong men, so they simply wiped their eyes and feigned insouciance.

Chapter 20: Pavel Nikolayevich's Demands

After receiving The American's instruction to wait outside the US embassy for another chance to kill Daisy Hallenbeck, Pavel Nikolayevich Alikhanov dressed lethargically and looked at himself in the mirror. With those dark rings under his eyes, he looked ill. And he wasn't putting on any weight, despite all the junk food. And – who knows? - maybe she wasn't the sort of girl who liked men with beards. Not that it would matter. Either the Turks would get her, in which case, she'd probably die without ever knowing he existed, or he'd have to do another stab-and-run job. In which case, she probably wouldn't even see his beard, let alone have chance to assess its sex appeal.

He unlocked the dressing table drawer and took out the carving knife he'd bought in Wandsworth.

Then he put it back, and lay down again on the bed.

No, he wouldn't go to the US embassy. What was the point? If the Turks didn't get her, he'd have no chance. It wasn't like the place wouldn't be heavily guarded. There would be a metal fence to keep terrorists out, and the car would drive inside the gates, and only then would she get out. If you were in a tree with a rifle, you might stand a chance. A man with a six-inch kitchen knife was completely without prospects.

The fact that The American apparently hadn't realised that showed he must be desperate.

Which suggested something had happened to him.

No point trying to work out what, though. He, Pavel Nikolayevich, was completely outside the loop, with no way of getting in. 'The American', 'The Brit' and 'The Turk' could be any three people at all, or even a variety of people; which was precisely the point, from their point of view. If Pavel Nikolayevich was caught, he'd know nothing. He couldn't offer information in exchange for a reduction in sentence. He posed no threat to them. They could use him like a landless serf and get away with it.

On the other hand, cooperating with them was his only way of getting to Daisy. In a city of nine million people, the chances of them meeting in a bar, or in some idiotic mix-up like in a romantic comedy, were negligible.

But he couldn't go to the US embassy. 'The American' was clearly in trouble, and he was casting about for solutions, one of which was, *I'll send the Russian on a suicide mission*.

Not today, thank you, sir.

He laughed as it suddenly struck him that this was Daisy Hallenbeck's *fourth* escape from death at his hands. Already – and he hadn't even left the room!

Or was it? Say she was killed by a Turkish marksman, then his own non-interference might count as him *indirectly* killing her; a kind of passive murder, committed simply in virtue of knowing what must now happen, and doing nothing to stop it.

In which case, since she was clearly his nemesis, the Turks *wouldn't* murder her. Something would intervene. Either none of them would turn up, or they'd all be captured, or they'd fire and miss, or their rifles would mysteriously jam, or the end of the world would come while they were taking aim, or the laws of physics –

He put his shoes on and picked a twenty pound note from his billfold. He went downstairs into the street. It was warm, and there was a scent of linden mixed with cooking oil and vehicle emissions. He walked three hundred yards to the off licence and bought a bottle of vodka. He went back to his bedsit, lay on the bed and drank from the bottle until he'd finished about a quarter. He tried not to think about Daisy.

But it was difficult to avoid thinking about the overall project of which she was a part. He was here to be of service in something very important to the Russian government. He might not know what it was, but he could see that he was failing. Yes, he'd killed the Englishwoman, then that guy on the bridge, but he seemed to have reached an impasse. And tonight would count against him in the same way the funeral had.

What did that mean? Obviously, they'd be displeased. And when those sorts of people weren't happy, they looked for someone to take it out on. In this case, him. And that would be fair, because it would be his fault.

Partly. He couldn't have foreseen that blubber pot after the funeral. He took another pull of vodka, then another.

Then he had such an overwhelming flash of insight that he almost dropped the bottle.

He was taking completely the wrong approach! In Russia, he'd been hugely successful. Look at the way his instructors in Moscow had talked reverently about his achievements. Abroad, he was much less capable, as experience had already shown.

But that was entirely consistent with his best interests! More, it was the *only thing* that could protect his best interests!

What he wanted: to live in his little log cabin in the woods in Krasnoyarsk, and occasionally venture out for a killing. That was the life!

What he didn't want: to be an international assassin.

But what would happen if he was successful over here? Say if he'd killed Daisy at the funeral, and then every other inconvenient person they sent him after? Obviously, when he got back to Russia, they'd praise him to the skies, but then they'd find other similar jobs for him. Success in Britain would be taken as evidence of achieved expertise. He'd be locked for ever into the hell of being a globe-trotting executioner.

But what would happen if, instead of being a roaring success, he failed miserably? Well, yes, they'd be displeased, but they couldn't be too hard on him, because they obviously needed him. If a horse is good at pulling carts, but it fails spectacularly on the racecourse, you don't have it destroyed, unless you're stupid. You revert to making it do what it's good at: pulling carts. Especially if good carthorses are hard to come by.

The great thing was, he was already doing a good job of failing in Britain. All he had to do now was continue in the same vein.

Thank God, after all, for that blubber pot.

Also, in retrospect, not turning up at the US embassy had been a good decision. Now all he had to do was make similar choices.

He could begin by ringing one of them back. He'd been told not to do that, so it would be evidence of a new type of incompetence: the inability to properly process instructions. 'The American', 'The Brit' or 'The Turk', which should it be?

'The American'? What would he say? *I understand you're in trouble* would be going a little too far, although it might have surprising results. If he helped an American traitor, he might get a medal.

Precisely what he *didn't* want. A serial killer with a medal, what a joke! *Oh, they knew he was a serial killer all right,* his fans would say, *that's partly why they decorated him.*

He had to think hard. Too much feigned incompetence might backfire. It could look as if his talents had gone bad generally. Everyone and everything had its shelf-life, and he might end up looking like he'd reached the end of his.

No, this wasn't going to be easy. Get it wrong, and the consequences could be severe.

He took another swig of vodka. He was falling asleep now. This place was probably freezing in the winter – there was no heating that he could see: no fire, no radiators – but it was pleasantly warm now, even at night.

For some reason, he couldn't think about *the precise level of incompetence* any more. It was as if, instead of his ruminations so far on the subject being the beginning of a more precise analysis, they'd actually been the end, and all he was ever going to think about it had already been exhausted. Instead, he kept returning to something he'd inserted along the way: the mental observation that *everyone and everything had its shelf-life.*

It began with him involuntarily recalling the two prostitutes he'd killed in London, in homage to Jack the Ripper. 'Kayleigh' and 'Phoebe', they'd been called. He'd killed them while they were entirely in role, so in a sense, he'd killed two people he'd never met. It was easy to feel relatively apathetic about it.

So different from his first killing, just four years ago, on that beautiful snowy evening in Labytnangi. He'd thought an awful lot about the victim, Anna Klimova, since. She hadn't been particularly attractive, nothing like Daisy, a bit rodent-ish really. But her killing had been an achievement: all the tons of excrement and urine she'd have expelled over the course of her life, that was all gone, and the planet was still benefitting every day. She'd have been twenty-seven now, had she lived.

And yet… increasingly, over the last year, he'd had the sense that maybe he was on the verge of a different, more disturbing view of her killing: a conviction that it was actually … *wrong*.

Everyone and everything had its shelf-life. He remembered when he'd first been released from prison, that interview with the three army officers in the middle of nowhere. How the middle one had said he was normal; he might even *grow out of* his 'criminal tendencies'.

He'd had more nightmares about that one little suggestion than he'd had about all the murders, the sobs and shrieks at the trial, the narrow escapes from capture, and the gang rapes he'd undergone in prison, put together. What if he was to wake up one morning 'cured'? Presumably, the horror would be indescribable!

Yet it was coming. He could sense its very, very gradual arrival. Kayleigh and Phoebe, my God, a small part of him even regretted *them!*

Didn't it? No, because while it was plausible that a strange new perspective was beginning to take hold of him, it was so far away on the horizon, it was barely a dot. It might not be remorse of any kind. It might not even be coming in his direction. No point fearing the worst.

He laughed out loud in the silence. The worst *was* coming, though! It *was!*

Perhaps – perhaps it was time for him to exit this world, before it struck. That way, he'd be the finished article. All those murders, described in prose worthy of Turgenev – because once he was gone, no one could stop his journal getting out – ending with the most spectacular murder of them all: the murder in which he and Daisy Hallenbeck were united forever. Even on the basis of what he'd already written, his future readers would have sufficient information to know that she'd been the love of his tragically short life.

He didn't care about overplaying the incompetence card now. Let them think what they liked. He picked up the phone. 'The American' was in trouble, so he'd be no use. 'The Brit' was probably best.

He pressed 'dial' and sat back, hardly expecting anything. But then there was a click. Someone – yes, it was 'The Brit' – said something in English.

"Hello, this is your assassin," Pavel Nikolayevich said, trying not to sound drunk.

Long pause. "My *God!* I thought you'd been told not to contact me!"

"I need something. I need equipment."

"Give – give me a few moments, yes, all right. I'll call you back."

Pavel Nikolayevich put the phone on the bed and drank more vodka. He had a vague feeling he was already in trouble. When the phone rang again, it would be someone at the Russian embassy with a 'how dare you'.

It started ringing. He looked at the screen. *The Brit*, but he shouldn't get his hopes up: there were many ways of assuming someone's identity on a phone.

He picked up in no particular hurry. "Hello, this is your assassin."

"What do you want?"

"I'm going to kill Daisy Hallenbeck."

"I *know* that," the fraught voice said. "What do you want me to *do* about it?"

"I'm only going to be able to succeed if I get very close to her and I put my own life at risk. I've just done a quick calculation of the probabilities, and I'm not even sure I'll come out of it alive. But she might. Then you've got no one left to do your killing."

"Just get to the point. I haven't time for a long exposition."

"I want a small machine gun – one I can conceal inside my jacket – and a hand-grenade."

"Oh, wow. Well, those two things are going to be very difficult to come by in this country."

"In that case, I can't do it."

"Can't you get them from the Russian embassy?"

"They'll say no. They've given me to you. They don't want any further involvement."

Sigh. "Okay. They'll probably have to be specially imported."

"That's fine. When can you give me them?"

"I'll have to call you back. In a few days."

"Don't leave it too long, my friend."

'The Brit' hung up.

On the other side of London, twelve MI7 agents began to close a wide circle around the US embassy. Annabel was the first to make a sighting: a man in a tree in one of the streets that led to the entrance. She pointed her gun at him and ordered him to come down in Turkish. He panicked and tried to turn his rifle in her direction, but it was too cumbersome, and he was too slow, and she shot his leg. He crashed ignominiously to the ground, and she called an ambulance.

But he must have given a signal. At almost the same moment, another man bolted from a thicket on the adjacent road. Phyllis tore after him, but Alec was hiding up front, and appeared at the last minute, tripping him so successfully that he seemed to fly a full two metres before crash-landing and skidding along the ground. He wasn't quite ambulance-worthy, so they cuffed him and hauled him to his feet in readiness for the van.

Edna flushed a third man from cover. He made an impressive run, but possessed nothing like her powers of acceleration, and she felled him in mid-flight with a rugby-tackle. His powers of recovery and fightback seemed to evaporate, and she handcuffed him with unexpected ease.

During the next ten minutes, nothing happened. A van arrived, courtesy of MI7 security, to take the captives away. Then it became clear nothing more was going to happen. The others – if there had been any – had all slipped the net.

But three was an excellent haul, and better than anyone had expected.

The US embassy was beginning to stir.

Chapter 21: The Poached Egg

Mordred had three hours' sleep on the sofa at the Barneses house, and set off to walk to Thames House at 5am. Since it was a four-hour journey, he expected to arrive roughly as everyone else was coming in for the working day. He couldn't take a taxi, because he had no idea who might be where: between dodgy Turks, dodgy Americans and very probably dodgy Brits, there were lots of possibilities for mishaps and, although the odds were heavily in his favour, he didn't want to leave anything to chance. He stayed away from the main thoroughfares as much as possible, and crossed parks, fields, estates and bands of wasteland. He stopped in Duckett's Green, at seven, for a mug of tea and a poached egg, and reached Hackney an hour later, where he boarded a bus: he was far enough from the Barneses now to make further precautions unnecessary. He arrived in Central London at 8.43.

"Has Phyllis arrived yet?" he asked Colin, as he signed in.

"Where's your mask, John?" Colin said.

"Sorry." He took it from his pocket and put it on.

"Welcome back," said Alec from behind. John swivelled to reply just in time to see Phyllis, several yards to Alec's rear, come in through the front door. She beamed and picked up her pace slightly to meet him.

"We understood from Kevin that you'd gone on the run with La Hal," Alec said.

"You're only half-dressed," Phyllis remarked.

"Unfortunately, Daisy's clothes were irretrievable," he told her. "They're probably being incinerated by men and women in hazmat suits."

Colin passed John a phone, plus a disposable wipe. "A call for you, John."

Ruby Parker. "Come down to my office," she said. "And bring Phyllis. We've a lot to talk about. The day's only just beginning, but you're already 'wanted for questioning', as they say, in Nine Elms."

"Coming straight down," he replied, as chirpily as he could, which wasn't very chirpily.

"Good luck," Alec said. He scribbled his name in the book and left to go upstairs.

Phyllis and John got in the lift.

She dipped in her bag and passed him his phone. "I recharged it for you."

He kissed her. "Thanks."

"Nice to see you again," she said. "I watched Ricky Gervais on Netflix last night, plus an episode of *Schitt's Creek*, and went to bed early. Had breakfast yet?"

"Not here. I walked from Enfield. I had a poached egg on the way."

"Er, how did that work?"

No time to explain. The doors swished open. They walked in step to Ruby Parker's office, knocked, entered and sat down.

"Welcome back," Ruby Parker said tartly. "So what exactly happened, John? I've heard something from Kevin already, and of course, we're cleaning that flat up, but I've only got a very vague story and I'd really like to hear the full and detailed version from the horse's mouth."

"And I'd be happy to oblige," he said. He recounted the events of the previous night, up till his departure from the Barneses house at 5am that morning. He told her about Daisy's recognition of the Albert Bridge assassin, her insistence that she was being framed, Mike's aggressive behaviour, his suggestion to Mike that Daisy and Angela had met up in London, Ree's plan to dye Daisy's hair and pass her off as a woman called Maddie.

"And you've actually *walked* all the way from Enfield?" Ruby Parker said incredulously, when he'd finished.

"To be fair," Phyllis said, "he did have a poached egg on the way."

Ruby Parker reached into her desk and took out a brown B5 envelope which, going by its size and shape and timely appearance, probably contained Mike's phone.

"Mr Rasmussen's phone," she said. "You probably won't be surprised to discover that it contains nothing suspicious. If the owner's in contact with anyone of a dubious nature, he must be using a different phone. Which, of course, is what we'd expect. You gave him no reason to think you'd passed it to us to examine. As far as anyone in the American embassy knows, you've still got it, and it's never been out of your possession." She upended the envelope, allowing the phone to slide gently onto her desk. "I'd like to keep it that way."

Mordred picked it up and put it in his pocket. "Switched off, I hope."

"And all evidence of it having been tampered with, erased," she said. "Now, I've got some good news and some bad news. First," she went on, without any indication that he had a choice, "the good news. Mike Rasmussen's gone missing. That probably indicates that he's got something to hide - your claim that Daisy and Angela met may have been the deciding factor - and he knows it's only a matter of time before he's exposed. The bad news is that the Americans think you're a kidnapper. At first, they thought you'd kidnapped Mike, especially given that Steve was discovered hammering on the inside of the boot of a car that belongs to them."

"I can see how they might have got that impression," Mordred said. "And technically, it is correct, although I only kidnapped him for a period of ten minutes."

"You held him at gunpoint," Phyllis said.

John laughed. "He started it!" He turned back to Ruby Parker. "You said, 'at first'."

"We were able to show them CCTV of the two of you going in opposite directions," Phyllis said. "And although you did nevertheless sequester his phone, the fact that he hasn't been back to report it means they don't know you've got it."

"Obviously, he might still decide to come back," Phyllis said. "He may be acting on the assumption that Daisy and Angela met, but the more time passes, the more likely it will look that you were bluffing. Otherwise, she'd simply provide the smoking gun that Angela supposedly conferred."

"I'd give it three days at the outside," Ruby Parker said. "After that, she'll look much less dangerous. But given her experiences in Istanbul, they'd be stupid to reduce her threat-level to zero. Ever. She has a story to tell, and who knows what new evidence might yet transpire with which her testimony – unverifiable as it might seem right now - will fit like a hand in a glove?"

"Anyway, what's the *bad* news?" John asked.

"The Americans do still think you kidnapped Daisy Hallenbeck," Ruby Parker said. "And that's going to be a little harder for you to deny."

"They don't just think you kidnapped her *last night*," Phyllis said. "They think you're responsible for her entire disappearance in this country. Everything since the funeral."

"From their point of view," Ruby Parker said, "it makes perfect sense. Otherwise, how would you have known where to find her? I mean, in Tower Hamlets?"

"Well, that should be easily solvable," John said.

Ruby Parker frowned. "Telling them we located her using CCTV would simply raise the question, why didn't we tell them where she was? She's not our agent, and America's one of our biggest allies. At the very least, it would look discourteous."

"I disagree," John said. "It's *we've found her on camera, now you go and deal with her* that looks discourteous. *We found her, we picked her up, we gave her an egg foo young, a glass of orangeade and a jet wash*: now that's courteous. After all, she is a friend of mine. A bit. It's not like she wouldn't want to see a friendly face, not if she's in trouble. We're just being kind."

"I take your point," Ruby Parker said. "I'm not sure the Americans will see it that way."

"I'd be perfectly happy to let her tell them the truth in person," John went on, "if not for the fact that some people in her own organisation are apparently conspiring to kill her. Let *me* ask a question now. Last night, in Mike's car, I was acting on the assumption that Mike had organised a bunch of snipers to bring Daisy down as soon as she got out of the car at Nine Elms. What happened?"

"You were totally correct," Phyllis said. "And we caught three of them. They're not talking, obviously, but that doesn't matter, because their very presence outside the US embassy, not to mention the fact that they were armed, speaks for itself. And of, course, given the present situation in Turkey, the British government's unwilling to authorise their release."

John scoffed. "And I suppose Mike had nothing to do with them? They just happened to be there at the precise time he was bringing her to where they were perched?"

"In principle," Phyllis said, "there's no reason to believe they hadn't been there since the funeral, in one form or another."

"Someone would surely have seen them in daylight," John said. "A sniper in a tree can't be that common a sight in Nine Elms."

"It's unlikely they'd present the same degree of unsubtlety at every point in the day," Ruby Parker said. "In any case, I'd be very surprised indeed if the Americans are ruling out the possibility that Mike had something to do with them. He's gone missing, and obviously that counts against him. The official explanation is that he's 'concussed', incidentally. My feeling is that the jury's still out on him, and we're not getting a lot of information on this side of the fence, because they're sufficiently annoyed with us to deem it none of our business."

"You mentioned 'the current situation in Turkey'," John said. "I haven't seen the news for a good ten hours."

"Things have escalated," Phyllis said. "The 'hostages' – that's what we're calling them now - "

"Because that's what they are," Ruby Parker put in.

" – Are being moved, we believe, to an area forty miles north of the southern coast," Phyllis continued, "near Anamur. Anamur's quite close to Cyprus, where there's a Royal Air Force base, which also hosts the ninth reconnaissance wing of the US Air Force. The Americans are still mooting the possibility of a joint rescue operation, Entebbe-style. Operation Entebbe, as you probably know, was a successful military operation by the Israeli Defence Force to rescue about a hundred hostages from Uganda. The only problem is, Turkey's not Uganda. It's a strong, aggressive, well-armed nation."

"However," Ruby Parker said, "the current President of the United States doesn't like being taunted. And the Turks are definitely taunting him. And as Commander-in-Chief, he's directly in charge of the United States military."

"The military itself may be more sceptical of him nowadays," Phyllis said, "given the recent Russian bounties-for-the-Taliban scandal, but it still has to obey him. And he might just think he can pull it off."

"Which could lead to a war," Ruby Parker said. "Or, at the very least, a major re-alignment of global allegiances, with the West as the likely loser."

"I take it we're still on the bad news bit," John said.

"The only thing I think we can do now," Ruby Parker said, "is cast the net as widely as possible for Mike Rasmussen. I'm going to call the Home Office in a moment, get the Met involved, and possibly other regional police forces. We've already got an All Ports Warning out on him. But, of course, he's a spy, and he'll be skilled at avoiding detection."

"Not if he's 'concussed'," Phyllis said. "Although the longer he remains at large, the more implausible that explanation becomes."

"Which will be scant consolation if there's a war," Ruby Parker said.

"I've a better idea," John said. "Firstly, I'll ring Hulusi Erkekli. If the killer on Albert Bridge was waiting for Daniel

Batsford, and those two Turkish agents didn't know anything about him, then someone may have – must have, I think – given them orders to shepherd him off the Tube and into position. That wouldn't be difficult for two agents used to working closely together."

"They'd have to have known they were doing it," Phyllis said.

"They wouldn't necessarily know they were setting him up to be murdered," John said. "And we didn't ask them whether they were told to manoeuvre him into position, because we didn't get a chance. Erkekli might be able to ask them, and more importantly, he might be able to find out who gave that order. If so, we've got a major lead."

Ruby Parker nodded. "It's definitely worth a try."

"Secondly, I need to go to the American embassy and bring them up to speed. I mean, right away. The longer we wait, the more suspicious they'll be, and the more difficult we'll find it to work together. Which we need to be doing right now if we're going to stop this thing."

Ruby Parker smiled thinly. "The first thing they'll want to know is, where's Daisy Hallenbeck? And as I understand the situation, you're not prepared to tell them."

"Nevertheless, I agree with John," Phyllis said. "If the Americans want to use RAF Akrotiri to launch a rescue mission inside Turkey, they can't afford to be too unforgiving. They might well meet us halfway."

"To be fair, though," John said, "they probably don't need our base in Cyprus. They've got their own bases in the region, and I wouldn't be surprised if there's an aircraft carrier nearby."

"The latter don't host transport planes," Ruby Parker said, "and yes they do have their own bases, but proximity's a determining factor in a situation like this. You're right, Phyllis."

"Sorted, then," John said.

"It's not a good idea for you to go to the US embassy on your own," Ruby Parker said. "You'll need to look like you've got the backing of your superiors."

John grinned. "So we're *all* going?"

"Why do any of us have to go?" Phyllis said. "We've got information they want, we've got John, we've got RAF Akrotiri. If we ask for an audience, or if we go over there, it'll look like we're coming cap in hand. It'll look like an act of penance, though we've nothing to feel contrite about. The better thing to do, surely, would be to give them a call, let them know the state of play, and tell them that if they've any further questions, they're welcome to come here. They'll almost certainly accept if they think there's a chance of talking to John. Then they'll be on our turf. They won't like it, obviously, but I don't much like the idea of us traipsing over there."

"That's a very good idea," Ruby Parker said. "John?"

"Ditto," he said. "I'll call Erkekli. You call Uncle Sam. Like you said, Phyll, they'll almost certainly want to come over, and probably within the hour."

"You'd better get some new clothes," Phyllis said.

"I'll second that," Ruby Parker said. "Go and see Amber. Tell her what it's for, and wear exactly what she gives you. Ideally, once you've briefed her, stop speaking."

"Understood," Mordred said.

Chapter 22: Nedrick to the Rescue

As soon as he got out of his meeting with his wife and Ruby Parker, Mordred took the lift to the top floor and looked for an empty seminar room. He had no idea why they were all called 'seminar rooms'. Pretentious, really. It wasn't like Thames House was a university. The University of Millbank, how depressing. And wasn't he a snob?

He loved Phyllis. In a TV drama, she'd have gone, *So you spent the night with that nasty little CIA whore, did you? No, don't deny it! Do you really expect me to believe your sorry tale about eating a poached egg on a four-hour trek from Enfield? What kind of fool do you think I am? You're obviously tired of me already! Well, I've got news, moron: it's mutual!*

And he'd have carried on protesting, because there really *wasn't* anything in it, but by then she'd have sown the seeds of self-doubt in his mind, and she'd throw him out, and he'd get drunk alone in a bar somewhere, and he'd go round to Daisy's and he'd say, *My wife's thrown me out, I need somewhere to crash,* and she'd be all, *Come in, ducky, take a shower,* and then they'd only half-accidentally have voracious sex, and -

Luckily, Phyllis was a grown-up.

He wouldn't say anything to her either: concerning how he'd noticed, halfway through their meeting a moment ago, that both she and Ruby Parker were inexplicably glowing.

Which – the peculiar *shade* of glow, more than anything - meant she'd got the job. She'd presumably been told not to tell him, which was also fine. When she did, he'd pretend not to have seen it coming, and he'd be delighted.

He wondered whether she'd been told he was transferring to Black. Not that it was a done deal. But Stella had been right about that. She'd need a blank canvas, one – professionally speaking - without him.

God, they were the perfect couple: totally boring.

Boring had massive advantages. It meant you could read books, watch films, do origami, keep a budgie, grow rhubarb, and have some kind of inner life. Most people didn't want a car-crash for a life, even when it included martial arts skills and rampant sex with someone who thought looking like a model was sufficient compensation for vacuity. He was no different.

H23, yep that was free. He went in, closed the door and scrolled down for the number he'd put in his contacts. *EK.* He pressed 'call'.

"Who is this?" a Turkish voice asked, fairly aggressively.

"John Mordred. We met in Victoria Tower Gardens for a brief chat."

Pause, then: "I *told* you you'd call me!"

"Well done, and apologies if I sounded sceptical."

"You realise I've got your number now? You must be desperate."

He chuckled. "From what I've heard, a war's on the cards, so I suppose everyone is."

He explained his theory about the two Turkish agents herding Batsford towards Albert Bridge and how whoever ordered them to do that must be linked to the assassin. "It's the only thing that makes sense," he concluded. "You and I are both certain the two agents knew nothing about the killing. But *someone* put the killer precisely there, knowing Batsford would turn up. Who else could it have been?"

"Coincidence?"

"Unlikely."

"That's the definition of coincidence," Erkekli said. "Okay, I'll definitely look into it. And could you do something for us? Three of our officers were captured the other night, trying to stop the 'war' you just mentioned. Maybe let your boss know why we're so desperate to eliminate Daisy Hallenbeck? You're British. You've got nothing to gain by colluding with the Americans. You're allowing Washington to play you."

"Even so: murder?"

"Kill one to save thousands. As you say, war may be 'on the cards'."

"I met with Daisy Hallenbeck last night, and she's doing the opposite of what you think. She's been continually presented with masses of documents whose purport is that Ankara's passing NATO secrets to Russia. She's consistently debunked them. And that's got her into trouble, because it apparently wasn't why she was hired. So whoever's been trying to use her has disseminated an allegation that she's the enemy of the Turkish people, in the hope that you'll do their dirty work for them. She's fairly junior, a woman in a still mainly male environment, and therefore easy to frame."

"And you believe her?"

"Absolutely. I've known her for several years now. Not intimately, but well enough to know that she's guided chiefly by her conscience, not by her perceived need to 'get on', or by money."

"I hope you're right. Do you know anything about the 'peace talks'?"

"What peace talks?" John asked.

"That's what *I* just said."

"No, seriously."

"Yesterday, the so-called JBL members were being moved to a spot near Anamur. It's on Turkey's southern coast. And then, about 1am last night, the whole operation stopped. The speculation, here in the Turkish secret service, is that diplomatic negotiations have begun. Maybe some sort of return-deal with the US and the EU and Britain. You give us our three agents back, we give you ... well, I don't know. Something."

"I haven't heard anything about negotiations. Neither has my boss."

Erkekli laughed. "Your 'boss'? Ruby Parker, you mean. Come on, John. We all know who she is. She's almost as famous as you are. In any case, it's been nine hours now. A long time to stop an operation like this unless you've got a very good reason."

"Well, let's hope there *are* talks. But let's work on the assumption that there aren't. I'm sorry, I'm going to have to get off the line now. The Americans are due to arrive in a few minutes. I've got to get changed and explain why I've kidnapped their agent and why I won't tell them where she is."

"I assume you're talking about Daisy Hallenbeck."

"The same. Someone in the CIA's trying to frame her. And if they succeed in doing that, they'll almost certainly succeed in framing Turkey too."

"Good luck, John."

"Thanks." He hung up.

My God, a hiatus. Maybe they'd pressed pause on the assumption that Daisy and Angela had met, and things were about to go pear-shaped. That seemed incredible, but...

Time to go and see Amber.

Amber Goodings, a stout fifty-two-year-old with frizzy yellow hair and red-framed glasses who ran MI7's wardrobe department, had already selected a brown suit and tie for him when he arrived, plus a shirt, socks and shoes.

"Ms Parker told me not to ask if you like them," she said. "You're just to put them on. I've got all your measurements on file, so they should be a perfect fit. However, before that, you need to get some food inside you, then get cleaned up. More orders, I'm just relaying them. Go to the canteen, then to Western Basement One for a shower and a shave. I'll have the suit sent down to you. Call me when you're dressed and I'll come and check the fit. See you later."

"Okay, yes, bye," he said. Sometimes, this place made him feel like a baby. *Ms Parker told me not to ask if you like them,* sheesh. As if she hadn't told him not to quibble already.

Perhaps he wasn't going to miss her after all. Mind you, Phyllis probably wouldn't be much different.

He'd assumed the Americans would be here by now. Shower, shave, more breakfast and a quick change would take at least thirty minutes. Their absence added plausibility to Erkekli's claim that negotiations had begun. Assuming any such talks were successful, the USAF wouldn't need RAF Akrotiri, and although the CIA might make a show of righteous indignation about him 'kidnapping' Daisy, firstly, they trusted him, so they already knew she was safe, secondly, she was a minor employee not a big shot, so they could afford to do without her for as long as it took for the threat to her life to subside, and for her to emerge from hiding at the Barneses. Which she'd have to eventually, anyway. In the meantime, they could 'break his balls', as they said in the USA.

So MI7 was back on the defensive. And that probably meant Nine Elms wasn't coming here, rather Thames House was going there.

No wonder Ruby Parker was so insistent about the shave, the shower, the suit and the breakfast.

He'd have another poached egg on toast. He'd enjoyed the last one.

He was mopping up a smear of yolk with his last corner of toast when his phone rang. *Ruby Parker.*

"The Americans are here, John," she said. "Room H8, five minutes."

The way she said it, it sounded like, 'The Dodge City Gang are back in town, Sheriff.'

Which wasn't a comparison that occurred to you when you weren't slightly delirious. He'd had hardly any sleep in the last twenty-four hours, and it was beginning to tell. He bought an iced coffee to supplement the American Cream Soda he'd just finished, timed himself drinking it, and set off for Amber with four minutes to go.

When he arrived at H8, he briefly considered knocking, but then thought better of it. He was the main attraction after all, and requesting permission to enter might make him look timid. Anyway, he looked magnificent in his new brown suit and matching brogues, they'd have to forgive him instantly. He took the door handle and opened the door widely and confidently.

Three men sat opposite Ruby Parker at a distance. They looked like they'd just been to a funeral – that's how seriously they took the 'kidnapping' – but also like they had concealed weapons and couldn't wait to use them. They all stood up.

Mordred had been to the US embassy twice before, but, from what he could tell, the authorities there kept changing the personnel. He didn't recognise this selection. One looked to be in his fifties, sandy hair, thick-framed spectacles and a prickly hairstyle; the other two were about ten years younger, blond haired, sporty types, distinguished mainly by the fact that one was slightly taller and had long sideburns, like a 1970s biker, and the other had a beard.

"Where's our agent?" the fifty-something one said aggressively.

"Please sit down, gentlemen," Ruby Parker said, in a tone that suggested she really didn't expect them to, and cared even less. Obviously, words had already been exchanged.

"You heard Nedrick!" the bearded one said. *"Where's our agent?"*

"Well, it's like this," Mordred said, "He held me at gunpoint outside a noodle bar in Shoreditch, but I managed to overpower him, then he chauffeured me - "

"Oh, *funny,*" the beard interrupted. "Listen to him. He thinks he's *funny.*"

"I am funny," Mordred said.

"John," Ruby Parker put in.

"I'll ask you one more time," the fifty-something said. *"Where's our agent?"*

Ruby Parker stood up and turned to face them. "We're supposed to be on the same side. If you intend to carry on like this, you might as well leave the building now. In that case, I'll call

Langley direct, and ask for someone a little less confrontational. Sit down."

They exchanged looks and complied.

"As I've already explained," Ruby Parker said, "and as you well know, we've taken your agent to a secure location for her own safety. Last night, had John not intervened, and our agents hadn't acted, she'd have been killed outside your embassy. You've got us to thank that she's still alive, so please don't get on your high horses. It won't work."

They looked at each other again, more calmly this time.

"Okay," the bearded one said, "but where is she?"

"What makes you think those Turkish agents had been outside your embassy since her disappearance?" Mordred said.

The fifty-something frowned. "What makes you think they weren't?"

"If they were for any length of time," Mordred said, "then you've got serious security issues. Fine, that's your problem. But then what makes you think you're capable of foiling a plot against Daisy's life?"

The sideburns guy scowled. "What makes you think it's any of your damn - "

"The truth is," Mordred went on, "that Mike Rasmussen set those guys to kill Daisy, and that's why he's gone AWOL. Because – unlike you, apparently - he knows that the *they'd been in place for days* defence just isn't credible. The US embassy in London must be one of the most heavily defended diplomatic outposts in the world, and you're sitting there, trying to persuade me that every single one of its security operatives could be oblivious, for days, to the presence of six or seven gunmen, poised to fire, within a hundred yards of its perimeter?"

Ruby Parker nodded. "I think John's point is that, unless you're willing to concede the possibility of Mike Rasmussen's complicity – and you've already given ample evidence that you're not – then we have to assume that you're on his side, not hers. And since she has evidence that may relate to the killing of a

British citizen, and since we're not holding her under duress, we're not morally obliged to give her up."

Mordred offered the fifty-something man a handshake. "Nedrick Sullivan, I assume."

The man didn't accept. "How – er, how did you know that?"

"Because Daisy told me about you. You and Mike were a team."

His mouth fell open slightly. "If you're implying, like I think you are, that - "

"But don't worry, because Mike didn't do anything wrong." He reached into his pocket, took out Mike's phone and slapped it into Nedrick's hand. "Although this phone may beg to differ. To be honest, I thought I might enter this room to find you being uncooperative, and I was right. Not that it matters. I don't need to talk to you, Nedrick, or you, Sideburns, or you, Vaguely Fashionable Beard. I've got much bigger friends in the CIA. Daisy's Uncle Frank, for a start. He's on holiday in the Everglades at the moment, but I imagine he'd be very interested to hear his niece almost got killed. I'm willing to bet you haven't told him. Or I could talk to Abe Mandelstrom. Or Marshall Hicks: he's a nice guy, and always happy to give the benefit of the doubt."

Nedrick smiled bitterly. "All you really need to know is that Daisy Hallenbeck's a Grade One fantasist. Good luck 'looking after' her, because that's a project that's likely to end with her in a mental institution." He turned to his co-workers. "I think we're done here, guys."

He led the way to the door and Beard left it open as he exited.

"Well, that was far more interesting than I expected," Ruby Parker said wearily.

He chortled. "I suppose this is the part where you tell me I'm an idiot, and why do I keep going overboard?"

"Usually, yes. But on this occasion, I'm glad you stood up to them. You told them a few home truths neither I nor they saw coming. And you're right: I'll be very surprised if the CIA's top men knew how Sullivan was intending to play it. I expect he'll have questions to answer when he gets back to base. You've actually strengthened our hand."

Mordred scoffed. "Unless he lies through his teeth."

"It's not as if they can't check the facts with us. And you've got an international reputation for probity, and the Americans have long first-hand experience of your truthfulness and reliability, going back at least to Libya. Whereas my guess is that, if Sullivan's like that with us, he's like that generally. That's usually how it works. They'll know who to believe."

"If that's true, you'd think he'd have been able to see it himself."

"Unfortunately, he dug himself into a deep hole by going on the attack too early. He should have taken time to assess your defences. He's probably acutely worried now. Especially since he probably *is* collaborating with Mike Rasmussen. Well done for spotting that, John. It was definitely the knock-out blow. I wonder where it leaves us?"

"What do you know of any 'diplomatic negotiations'?" he asked.

"You mean, between the Turkish and JBL's various countries of origin? Only rumours, I'm afraid. Where did *you* hear it?"

"Hulusi Erkekli. Although he'd only heard it as a rumour too."

She drew her eyebrows together. "I wonder what's going on? I know the whole thing's being kept under wraps as far as possible, but if there was anything in it, I'd have heard something through official channels by now. How did Erkekli react to your theory, by the way?"

"He said he'd investigate. He's a Turkish patriot, and he doesn't want to see his country sold down the river. Which he thinks is what could happen if he doesn't keep a hard eye on things."

"There's certainly been a pause, for want of a better word, by the Turks. They were clearly bent on taking those hostages to within USA-baiting reach of the sea. And now they seem to have halted. And no one knows precisely where they are. I hope it's not evidence of something sinister. The prisoners could have attempted a break-out and Erdoğan could have ordered a mass execution. I wouldn't put it past him."

John laughed. "I wonder what Allah thinks of him."

"Nothing good, I imagine," she replied, surprising him by not interpreting a serious question as flippancy. "The Muslim god is the same as the god of the Bible. He requires mercy, not sacrifice. Converting Hagia Sophia to a mosque is unlikely to win him a place in paradise. And of course, the Russians will hate it, although they'll probably keep quiet for the time being. I can imagine a Russia-Greek axis sometime in the not too distant future, based on a common Christian Orthodoxy, with a particular conception of 'Constantinople' in common, and with Turkey besieged on all sides. I'm sure it's also one of the things that keeps Hulusi Erkekli awake at night: the idea that President Erdoğan may be inadvertently engineering his country's ultimate humiliation."

John nodded. Bloody hell, she was far-sighted.

He wondered how MI7 could possibly get along without her.

"I know this is perhaps a little off the wall," he said, "but it occurred to me that maybe Mike's more central than we supposed. Maybe he's spread the word that Daisy met Angela, and that Daisy may therefore be in a position to put a ton of gelignite under whatever they're planning. Maybe they've decided to cut their losses. Or they're waiting to see if I was bluffing."

"You're making a huge speculative leap," she replied. "But I suppose it's not impossible. If you're right, it simply means we've won a reprieve. It's up to us to use it to good effect. Apart from that, of course, it changes nothing."

He nodded. "I'll go and give Amber the suit back."

Chapter 23: Baddie Issues

Walter Doyle was sitting at his desk in the Foreign Office when he heard his phone ring. He stopped writing to pick it up, then he realised, with a lurch that was strong enough to feel like a sudden falling into the abyss, that it was his 'burner'.

He scrabbled about in his desk and answered.

"Hello, this is your assassin," a slurry voice said.

Doyle needed an extra breath. Then realised he was angry. "My *God!* I thought you'd been told not to contact me!"

"I need something. I need equipment."

"Give – give me a few moments, yes, all right. I'll call you back."

He ended the call and put his head in his hands.

What to do with a 'burner' phone? TV and the movies made it look simple. You memorised your contact's number, you called him, had a chat. Afterwards, you removed the battery, snapped the SIM card, and bought another.

In practice, it wasn't that simple. What if your contact needed something urgently? He'd have to call you. What if there was an emergency and you couldn't find a phone shop? After all, you couldn't keep going into the *same* phone shop, continually asking for yet another pay-as-you-go. Everyone had seen *The Wire*. It looked suspicious. And if you were an Under Secretary at the Foreign and Commonwealth Office, how soon would it be before MI5 got to hear?

So there was no ideal solution. Doyle was constrained by his job. He told himself that he only needed one 'burner'. When all this was done, he could drop it in the Thames, plus the snapped SIM card, and he'd be no worse off than any of those fellows in The Hood.

He both had, and hadn't, reckoned with the 11pm phone call from the Russian assassin. He had, insofar as he'd expected emergencies. But he hadn't put that together with the fact that there might be an emergency *while he was at work*. His earlier decision to keep the same 'burner' hadn't budgeted for that.

He should have kept it at home. But then, it would have been beyond his immediate oversight, thus insecure. And if there had been an emergency, he wouldn't have been there to deal with it.

His mind raced. The Russian was expecting a quick return call: 'a few moments', he'd told him.

Should he leave the building? He didn't know anything about phones. A mobile mast would have picked up the incoming call, surely? Surely the FCO was the sort of place where MI6 wouldn't allow any call to go unregistered? Common sense suggested there had to be *some* mechanism for automatically logging them. And when they'd been logged, they'd be passed to GCHQ. And they'd say, *Anomalous phone call to Walter Doyle's office, 11pm? Hmmm.*

So it was already too late for preventative measures. Leaving the building to return the call wouldn't achieve anything.

He was probably finished. Probably.

He called back.

"Hello, this is your assassin," a voice said in Russian.

His own Russian wasn't perfect, but it was good enough. "What do you want?" he asked weakly.

"I'm going to kill Daisy Hallenbeck."

"I *know* that. What do you want me to *do* about it?"

"I'm only going to be able to succeed if I get very close to her and I put my own life at risk. I've just done a quick calculation of the probabilities, and I'm not even sure I'll come out of it alive. But she might. Then you've got no one left to do your killing."

He scrunched his eyes shut and pressed his forehead hard with three fingers. "Just get to the point. I haven't time for a long exposition."

"I want a small machine gun – one I can conceal inside my jacket – and a hand-grenade."

Doyle laughed deliriously. "Oh, wow. Well, those two things are going to be very difficult to come by in this country!"

"In that case, I can't do it."

"Can't you get them from the Russian embassy?"

"They'll say no. They've given me to you. They don't want any further involvement."

He sighed. "Okay. They'll probably have to be specially imported."

"That's fine. When can you give me them?"

"I'll have to call you back. In a few days."

"Don't leave it too long, my friend."

He hung up contemptuously. He flung the phone in the drawer and took out a hip flask only quarter-filled with Scotch whisky. He drained it, wept, then got up, put his coat on.

He was finished. Kaput. Well, it didn't matter. His aim was true, as Elvis Costello would have said. There had to be an off-licence open somewhere.

Then he had a brainwave.

It would make the other conspirators furious with him, though... until they realised what he'd achieved.

He still had access to some of the papers Daisy Hallenbeck had discredited in Istanbul, and which Nedrick Sullivan was disingenuously claiming had all been shredded. He should leak them to a British newspaper, along with Daisy's name. At such short notice, she'd almost certainly be the only person the editors would trust to examine them. If she had any shred of decency at all, she'd then have to come out of hiding.

And that would provide the perfect opportunity to kill her.

It took four days for 'The Brit' to source some weapons. Pavel Nikolayevich lay on his bed, remembering the men and women he'd killed, and worrying about being killed in turn. He had no other option: he'd been warned not to go out too much ('ideally, not at all'), he couldn't speak or read or write English, and, as far as he could tell, there was no way of accessing anything at all in

Russian: no TV, movies, newspapers, books. His reflections became increasingly obsessive, and the borderline between sleeping and waking became thinner and thinner.

All his worries about being killed focussed on the drunken phone call he'd made. He could tell 'The Brit' hadn't liked it. Enough to report him and have him replaced? Possibly. The moment he knew for certain would be the moment he died. And since there was nothing else for him to do in this country, he might as well await the executioner's blade with dignity.

Yet he worried that death wasn't the end. What sort of an afterlife awaited him?

On the night of the phone call, he had a dream that later became recurring. He was walking through a driving snowstorm to a brightly-lit mansion, where all his murder-victims were having a party. When he entered the sumptuous ballroom where they were socialising, they cheered. They took his coat, they slapped his back, they shook his hand, they embraced him. They'd made him a huge cake, and hired a band in his honour. All because, as one of them – Lyanka Isakova, actually, whom he'd murdered in broad daylight during an Easter parade in Novosibirsk - put it, 'Being alive used to be miserable, all that trudging about every day, worrying about bills, getting older and more infirm, having to put up with the stupid, thieving authorities.' For all of them, death had been a happy release.

But then, in the middle of the dream, a messenger arrived from a distant province with an urgent telegram. He passed it to Anna Klimova, and the life seemed to go out of her eyes. She passed it to someone else and, as it made slow progress through the guests, the celebrations progressively petered out. People stopped dancing, and one by one the musicians broke off. It reached Pavel Nikolayevich last. Its gist was that the victims' relatives were trapped on earth, and they were incalculably grief-stricken.

Somehow, this was more than enough to ruin everything. By the time he'd finished reading, the party was over, and he found himself alone in a dilapidated hall that, by some strange quirk of the laws of physics, had been abandoned centuries ago. And he'd remain on his own for ever now. Meanwhile, the snowstorm outside was getting heavier and heavier -

He awoke.

Afterwards, he no longer thought about his victims – what they'd been wearing when they'd died, that last little snort of surprise when the knife went in, the look in their eyes as they'd realised their own death was actually *here, now* – but only about their friends and families: faces of men and women he'd never seen before, and which probably had no counterpart in reality, all crumpled in anguish.

It had to end. He couldn't keep doing this.

He finally realised why he'd been plucked from prison. The Russian killings had been a mere trial run. They weren't something they'd let him go back to, once this job was over. He'd be an 'international assassin' for ever now.

He remembered a few years ago, when the Kremlin had wanted Sergei Skripal killed. They'd assigned two men to the job. But the British managed to match their faces to some kind of GRU directory somewhere. The cat had been out of the bag long before that, but somehow the military intelligence link had confirmed it. Guilty, guilty, guilty. Russia is a *liar*.

But that was the wonderful thing about Pavel Nikolayevich Alikhanov. He was a complete nobody. If he was killed over here, no one would ever know he'd even been Russian. He'd certainly never been in the GRU. He hadn't even been in the army. And he had no connections. He hadn't seen his father for years: the alcoholism had probably killed him by now. If his mother was still alive, she might not even recognise him any more. She definitely wouldn't be able to identify his corpse on TV, thousands of miles away, with the words 'international assassin' on the news ticker. In any case, even if she did, they'd tell her to shut up. And, when he thought about it, she was probably dead, too.

He wished he hadn't asked for the machine gun and the hand grenade now. What the hell had he been thinking? It was the sort of thing a lunatic did: ring the shadowy guy in the middle of the night and ask for something completely insane.

He kept expecting the door of his bedsit to open. Hopefully, his end would be quick, clean and professional.

And why wouldn't it be? He'd done nothing to inspire feelings of revenge in 'The Brit', or in anyone else connected with this whole weird project.

The door would open, apparently of its own accord, or there would be a polite knock. Then, when he showed himself, there would be two little phuts, like air released in quick bursts from a tyre. He wouldn't even know it had happened. The assassin would replace his gun inside his leather jacket, leave by the external fire escape with his hood up, then call base to report mission accomplished. And the next day, someone would discover the corpse. Because he'd been shot, he'd probably be on the local news, but the emphasis would be on the proliferation of guns, not on the victim. Halfway across the world, in Yamalo-Nenets, his parents – if either of them still existed – wouldn't even get to hear about it. And as for him, he'd be walking up to that brightly-lit mansion in the snow…

He was a coward, that was his problem, and that made him totally unsuited for the profession of international assassin. Now he had chance to think about it – no, now he'd been *forced* into a situation where he could do nothing *but* think about it – the truth was undeniable. A good international assassin would suss out his likely opponents on any mission, and he'd go to extraordinary lengths to destroy them. But there was no way he'd be prepared to pit himself against someone of equal, or greater, strength. He'd always told himself that serial killing was a sport in the sense that shooting animals was a sport. He saw now that, somehow, that also defined his own limitations.

On the fourth day of his self-internment, his phone rang. As before he jumped before he looked at the screen. 'The Brit.' He looked at the door, because this was one of the scenarios he'd envisaged. They'd busy him with a call, then the door would fly open, phut, phut, bye-bye.

He picked up and said hello in what he hoped was a contrite voice. Although, either way, it was probably too late for that.

"We couldn't get you a machine gun of the appropriate size," the voice said. "But we managed to get you two hand grenades. They're in a red carrier bag at the top right-hand side of the first wheelie bin, on your left, that you come to when you leave your building by the fire escape. Inside the bag, you'll also find a map, a T-shirt, a face mask, and a security pass for a newspaper building. We need you to be ready tomorrow morning. Daisy Hallenbeck will be coming to you. She'll probably be heavily guarded. You need to do whatever it takes to kill her. No mistakes this time."

"Okay."

"Expect a call tomorrow morning. Then you simply need to follow the map and take the pass. Enter the building. You're registered as a cleaner called 'Jaroslav Voskovec'. There's a basic disguise for you in the bag too. Go inside the building, and get in role if necessary, access the roof, and keep an eye on the entrance."

"Okay… And thank you."

"What for?"

He wanted to say, *for not killing me*. But it sounded pathetic.

"For the hand grenades," he said.

Chapter 24: The Mysterious Five Day Hiatus

Five days passed. All the best prognostications were called into question. According to every report, the thirty-five JBL members, originally destined for somewhere near to the coast as an exercise in taunting the Americans, had inexplicably stalled a long way inland. No one outside Turkey knew precisely where they were, but there were definitely no diplomatic discussions under way. It became increasingly unclear when, or if, they'd start moving again, or even when they'd next appear. The whole thing felt weirdly like a phoney war.

Daisy remained in hiding with the Barneses. Frank Hallenbeck had returned from holiday, marshalled a few allies, and the CIA and MI7 were now singing from roughly the same hymn sheet. One which didn't include Nedrick Sullivan.

Not that Nedrick Sullivan was remotely cowed. He and his men had returned to Istanbul, from where they continued to muddy the waters. They'd never been sceptical of Daisy Hallenbeck's skill at authenticating documents, they said. Those she *had* discredited had all been destroyed, because what would be the point of keeping them? That didn't mean there weren't genuine ones out there, or that she hadn't missed them. That was precisely the way to get something like that through a rigorous filtering process: you put one genuine article among a thousand fakes in the hope of wearing the sifter down. At the very least, she should have had more stamina and been less neurotic.

But perhaps she *hadn't* missed them. Maybe she'd deliberately suppressed them.

And the mudslinging didn't stop there. According to Mordred's own account – 'her greatest supporter!' – she'd left Turkey without notice after apparently learning that Angela Barnes was in Britain. How did she find out? Contrary to what she allegedly claimed, no one else in the substation knew. Was it even possible that *she herself* was Angela's killer? Could she, for example, account for her movements on the night of the murder? She definitely had questions to answer.

Meanwhile, Mike Rasmussen was still nowhere in evidence.

Then, four days after they'd apparently fallen off the map, the thirty-five members of JBL re-appeared on a convoy of trucks moving towards the coast. They ended up, ten hours later, in what satellite pictures showed to be an absurdly poorly-guarded prison compound ten miles north of Anamur in southern Turkey. Of course, most analysts concluded, its insecure appearance was obviously meant to deceive.

Overnight, emergency restrictions were declared in southern Cyprus, and a USAF Lockheed MC-130 appeared in RAF Akrotiri. Two aircraft carriers - the USS Abraham Lincoln and USS John C Stennis - arrived four miles from the southern coast. Military analysts believed that, if war broke out, Cyprus would almost certainly play host to its first engagements, and that they would probably be fierce.

The horrible thing was that there was no need for a war. Everyone knew that. But they also knew that wars can be used to unite electorates behind a faltering leader. With established politicians everywhere taking the blame for coronavirus, this might be seen as one way, in several places, of obviating the censure, bringing people together, and engineering an incumbent's surge up the polls. Apart from that, it began to feel like a twenty-first century version of the Cuban Missile Crisis.

Then two things happened at once.

Firstly, Hulusi Erkekli had 'a real breakthrough.' He called Mordred to disclose that yes, those two Turkish agents *had* been ordered to place Daniel Batsford on Albert Bridge, and the man who'd issued those orders was a 'Colonel Tuncel Alasya', whose name Mordred recognised from the list appended to the footage of mourners at Angela's funeral. Alasya had left Britain shortly afterwards, but he'd not only been in charge of the operation to capture the thirty-five members of JBL; he'd also initiated, and overseen, their transport to Anamur, where he was still in charge.

MI7 and the CIA began frantically pooling everything they knew about him, and gathering every scrap of new evidence, especially about his recent sojourn in London.

As regards the latter, nothing much came to light, but it appeared that, four years ago, just after the failed Turkish coup in 2016, he'd had several meetings in Ankara with Nedrick Sullivan, and Walter Doyle. The substance of those meetings had gone unrecorded, except for the vague declaration that they had concerned 'trade'.

The combined US-UK intelligence operation placed Doyle and Sullivan under close surveillance with immediate effect. Watching their movements, digging into their backgrounds, monitoring their communications, became its top priority.

The second major development happened almost at the same time. Ruby Parker called Mordred at 1pm, when he was in the middle of re-examining a piece of CCTV at Thames House, and told him to make his way over to *The Guardian* building on York Way. Someone had passed a tranche of classified documents to its foreign affairs editor, and they apparently 'proved' that Turkey had been passing NATO secrets to the Russians in return for substantially discounted military hardware. But before they went to press, *The Guardian's* senior editorial team urgently wanted to speak to Daisy Hallenbeck.

"How do they even know she exists?" he asked.

"I don't know," Ruby Parker said. "Stella called me and I called you. We're both stuck in different meetings right now, and Phyllis is with me, so you need to deal with this on your own. What I can tell you, John, is that, ludicrous as it might sound, we may be on the verge of a war. What happens with those documents could be the nudge that either pushes us into the abyss, or brings us back from the brink."

It took four days for Doyle to source some weapons, during which the entire operation had to be put on hold, since everything had to come to fruition simultaneously. Ever since the assassin had called him, he'd expected to encounter material evidence that MI7 had him under observation. Yet he knew the rule: when you looked hard enough for something like that, you'd find it whether it was there or not. Everyone who slowed down as they passed him in the street, or seemed to appear twice within a few minutes, or stood unmoving on a corner, or made eye-contact, or avoided it, became a possible MI7 agent. And there were lots of them. Had he been a full government minister, it might have been explicable: half-recognition, from the TV maybe. But no one half-recognised an Under Secretary.

They were poised to take him down, and the ludicrously difficult task he'd been set – finding terrorist-coveted weapons – made it almost certain it'd be sooner rather than later. He had no option but to keep using his 'burner'. Since he was desperate, he called the Russian embassy. He asked for a pistol too. In for a penny, in for a pound, and he had a presentiment he might need to defend himself. And they were so nice about it, he felt like falling on his knees and embracing their legs. *Leave it to us,* they said. *We'll do everything we can. And we'll pause the whole enterprise while we find you your equipment. We can do that, no problem. Have a nice day, Walt.*

Walt, they called him Walt, like they already knew how grateful he'd be, because he was their big friend.

The pistol was apparently easy to obtain; it must have been, because it arrived the next day, enclosed in a padded envelope and deposited in a left-luggage locker on Belgrove Street, across from King's Cross station. He did everything he could to avoid his possible tails on the way there, including several false trails, a detour, a little jogging, a sudden sprint, and a quick change in the public toilets in Charing Cross Station. What should have been a ten-minute journey took an hour and half.

But it didn't matter. He had a gun now. He didn't know anything about guns, but it looked like a good one. He worked out how to remove the safety catch. He checked it was loaded.

Where should he hide it? Well, if MI7 was after him, there was no such thing as a safe place. In that case, he was doomed anyway. *Where did you get it? I don't know, someone must have planted it on me, what would I, a junior government minister, need a gun for?* He decided his best bet was under a mound of disused stationery, press cuttings and unread internal policy files in the bottom drawer of his desk at the Foreign Office. He didn't want to take it home in case his children or his wife found it. And the FCO was probably the last place MI7 would look. Which didn't mean they wouldn't look there; of course they would. But only *eventually*. And right now, it was about buying as much time as possible.

The Russians called him on his 'burner', at home, two days later. The machine gun was impossible, the disembodied voice said in a cheery tone, but the great thing was, they'd got him two grenades! It hadn't been easy, because of course, they had to be untraceable, but they'd done their absolute best, because they had great respect for him: if he said he needed something, they believed him. Same arrangement as before: pick them up from a secure storage locker in central London.

After he put the phone down, he laughed hysterically. *Where did you get these? I don't know, someone must have planted them on me, what would I, a junior government minister, need two hand grenades and a gun for?* Perhaps he should ring back and ask them for a bazooka and a ground-to-air missile, just to complete the Pythonesque potential. After all, if he said he needed them, they believed him.

He felt unbearably tense. He'd been under too much pressure for months now, ever since this thing was first initiated. But what was happening now took stress to the nth degree and added lead weights. He was going insane.

Whisky helped because it made him think insanity was good; it spelt freedom. He was doomed, so he could do whatever he liked. He could go downstairs into Moira's office. He could whip off his jacket, and show her he was wearing a bra. Then he could whip off his bra, and there would be two hand grenades parcel-taped to his nipples. And she'd say, what are those, sir? And he'd just stand there. He wouldn't even pull the pins out. He'd just stand there. And eventually, she'd call someone, and they'd say, Don't get too close to him, he's got bombs on his chest. And he'd go back upstairs, get dressed, and the next day, the Foreign Secretary would call him into his office and say, Are you okay, Walter, because I heard that yesterday, etc. Ending with, perhaps you should take a little holiday.

It occurred to him when he was drunk that the Russian assassin, whoever he was, was in the same situation as him, and quite possibly feeling stressed too. When he'd called the other night, he'd definitely sounded drunk. That slurry, *Hello, this is your assassin*.

And he was Russian, and the Russians were nice people. He'd recently wanted to embrace their legs.

He and the assassin were probably the only people in the world who could truly understand each other right now. The assassin was probably as on edge as he was. And they were both doomed. *I'm not even sure I'll come out of it alive,* he'd said. *But she might, then you've got no one left to do your killing*.

They should team up. Together, they might even pull off a great escape.

Separately, they had no chance.

What would his wife and children say, though?

The time for that consideration was well past, but they needn't feel ashamed. He was a patriot. He loved his country, and although people might well queue up afterwards to assert the opposite, still, there remained at least *one* interpretation in which he was vindicated. *At least* one; probably more. And in the end, that was all history was about: interpretations, and fashions in interpretations. There was no 'truth of the matter'.

All his wife and children had to do, if they loved him, was to cling to that one interpretation. Not too much to ask, surely.

But it might not come to that. Not if he and the assassin could bring Daisy Hallenbeck down. And bloody John Mordred, he was in there somewhere too.

And he had a brilliant plan. So brilliant, in fact, that it even looked good in the harsh light of total sobriety.

Now he had the grenades and a gun, he needed to get a copy of those Istanbul documents and send them first class to a respectable broadsheet. His brother-in-law owned the commercial cleaning company contracted to *The Guardian* HQ at Kings Place. He could get access.

And when Daisy Hallenbeck and Johnny Mordred turned up there – as they'd have to – they'd be sitting ducks. Her first, obviously. Keep to the initial plan.

Which definitely wouldn't be enough to save him now, at least not in the short term. MI7 had his card marked.

But at least it would tie up one loose end. And it would prove he was no coward.

He called the assassin the night before he was needed. He explained that he'd be posing as a cleaner in order to get into *The Guardian* building, where the killing would take place. He didn't tell him that he wouldn't be going alone. He wanted that to be a nice surprise.

Chapter 25: Journalist Meets Spy

The Guardian building stood on an unremarkable street in north London, not far from where John and Phyllis lived. It was fronted with stylish-looking tinted wavy glass, as if to ameliorate the surrounding monotony. At the same time, it looked as if the tinted wavy glass had merely been clipped on: as if it could just be taken away, and clipped onto something else, if fashions in exterior design didn't turn out as expected.

Mordred put his mask on and walked into the reception area, gave his name to the man at the desk, and asked for Neil Absolom, the foreign affairs editor. The man asked him to take a seat.

Absolom appeared just forty seconds later. Tall, mid-forties, with a long face and lank hair, he wore a mask and a suit, and approached his guest at a brisk pace with a smile and both hands together in a *namaste*, one conventional alternative to shaking hands nowadays.

"Shall we go outside?" he said, when they'd exchanged introductions. "It's a pleasant day, and obviously, I'm a little hesitant to show a member of the state security services around the interior. It wouldn't make me very popular with my colleagues. Please don't take that personally."

"I understand," Mordred replied. "And I'm relying on you to treat our conversation as strictly confidential."

"Of course."

Absolom held the door for him. They walked outside, turned left and began to saunter.

"How much do you know about what we've got?" Absolom asked.

"You've come into possession of a pile of documents that supposedly 'prove' Turkey has been passing NATO secrets to the Russians in return for money-off vouchers on military hardware.

And I believe the name 'Daisy Hallenbeck' appears somewhere in the chain of evidence."

"Does it ring any bells with you?"

"Yep."

"So who is she?"

Mordred smiled. For a moment he was tempted to suggest a trade: for *who gave you the documents*. But he reconsidered. Naturally, Absolom would cite press privilege, and that would be that. But there was another, equally interesting question, and, conveniently, it was also the most glaring one. "Why do you want to know?"

"Okay," Absolom said, in the manner of someone who'd spent at least half an hour rehearsing what he was going to say, "it's like this. We've got two hundred and fifty documents – receipts, transport dockets, letters of recommendation, supposedly top secret communiqués – all of which look entirely kosher. The trouble is, these are very, well, *niche* items, and, although we've got freelance and in-house 'experts' in document authentication, none of them can pronounce with more than about seventy percent certainty. They've achieved a certain unanimity, but even so - "

"Who gave you the documents?"

Absolom laughed. "Oh, come on, John. You know you can't ask *that*."

"I don't mean, 'please could you tell me', I mean, 'Do you think your provider is trustworthy'? I suppose you must do."

"Mostly, these things – and I'm not saying that's the case in this instance – are forwarded by anonymous whistle blowers."

"Fair enough. Let's get back to Daisy."

"As I just said, as of now, we've got a seventy percent approval rating. Is that good enough to go to press with? Maybe. If we *don't* publish, probably later today, some other broadsheet – *The Times*, say, or *The Telegraph* – will get a similar wad of documents and they might well be less punctilious. After all, for some of our rivals – and I'm not necessarily accusing either of those two – it's principally about selling papers, not serving the public. I like to think we're slightly more conscientious."

Mordred laughed. "Now say something about Daisy Hallenbeck."

"Oh, yes, that's right! Well, I'm not about to appeal to you for some of your own document authenticators, although I'm sure you do have qualified employees who could do that sort of thing, and do it well. We've made a firm decision not to let anyone from the CIA or MI7 or Turkey look at them, for reasons that are probably obvious. Nor will we allow the documents out of the office, nor will we permit them to be photographed, or otherwise duplicated; meaning Zoom's also out of the question, since it creates that possibility. But some of them have come with handwritten notes appended – obviously part of a prior, expert analysis – declaring them 'NOT genuine', and signed by one 'Daisy Hallenbeck'. So that's why we'd like to speak to her. We want her to explain to us why she reached the judgement she did. I'm not saying we'll concur, but it's currently our number one preferred next step."

"It may or may not surprise you that Daisy's a CIA agent."

"It doesn't. She'd have to be someone within *some* security service to be dealing that confidently with those particular documents – and her name suggests she belongs to a primarily English-speaking nation."

"Her being CIA doesn't bother you?"

"Not in the slightest, because she's obviously already reached her verdict in a technical environment comprising her professional peers. Obviously, if she changes it now, yes, there's a problem. We'd be suspicious. But I don't see why she should. All we want her to do is explain her reasons in the presence of our own experts. We actually *want* them to be fake, John. I don't know what's going on in the eastern Mediterranean right now, but there are some very scary rumours flying about."

"It may interest you to know that Daisy's in hiding. Until very recently, she worked in Istanbul. That's where she appended those handwritten notes. There were several unsuccessful attempts to kill her, and she came to me for protection – or rather, I found out where she was staying and arranged for her protection. She's in a lot of danger."

"Oh, dear. So I suppose that means you can't - "

"I do know where she is. And I can find her and bring her here, probably within two hours, if need be. The problem is, I'm beginning to think someone's setting her up."

Absolom did a double-take. "You mean" – he pointed to himself, incredulously – *"me?"*

"Not you. Not anyone who works for *The Guardian*. No, I mean, whoever sent you those documents. It seems like a very good way of flushing her out."

"You think that same person could be planning to kill her?"

"I think it's worth seriously considering."

"We could get the police in, give her a bit more protection. Or *you* could. If anyone was thinking of picking her off with a rifle – well, there would have to be several of them, at least two, because there are at least two ways of approaching the building. Four, if you count Crinan Street and Goods Way. And of course, there's King's Cross Station, about two hundred metres across the way from us – behind those buildings: you can't see it from here – and its approach passes parallel to us, so that probably means lots of possible hiding places. And St Pancras, obviously. My God, a total bloody nightmare, when I think about it! Maybe that's why they *chose* us! I mean, why they chose *The Guardian!* Not because of our passion for truth and justice, but only because there are lots of places from which to aim a rifle! Sorry, I'm just thinking aloud."

"Be my guest. You're saving me some of the effort."

"I suppose you could bring her here in a bullet-proof car. But could you get one at such short notice?"

"It would save a lot of time and effort," Mordred said, "if you'd just allow those documents to be taken out of the building."

"Sorry, non-negotiable, I'm afraid. I'd never be able to sell that to my colleagues. They'd point out that I was following the

189

advice of an MI7 officer, and taking the documents to a CIA agent. You can probably imagine why, in their minds, that might add up to 'We'll never see those documents again'. A lot of them don't like the security services very much. Personally, I'm agnostic, by which I mean, I judge you on a case-by-case basis."

"Thanks. So we have to bring her here, yes?"

"I'm afraid so," Absolom said. "If we get her a bullet-proof car, we can drop her on the pavement outside the front door. Then she can run from the car into the building. Hardly any gap at all. I'll be on hand to accompany her upstairs, and of course, once she's confirmed her original analysis, explained it, and our experts have concurred, she'll probably no longer be in any danger. From what you've told me, the only reason she's in danger now is because someone doesn't want her verdict on the documents to stand."

"That's correct."

"Any idea who it might be?" Absolom asked. "You must have."

"Theories, that's all. But I'm pretty certain it's connected to what happening in the Med."

"Has it occurred to you that she might be wrong? Or even trying to mislead you? I mean, maybe these documents *are* kosher. *Our* experts seem to think so. With the usual arcane qualifiers of course, but you know what academics are like."

"I trust her, but I admit, she could be mistaken. I don't think she is, though, simply because I happen to know she was placed in a situation which, structurally speaking, seemed designed to pressure her into reaching a specific conclusion: 'genuine'. If she'd been examining the real McCoy, that wouldn't have been necessary."

"Point taken," Absolom said. "So what's the plan?"

"We'll need to do a lot of preliminary legwork. Obviously, Daisy Hallenbeck can't be part of any news report, nor can you take any pictures of her, nor can you mention that she was ever anywhere near the building, nor can you etcetera, and it'll all need to be agreed upon between our lawyers and yours, and drawn up in binding contracts, which you and she will have to sign. I'll arrange for our legal department to get in touch with you as a matter of urgency."

"We're used to doing that sort of thing. With sufficient good will on both sides, it never takes as long as you might think."

Mordred looked at his watch. 2.15pm. "And we'll have to get the police involved. As you say, there are lots of ways in which something like what we're mooting could go wrong. Again, we can make that a matter of priority. How long before you have to go to press?"

"We've got to get the final pages over to the print centre in Stratford by nine. *In extremis,* we could leave it till ten, but I'd prefer not to cross that bridge unless we come to it."

"With all the red tape to be cleared, it's unlikely we'll be able to get Daisy here before seven. But I'm sure whoever's behind this intended it that way."

"You mean, it limits your window of options, in terms of when she has to appear. I can appreciate that, yes. We have had the documents since this morning, but there are a lot of them, and it's taken us a while to make sense of what we're seeing. I hope you understand. They were delivered by Royal Mail, so they may be untraceable."

"We need to work quickly. Let's exchange numbers. You'll have to delete mine afterwards, but I'm required to change it every eight weeks anyway."

"No problem. Good luck, John."

As he walked away, Mordred looked up at the building and then reviewed its surrounds, trying to assess its points of risk. He couldn't. Any angle from down here on the street would only ever give a partial, and possibly a distorted, result. He needed to call Annabel, Alec and Edna, get them to come over now and do a proper recce.

Absolom was right: the gap between a car pulling up flush with the pavement – or even *on* the pavement: that would probably work - and the entrance was virtually negligible.

And yet, for some reason, nothing felt right.

Chapter 26: An Unusual Couple

Eleven hours before John Mordred met Neil Absolom at *The Guardian* building, Pavel Nikolayevich lay in bed having yet another dream about the party in the mansion. He'd begun to anticipate the telegram now, and when it arrived, he tried to neutralise its effect with increased jollity. When the phone rang, he thought it was part of the dream. Only after the third ring did he grunt awake, look at the screen – *The Brit* - and pick up.

Yes, that's right. This was the day he was going to die.

"Are you ready to go?" the Brit asked. "It's time."

"Are the – are the grenades where you said they'd be?"

"Everything's in place. Get dressed quickly, then go downstairs and pick it all up, before it gets stolen."

"Right, yes."

"And good luck," the Brit said.

There wasn't much chance of that, given Daisy Hallenbeck's consistent good fortune, but it was a nice thought.

"Thank you," he said.

He was supposed to be posing as a cleaner, so he probably wouldn't be allowed to take much in with him. No knives, he wouldn't need those. He might be able to smuggle some vodka past security if he put it in a soft drink bottle. But it was a hot day, so he'd probably need water too.

He laughed for no reason as he pulled his trousers on. He donned a shirt, and his jacket. He needn't bother with a shave, since he was probably going to be shot dead.

He transferred some vodka to an empty coke bottle, thrust it into a fabric bag along with his phone, and went downstairs, relocating to the external fire exit on the second floor down.

He found the wheelie bin where The Brit had indicated. He went inside and found the red carrier bag with the map, the T-shirt, the face mask, the grenades and the security pass inside.

He'd never seen hand grenades before. They were bigger than he expected. He checked his pass. Not a bad photo of him, but all photos of him were a bit dated. He wondered whether 'Jaroslav Voskovec' was a real person, or whether they'd just invented him for the purposes of the assassination. What would happen if he met any of the other cleaners? How would he understand them?

His phone rang. *The Brit.*

He hoped this was the *mission aborted* call. He already felt nervous. He was a serial killer, that's all. First, they'd tried to make him into an international assassin, now they wanted to make him into a con man! *He wasn't cut out for any of that!*

He picked up. "Yes?" he said irritably.

"Turn around."

His obedience was so instinctive, he didn't even have time to recall his anxiety about being shot.

He found himself facing a small man of about fifty with a broad face, narrow eyes, ruddy cheeks and a few strands of red hair covered by a baseball cap. The man smiled and gave a little wave.

It took Pavel Nikolayevich a full two seconds to make the connection. *The Brit.* But then all his anxieties about being shot returned.

"Allow me to introduce myself," the man said, in his heavy British accent. "I'm 'The Brit', and I'm coming with you."

Pavel Nikolayevich thought he was going to faint. "Er, what?" he said weakly.

"I'm coming with you. This is a complex operation, and you may need backup. Get changed into the T-shirt and the face mask. That's important."

He complied. "Who really are you?" he asked as he thrust his arms through the holes and pulled the hem down.

"I've just told you. I'm 'The Brit'. The person you've been speaking to on your phone. You don't need to know my name…

but, what the heck: I might as well tell you anyway. I'm Walter Doyle. You can call me Walter, if you like. And you are?"

"Pavel Nikolayevich." He cleared his throat. "Alikhanov," he added, as if it might be useful.

"Well, Pavel Nikolayevich, we're going to do this together. Unless you've any objections?"

The Russian shook his head. He didn't know whether he had any objections. He didn't really know what was happening.

'The Brit' put a face mask on. "Come along, then!"

Half an hour later, they stood on the pavement outside a large, sinister-looking building in an otherwise unremarkable road, with cars and lorries passing leisurely in both directions.

"It's important not to break stride as we go in," Walter said. "Obviously, they'll check us at the front desk: our ID's and so on. There's a cleaners' entrance round the back, but I'm going to tell them that we were called out of bed at short notice to cover, and they'll either send us there, or let us proceed with a set of verbal directions."

"Why won't they just send us home? I mean, since we're late."

"They're not authorised. Only the cleaning company can do that, and they won't have a representative at the front entrance. Anyway, if we have to go round the back, don't worry: I know what to say. Once we're inside, we've got to get to the roof. I know about that too. You're in good company, Pavel Nikolayevich!"

"Won't they search our bags?"

"Stop worrying. Think of the virus. They probably won't have gloves and they're not going to want to touch the inside of two bags belonging to *cleaners*. Who knows where we've been? Anyway, the real cleaners have been inside for a while now. They're probably close to clocking off. And most of them wouldn't have been searched at reception. It's not like *The Guardian* building's an important landmark, anyway. You might get searched at The Shard or The Walkie-Talkie. Not here."

"What if we are?"

"Wrap the grenades in the fabric bag you brought, and put it inside the carrier bag. The carrier bag has 'Clitheroe' written on, which is the name of the cleaning company. Why they have their own carrier bags is anyone's guess: it's not like they're a supermarket. And of course, your T-shirt says 'Clitheroe'. So you've got the crappy bag, the crappy uniform and the fake identification card. They're not going to want to search you, believe me."

Pavel shrugged. "Okay."

They went inside. They showed their cards at reception. Walter smiled and told the receptionist something in English. They shared what looked like a little joke and chuckled.

"Just follow me," Walter said, when they were through. "I know where I'm going. Are you okay, Pavel? Would you like to go to the toilet before we go upstairs to the roof? Because we're approaching the gents' now."

They were both feeling nervous, so they both took a sharp right turn into the toilet. They locked themselves in the cubicles. Pavel emptied his bowels and drank vodka at the same time.

Five minutes later, they emerged simultaneously. Pavel caught sight of their faces in the mirror. They both looked ashen.

"Now let's wash our hands and sing Happy Birthday," Walter said solemnly.

Five minutes later, they were on the roof, which was very different to how Pavel Nikolayevich had pictured it in his imagination. He'd envisaged a slope made of brick tiles with a sheer drop in front, and a pinnacle above and behind, and them clinging to something to keep from falling. In fact, it was flat and spacious, with a path to different areas. If you stood on something, you could see over the curvy glass frontage into the street. Walter sat down on the path with his back against something vertical covered in roofing felt. Pavel Nikolayevich sat next to him. The sun shone with such intensity that the birds had fallen silent, but up here there was a cool breeze. Cars susurrated in the streets below; a train parped.

"Do you want to know the plan?" Walter asked.

"Why have you come with me?"

"I've told you, you can't do this on your own. The way the whole thing's supposed to work, it needs at least two people."

"So it's not that, once I've done the job, you can kill me?"

"I'd be in deep trouble with the Russian embassy if I did. Besides, if I wanted to kill you, I could have arranged to meet you afterwards. I've actually got a gun."

Pavel Nikolayevich gasped. *"With* you?"

"Yes, *right now!"*

"Can I *see* it?"

Walter reached into his bag and took it out. He turned it round in his hands. "It's loaded and ready for action."

"What type is it?"

Walter laughed. "I was hoping *you* could tell *me! You're* the international assassin!"

"I don't know anything about guns. I'm not actually an international assassin at all. I'm just a simple serial killer. I use knives, mainly."

Walter drew back. "A *what?* A - *serial killer?"*

"That's worse than being an international assassin?"

"Well… well, I don't know. No, I suppose not." He laughed nervously. "You're not going to kill *me,* are you?"

"No." He sighed. "I mainly kill women. I've come to realise recently that it's not… I don't know: that there's something *not right* about it."

"You mean, morally?"

Pavel Nikolayevich shrugged. "Maybe."

"I mean, do you do it for pleasure? Don't take this the wrong way, but that would be worse than being an international assassin, because in the latter case, you'd be doing it for professional reasons."

"Why would it be better to kill someone for 'professional reasons'?"

"Well, it would imply more self-control on your part, I suppose."

"Why is that better?" Pavel Nikolayevich persisted.

"Because then it would be just a job. You could give it up if you found something with better pay. You'd be like the rest of us: simply trying to make a living. But with a serial killer, you think they could *never* give it up, because it's what drives them."

"Maybe I do enjoy it. Or not. That doesn't mean it drives me."

"So what makes you think there's something 'not right' about it?"

"The people who get left behind. The way it makes them sad."

"What about the people you've, er, murdered?"

Pavel Nikolayevich frowned. "Once they'd been killed, they don't exist any more. Unless there really *is* life after death, who knows? If they don't exist, there's no one to feel sorry for. It would be like feeling sorry for Sadko the minstrel."

Doyle laughed. "You know who you remind me of? Serial killer turned international assassin? Villanelle from *Killing Eve!*" The smile dropped from his face. "Sorry, I don't expect you've seen that. Or read it. Novel, then TV show, both fairly recent. New things probably take a long time to reach Russia nowadays."

"I've heard about it."

"Maybe we should change the subject."

"Okay." He reached into his bag and produced the plastic bottle. "Vodka. Drink?"

Walter produced a hip-flask from his pocket, then a second hip-flask from his bag. "Great minds think alike!" He reached into his trouser pocket and took out a packet of cigars.

"Oh, *wow!* That's *great!*"

"*And* I've got a lighter!"

They stopped talking. Walter yawned and examined his gun. Pavel Nikolayevich sat with his palms flat on the floor and closed his eyes and sniffed the breeze. They drank vodka and smoked a cigar each.

"What's the plan?" Pavel Nikolayevich asked eventually.

"I thought you'd never ask."

"This is weird. When is she actually coming?"

"Not for a good long while yet. We had to get here several hours in advance, because our only way of entering was with the cleaners. By the time she arrives, they'll have forgotten all about Clitheroe."

"So a long time. How will we know?"

"We'll notice an increasing commotion in the street. And it'll build to a crescendo, and a car will come here quickly, because they're probably expecting a sniper or two. That'll be her. Then, you go downstairs in the lift. When I see her get out of the car, I'll pull the pin from one of the grenades, count to three and then let go. It should explode about halfway down, long before it hits the ground. That'll blow the window in and create a panic. Daisy Hallenbeck will be inside the building then. You grab her, put my gun to her head and bring her up here."

"Why don't I just kill her then?"

"Because then they'll just kill *you*, then *me*. No, bring her up here, lock the door so they can't get in, *then* we kill her, *then* we escape via the rear of the building. I've brought two ultra-thin ropes. We'll attach them to the eastern parapet in a minute, so they're ready. We'll abseil to the ground, and there's a canal basin just across a barrier down there, where I've put a hired speedboat ready. The basin leads straight on to the Regent's Canal."

"Oh, wow. Do you *really* think we can get away?"

"I very much doubt it. But you should never underestimate the incompetence of the British police force."

"Well, I wasn't planning on getting away. I don't want to live any more. There's a mansion, you know, on a slight hill in a snowstorm…"

Doyle chuckled nervously. "I don't know which, er, 'mansion' you mean, Pavel Nikolayevich. Tell me later, eh? Another cigar?"

"No, thank you. I don't really smoke."

"Someone will be up here at some point to check the roof for snipers, so we should keep on our toes. We just have to hide behind the air conditioning units. If we keep moving, we should be okay. If the worst comes to the worst, we can go down into the concert hall. *The Guardian* isn't the only business with premises in this building."

"How long do you think we'll have to wait before they do the inspection?"

"Oh, hours yet. We'll have a look around, check out the best hiding places, then, if you want to get some sleep, we can take turns keeping watch, and I'll wake you up if I hear anything."

"That would be lovely," Pavel Nikolayevich said.

They split up to locate the best places of concealment. Walter lit another cigar.

Chapter 27: Elon Musk or Not?

At 5pm, John was at in H18 on the top floor of Thames House signing papers. Ruby Parker sat at a desk, countersigning. Two middle-aged lawyers in dark suits stood on the other side of the room, looking obsequious, and fetching and carrying documents at half-minute intervals. They all wore masks.

His phone rang. *Edna*.

"John, I'm at *The Guardian* offices," she said. "They're not going to let us do a search of the roof, because it would give MI7 access to the building, and that's a bit of a no-no at the moment."

"What about the police?"

"The police are happy for them to use a private security firm. If you're not okay with that, we can get access to the roof by other means. *The Guardian* shares the building with some sort of music company."

"I'm not happy with a private security firm: we don't know how good or bad they'll be. I can just about understand them denying us access. *Just about*. Tell them it's got to be the police, and it's got to be now. We're wasting time. If they can't cooperate, tell them, we're not bringing Daisy."

"I get the distinct impression everyone here thinks we're paranoid. Not just the journalists, but the police. I just overheard two WPCs moaning about 'bloody spooks'. The Met's done a wide sweep already, apparently, and found nothing. And let's face it, they've never liked us that much anyway."

"Let me guess: *bloody MI5, always inventing threats to justify their own existence.*"

"Roughly, yes. And of course, the journos think the same thing, only squared."

"I like the way *we're* paranoid but *they* won't let us up on the roof because it might be a sneaky plot."

"Paranoia cubed, then. Even if the police do go up there - "

"Which they will, after you've issued your ultimatum..."

" - I'm not sure they'll do a thorough job. It'll just be a box-ticking exercise."

"Tell them you want the names of the officers assigned. That should keep them on their toes."

"Will do." She hung up.

"This is the last official form," one of the lawyers said. "After that, you're free to go ahead."

"John, call Frank Hallenbeck," Ruby Parker said.

The plan was that two CIA agents – Frank Hallenbeck and Elmer Flood - would take charge of Daisy's transfer to *The Guardian* building. They'd come over to Thames House, and Kevin would take them and John over to the Barneses in Enfield. A fleet of four bullet-proof cars with blacked out windows – two British, two American – would meet them on their way back to Central London at Tottenham Hale. At that point, Daisy, Frank and Elmer would change vehicles. At Tottenham Hale, John would stay in the original car to be joined by Ruby Parker. Theirs would then become the foremost vehicle in the convoy.

"Hi, John," came Frank's voice. "All systems go?"

"We're ready when you are. I'll call Daisy."

He hung up. Ruby Parker preceded him out of the room. They went leisurely downstairs, where four agents – three men and a woman – were waiting with grim expressions.

"We'll meet you at the rendezvous point," Ruby Parker told him. She left the building without breaking stride or wishing him good luck. The four agents followed her.

"Excuse me, John," Colin said quietly, from the desk. He solemnly passed a fat brown envelope over. "Your 'piece', as the Americans say. And the best of British."

"Thank you." He signed out by way of showing his gratitude. He took the gun from its covering and put it in the inside pocket of his jacket.

"Please let me know if I'm out of line," Colin said, "but that really deforms your jacket. It's probably not very safe that way either, and I wouldn't want you to get shot. I've got a shoulder holster under the desk here if you want it. I can even help you put it on, if you like. Sorry, if I'm speaking out of turn. I'm just thinking: we wouldn't want to lose you."

"That's very kind of you."

Colin came round with what looked like a small bundle of straps. John took his jacket off and Colin fitted it like he was a gentlemen's tailor. Mordred thanked him, took out his phone, then wandered to the door and called Daisy.

"John?"

"We should be with you in about forty minutes," he said. "Are you ready to go?"

"Yep. Nervous, but at least we're going to get it all over with. Then it'll be back to boring normality. I hope. Am I coming back here afterwards?"

"I doubt it. The CIA badly wants to debrief you, and once those documents are proved to have been fabricated, Nedrick Sullivan's going to have a lot of explaining to do."

"I'm going to miss Tony and Ree and Sandra. I might come back and see them a bit, if I'm allowed. They've been really nice. Obviously, Tony and Ree haven't even begun to get over Angela yet, but they're putting on a brave face, just for me. And Sandra's been shopping and doing the garden. They won't let me go out at all, even to look at the greenhouse. We play Rummy at night and drink sherry and watch TV. I say 'at night': after six: we go to bed at ten and read. But I feel guilty all the time, like I should be doing something to help them. Yet I love their normality, you know? Tony and Ree are like *my* mum and dad. I'm serious: I've half begun to wonder whether I shouldn't be a History teacher, after all. I could probably *get* to like kids. I wouldn't want to put my parents through what Ree and Tony are going through."

"To be fair, document authentication isn't usually as dangerous as it's been for you lately."

"I don't see why not. I've already told you it can make or break governments. And the world's a hell of a lot leakier nowadays than it was even twenty years ago."

"And so people in power have learned a new tactic: to just keep claiming it doesn't matter. And then the media, and public opinion, inevitably moves on, because it has to."

"Well, that didn't happen in this case. Perhaps the baddies are wedded to an old-fashioned idea of truth. Namely, that there is such a thing, and it makes a difference."

He laughed. "Good old baddies. Our last hope for a decent world."

"Would you like to speak to Tony? He's here."

"Please."

"Hello, John," Tony said. "Should we put the kettle on?"

"It'll be a straight-to-the-car job, I'm afraid. Daisy's Uncle Frank will be coming with me, so we'll reunite her with him and another CIA agent, then it'll be direct to Central London. The whole thing shouldn't take very long."

Frank and Elmer entered, dressed in suits slightly sharper than any he'd hitherto seen on them.

"I've got to go," John told Tony.

"See you soon," Tony said. He passed the phone to Daisy, who said bye and hung up.

Frank and Elmer each took a turn at shaking John's hand, as if they were competing to see who could pump his arm the hardest.

"See you're wearing a gun," Frank said.

"I'll try not to shoot myself," John replied.

Elmer chortled.

"Let's get out of here," Frank said.

They exited. They descended the steps. They put their masks on as they got in Kevin's car, like they were off to a bank robbery. John sat between the two CIA men on the back seat.

"Good news," Frank said when they pulled out into the traffic.

"Strange use of the term 'good'," Elmer said, before his colleague could say what it was. "I happened to like the guy."

"Would you have liked him as much if he'd managed to put my niece in a coffin?" Frank replied drily.

"I thought those guys had been outside the embassy for days," Elmer said. "I thought they weren't any of Mike's doing. That's what I was told."

Frank hooted. "Well, here's the truth, Elm. Mike put them there. All that stuff about him being 'concussed' was A-one garbage. We were hoping he'd buy the idea that we were giving him the benefit of the doubt, and come sneaking back. But it turns out he knew we knew. To be fair to the guy, how could we *not* know?"

"Sheesh," Elmer said. "No one said. In that case, I guess it *is* good news!"

"What's happened?" Mordred put in, as politely as he could.

Frank folded his hands in his lap. "Mike Rasmussen put a gun in his mouth and shot the back of his head off. In Vienna. On his way to Istanbul, apparently."

"It's what you might call *breaking news*," Elmer said. "Happened about thirty minutes ago."

"Whoa," Mordred said, with less enthusiasm than Frank was probably hoping for.

"Hey, don't get me wrong," Frank said, apparently catching something of the reaction's tone. "He was a human being. I'm sorry he's dead. But it's the better of the two possible outcomes."

"He could have come back and begged for mercy," Elmer said. "That would have been a third outcome and it'd have been much better than him committing suicide. Poor Mike."

"My ass," Frank said. "Anyway, John, since it's – like Elm just said – 'breaking news', we don't have any hard facts yet, but some people are saying he tried to get in touch with Nedrick Sullivan, and Sullivan gave him the brush off. In return, Rasmussen penned a confession, naming names, and left it on the bed for us to discover."

"So the case could be over?" Mordred said. "I mean, assuming it *is* a confession, and that it's true, and can be substantiated?"

"Could be," Frank said. "That's a lot of maybes, though. Let's just concentrate on getting Daisy into this building, yeah? Then we'll see how the chips fall. In any case, you'll get to take chief credit, yet again. Without you, Mike would still be walking the streets."

Mordred nodded ruefully. Putting it that way didn't diminish its sadness, quite the opposite. They fell into a prolonged silence.

"Don't tell Daisy," Frank said, an hour later, when they pulled up at the Barneses. "About Mike, I mean."

"Why not?" Elmer asked. "I thought you said it was good news?"

"Women don't like that sort of thing," Frank said. "Call me a sexist, but in my experience, they tend to get teary and start crying. Even when the guy was a first-rate douche bag. Last thing we want is her having a breakdown on her way to something like this. You know what journalists are like. They'll think we've been pressuring her to tell them a story entirely of our own making."

"She's not going there to tell them a story," Mordred said. "She's going to apply her expertise in a situation where she'll be surrounded, and possibly judged, by her professional peers. But I take your broader point: she's already nervous. Telling her about Mike's death probably won't help. She's only human."

They pulled on to the Barneses drive. Mr and Mrs Barnes came out with Daisy. She looked nothing like the last time John had seen her. She had short blonde hair and an Alice band, and she wore a suit slightly too small for her and a pair of brown Hush Puppies. She hugged Tony then Ree for what seemed a very long time. Then Sandra came out, and there was another long hug. Meanwhile, Frank, Elmer and John stood by the car, not coming too close for the virus's sake, but not wishing to look impolite by no gesture of gratitude.

"Thank you!" Frank called, when Daisy finally came over. "You're magnificent people!" He lowered his voice. "Elmer, you sit shotgun. Daisy, you get in the middle, between me and John."

Daisy got into the car wiping her eyes. "I'm going to really *miss* them," she said. Then, when the car pulled off the drive: "My God, I'm *so* nervous. I might need to throw up on the way. Hi, Kevin. Thank you for the other night. John told me everything. You were brilliant."

"No problem," Kevin said.

"I really, really hope they catch Mike. 'Nuff said. Sandra gave me some freezer bags to be sick in. They're airtight. I probably *will* be sick. No pressure, but the fate of the world hangs on me getting it right. And what if I'm not? What if I'm wrong? What if I've been wrong all along? Or what if I *am* right, but the others won't accept it? You know what academics are like: they don't like being gainsaid, or they see it as an opportunity for an abstruse discussion. And I'm young. They won't like that. And I'm not a professor. And a lot of them probably don't like the CIA. We're always the villains. What if I end up looking like a total dumbass?"

She yanked a freezer bag from her jacket and vomited. Frank rubbed her back and said, "Don't worry." Kevin pulled into a layby. Mordred got out so she could run to the bin.

"I'll sit next to the door," she said with forced cheeriness, when she came back. "You sit in the middle. Don't worry: I've got plenty of bags!"

After half an hour, the car pulled in at Tottenham Hale. Daisy, Frank and Elmer got out and transferred to a CIA car. She'd been sick five times now and they'd been getting used to it.

Ruby Parker got in the car next to John. "You were slightly longer than I expected," she said.

"We've had a few stops to discard freezer bags full of vomit," Mordred said. Probably not the excuse she was expecting, but it both had the ring of truth and was true.

"Understandable," she replied. "Let's hope she knows her field as well as she says she does. I really want this to go well, for her sake."

She seemed to have put Mordred's own, hitherto unrecognised, anxieties into words. He wished *he'd* brought a few freezer bags now.

Twenty minutes later, they turned off the A503 onto York Way, Ruby Parker called Edna and put it on speaker.

"It's all clear," Edna reported.

"What about the roof?"

"Two PCs went up about an hour ago. Nothing to report. They say the sight-line's useless up there, anyway. To get a good shot, a sniper would have to go through the glass or stand above it."

"That's reassuring," Ruby Parker said without conviction. "Well, we'll see. We're about ten minutes away. Let everyone know."

"There are lots of *Guardian* people here to welcome her. And others, for some reason. Quite a crowd."

"Well make sure she's got a clear entrance, and that the police do their job and cover her on the way in. If necessary, tell them to pretend coronavirus doesn't exist for just thirty seconds. That's all it'll take."

"Yes, ma'am."

Mordred took a deep breath. He suddenly felt anxious for everyone. Edna, Annabel – Phyllis was supposed to be there now too – Alec, Ruby Parker. This was Ruby Parker's last case. *Just one last job before retirement…* It might even be her they were after.

If anyone was after anyone. The police weren't idiots. Mostly – you should never over-generalise - they didn't like MI7, but they knew what they were doing. Maybe nothing would happen.

And if Mike Rasmussen really had written a comprehensive confession, that might be it. The least exciting end to a case ever.

He wondered if Ruby Parker knew about Mike Rasmussen. He should have told her earlier, but he was too focussed on Daisy.

Not that it could have made any difference. He'd tell her later. He could see she was as on edge as he was.

When they came within view of the building, it became obvious that Edna hadn't been exaggerating. There really was a large crowd. It became clear later that a heavy police presence and a lot of anxious-looking journalists had persuaded everyone that a celebrity was about to arrive. Then, for reasons no one was subsequently able to discover, the celebrity became Elon Musk, then Mark Zuckerberg, then Kristen Stewart, then Elon Musk again. Eventually, people were making detours from sightseeing in Central London just to see the mystery visitor. Police efforts to move them on, gradually created a rumour that a terrorist attack was expected, and since this had some of the required dispersal effect, and wasn't a million miles from the truth, no one in charge made strenuous efforts to deny it.

Mordred's car pulled up at the kerb. He and Ruby Parker got out. Ruby Parker went into the building. Mordred tried to find out who was in charge of security. Daisy's car pulled up. She got out, with Frank and Elmer trying to keep hold of her. People were pushing and shoving. A clutch of journalists awaited her in the foyer, looking slightly horrified by what they could see was happening, but couldn't fully comprehend. Two of them half-expected Elon Musk.

She passed the reception desk. There were so many people around her now, all seemingly talking at once, that Mordred temporarily lost sight of her.

Then total chaos erupted.

Someone shouted something about a bomb. A cacophony of screams. A huge surge of bodies that seemed to carry everything outwards. Men and women collapsed, either accidentally or to avoid the expected blast, or as others tried to get past them.

A man yelled, *'It's a grenade!'*

The shouting and screaming intensified. The general flight, from an epicentre just outside the front door, was abruptly turned back in on itself by the limits of space and the numbers.

Men and women fell, or were shoved or pointlessly yanked to one side. Things got broken. Mordred was pushed over from behind and landed on a woman in a suit who looked terrified. People started trampling each other.

And yet… there was no blast.

Frank and Elmer emerged from the melee for a second looking shocked – and empty-handed. They scanned the area frantically, trying to see through the pandemonium, though they were still being controlled by it. Everyone was. Nevertheless, their faces gave the situation away as well as anything could.

They'd lost Daisy.

Chapter 28: We Love You, Kristen

When a couple of police officers emerged from the doorway onto the roof, Pavel Nikolayevich and Walter Doyle evaded them by simply separating keeping quiet and staying one step ahead. By this time, they knew their surrounds intimately, and they hardly had to try. Nevertheless, they couldn't believe their luck when the duo decided they'd done a good enough job, and returned the way they came. They were alone again. Pavel Nikolayevich still had a little vodka left, so they celebrated by finishing it. It was a perfect summer's night, and despite the getaway speedboat, neither of them expected ever to see another sunrise. They were both drunk now, but they agreed: you were generally luckier when you were more risk-averse.

Doyle asked Pavel Nikolayevich whether he'd ever heard of John Mordred.

Pavel Nikolayevich shrugged. "Who is he?"

"A British secret serviceman. Your worst enemy. If anyone's going to stop you, it'll be him."

"We've got two hand grenades and a gun. He'll have to be Superman to get past those."

"Let's hope he's not."

Pavel Nikolayevich sniggered. "Is he as good as your famous James Bond?"

"Obviously, no one's as good as James Bond. But he might be one day. He's got two novels based on his exploits. Knebworth Jannison, he's called. I mean, in the novels."

"Why are you telling me this?"

"He'll probably be Daisy's bodyguard today. To get to her, you'll probably have to get past him."

"So... have you got any tips?"

"None whatsoever. I don't really know anything about him, except that he's famous."

They both laughed uncontrollably, though they had no idea what was amusing them, except perhaps fear.

"So he's famous, yes?" Pavel Nikolayevich said eventually.

Doyle suddenly became serious. "That's right. And as I understand, from what you've been telling me, you only ever wanted to become a serial killer so you could be famous. You wanted to do what other serial killers had done, but better. You wanted people to go on Pavel Nikolayevich Alikhanov tours, yes?"

"They will."

"That's why you've written that journal."

"It is."

"Well, I've got good news," Doyle continued. "If you kill John Mordred, you'll be more famous for *that* than for all the other murders you've committed *combined*. Put it this way, who's more famous: Lee Harvey Oswald or Jeffrey Dahmer?"

"Lee who?"

"Harvey Oswald. He assassinated President Kennedy."

"Yikes."

They laughed again.

"So if I kill 'John Mordred' today," Pavel Nikolayevich said eventually, "you're saying I'll be more famous for *that* than for every other murder I've committed *combined?*"

"Those were virtually my exact words, yes."

"Oh, wow. This is sounding better and better. How can we fail? We've got two hand grenades and a gun. What's he look like?"

"Tall, curly blond hair, clean-shaven, mid-thirties. You can't miss the hair. It's almost golden. The man with the golden hair. Looks like it's been dyed, but I'm fairly sure it hasn't."

"And if I kill him, I'll be more famous for that *one killing* than for every other murder I've ever committed before?"

Doyle nodded. "I genuinely believe so."

"Combined?"

"Yes!"

"Oh, boy! Oh, wow! We can't fail. We've got two hand grenades and a gun. But you will let *me* kill him, won't you? *You* won't try to kill him?"

"I can't make any promises. We have to see how it pans out."

"You say he's a secret agent. That means he must have killed people before, yes?"

"I imagine so. He kills lots of people in the Knebworth Jannison books, and they're supposed to be based on him. What are you driving at? That you somehow inherit all his kills in the act of murdering him? That they become your property?"

"No, it wasn't anything like that." Pavel Nikolayevich said.

"What then?"

He explained his dream about the mansion. Doyle listened sympathetically and, at the end, said, 'It's only a dream.'

"No, I think it's a premonition," Pavel Nikolayevich said. "And I'm going to go there today. But if I kill this 'John Mordred', he'll be there too, in the mansion. He'll be added to the guest-list. But if *he's* killed people too, then *he* won't be able to get out either! So I won't be alone. We might not like each other at first, but over the course of a long time, we could become friends."

Doyle took a slight breath. "It's – it's not impossible."

"I've never really had a friend before."

Doyle patted his thigh. "You've got me."

"Can I have another pull on your hip flask?"

"Cheeky." He passed the hip flask over. "We'll take one more drink, then we need to go and watch for Daisy Hallenbeck arriving."

"Cheers."

They went to the front of the building and peered through the smoked glass for the tenth time that day. The whole road was full of people now. It had been busy when they'd last looked, an hour ago, but nothing like this.

"What do you think's going on?" Pavel Nikolayevich said.

Doyle shrugged. "I don't know, and I don't like it. There shouldn't be this many people."

"What's it say on that home-made banner?" Pavel Nikolayevich asked, pointing.

"It says, 'We love you elon'."

"What's it mean?"

"God knows. There's another one there. I don't actually know what an *elon* is. It's not even an English word, as far as I'm aware. Mind you, they've probably misspelled it. That wouldn't be surprising, given the general standard of literacy in this country. But I don't even know what it's *meant* to be."

"*Elon* sounds a bit like *Hallen*. As in Daisy's surname. Elonbeck. Maybe they're foreign, like me."

"I don't suppose it matters. Except that it might explain the crowd. There's another: 'We love you Kristen'." He sighed hopelessly. "There's no point in trying to make the least sense of it. In cases like this – and, believe me, you encounter them every day in politics – it helps to remember that the great British public is mind-bogglingly stupid. If you try too hard to make sense of its behaviour, you end up weeping with frustration. 'We love you, Kristen': God help us, you bone-headed morons."

"I think I can see them coming!"

Doyle looked. "My God, yes, that must be them."

A convoy of five cars approached at speed. To clinch matters, the blacked-out windows of the foremost was visible even through the tinted glass of the building's frontage.

Both men felt light headed. Here were their deaths. In cars. On an otherwise ordinary summer evening.

Doyle turned to Pavel Nikolayevich and shook his hand emotionally. They hugged. Doyle gave him the gun.

"Go to the lift," he said, "count to ten, and get in. Remember, don't rush. Everyone else will be panicking. A lot of them will probably die – possibly including her. If she is killed by the blast – if you're sure – and you think you've got a clear means of exit, then do whatever you have to in order to get away. Otherwise, bring her up here. Don't kill her till we're together, otherwise you'll leave yourself totally exposed. We'll kill her when we've got her up here and the door locked, then we might – just might – get away."

Pavel Nikolayevich swallowed, nodded and left.

Doyle took a grenade from his bag. He weighed it in his hand. Grip the lever, pull out the pin, count to three, drop. It should explode halfway down, blowing a great hole in the window and showering everyone with glass and fire.

My God, that he should have come to this!

He climbed on an upturned flowerpot he'd put there for the purpose and looked down into the street. He saw a blob of blond hair exit the first car at speed. He took a sharp breath. Then another car pulled up. Two men flanking a woman in an Alice band.

Her!

He squeezed, pulled the pin, counted, then dropped.

He was so elated, and high on adrenalin, that the danger of watching didn't occur to him till a few seconds afterwards. The grenade seemed to fall in slow-motion, down, down…

Then it landed on the pavement in between two people.

Someone shouted something about a bomb. A few people screamed. There was a huge surge of bodies. People collapsed, either accidentally or to avoid the expected blast. A man yelled *'It's a grenade!'* The yelling and screaming intensified.

But no explosion… Then *still* no explosion.

He involuntarily took a deep breath. My God, they'd given him a *dud!*

Pavel Nikolayevich got in the empty lift and pressed 'ground'. He thrust the gun, trigger-first, beneath the waistline of his trousers, and waited for the slight arrival-judder.

The doors swished open to reveal complete havoc – people screaming, clambering over each other, pushing and yanking - yet much less mayhem than he'd expected. No dismembered bodies, shattered glass, zombie-like victims covered in blood. Just a horrendous all-directions stampede.

He realised at once what must have happened. The grenade had failed to go off.

Which meant it still could, at any moment. The intensifying panic indicated everyone else thought the same.

He spotted Daisy, several metres in front of him, crawling on the ground. She looked like she thought the earth had opened and tried to bite her in two. He strode over several bodies and put his hand out to help her. Their eyes met. She was in shock. He could take advantage of that, by looking composed.

Not too difficult. The explosive could go off at any moment, but he was the only one here who really knew what was happening.

She accepted his hand with apparent docility. He pulled her towards the stairs, and kept tight hold of her. Then he almost dragged her up behind him. He could hear a wave of panic-stricken people fleeing behind him.

She was probably too traumatised to know what was happening. Even if she stopped to think about it, though, him bringing her up here at speed wasn't unreasonable: the further away from the possible blast, the better.

He thrust her through the doorway on to the roof. Doyle stood waiting for them. His anguished look turned to a grin of triumph when he registered that *this was her*.

"Well *done*, Pavel Nikolayevich!" he yelled feverishly. He shook both fists in the air and leaned back to thank the heavens. "Now kill her! *Kill her!*"

Mordred clambered to his feet just in time to see someone apparently leading Daisy upstairs and out of harm's way. It took him a split second to realise something wasn't right in the guy's expression – like he'd caught his prey, and now it was only a matter of time – then another split second to recognise the killer from the Albert Bridge video footage. He tried to get to his feet, but there was another surge forwards, and he found his arm being gripped by what looked like a security official. "Let me get you to

216

safety, sir," the man said, like it was a command more than an offer of help.

In fact, everyone was surging at the stairs now. Whoever he was, the Albert Bridge assassin must have arrived on the scene at precisely the right time.

Mordred yanked himself free and put all his strength into getting to the front of the surge. He grabbed a woman in a suit, then a man in a bomber jacket, and threw them out of the way. He stepped over a man he vaguely recognised as Neil Absolom. He trod on someone's hand, and absently said sorry. He quickly became a new general source of disturbance, one that was far more indignant than afraid.

The security guard caught up with him when he was almost at the front of the ascending stampede. He grabbed him more roughly this time. Mordred turned and punched him in the mouth. He recoiled and released his grip, then came back for a second attempt.

But by this time, Mordred had drawn his gun. The guard yelped, slammed on the brakes and fell over backwards. The people at the front of the crowd screamed angrily, then – as they each registered the gun - in renewed terror, and the whole mass turned about and began to stampede back downstairs.

Mordred bounded two stairs at a time to the top, where he found a closed exit door. He shoulder-barged it. It opened with a bang on the second attempt and he fell on to the flat roof.

He got up quickly.

Twenty yards away, Daisy stood three feet in front of Walter Doyle, who had a handgun aimed directly at her head. He was repeatedly pulling the trigger to no effect. Both he and Daisy looked like their worst nightmares had come true.

To one side, the Albert Bridge assassin stood casually squeezing a hand grenade with the pin in his mouth, obviously for exhibition purposes.

"Keep the lever compressed, Pavel Nikolayevich!" Doyle said, in Russian. "Bloody, *bloody* - !" He hurled the gun at the sky.

It arced for about thirty metres then descended till the parapet obscured it. He grabbed Daisy and held her in front of him. "If you shoot either me or him," he told Mordred, in a gasp, in English, "then he'll release the lever, and we're all finished. This wasn't how I planned things, but we can all still get out of here alive, if you do what I say. Put your gun down, close the exit door, and stand with your back against it."

Mordred noticed Daisy wasn't as frightened as she looked. In fact, she was more angry than scared. "Release Daisy," he said. "Send her over here, and I'll put the gun down."

Doyle shook his head. "Not a chance. You put the gun down first."

Having successfully created the impression that negotiations were under way, Mordred shot the assassin through the chest. Doyle yelped. Daisy yanked away, grabbed the grenade and threw it high into the air over the side of the building. It seemed to rise for even longer than the gun had, and Mordred kept expecting it to explode in mid-ascent, but it finally lost momentum, and then it fell like a boulder. It disappeared beyond the parapet. Then silence.

Doyle fell to his knees. "Bloody, bloody *crappy JUNK!*"

The door behind Mordred burst open. A flood of policemen in flak jackets entered with guns, shouting 'on the floor!' Probably because everything else had been so surreal, it felt like some kind of weird street theatre.

"Whoo!" Daisy said, above the men's voices. She sat down and leaned back on her palms. "I probably won't be a History teacher now, after all."

His phone rang. *Ruby Parker*.

"I need all the information you can give me," she said, when she'd received a twenty-second report, "and you need to get Daisy Hallenbeck down here as quickly as possible. She's still got crucial work to do. A US Air Force exfiltration plane has just taken off from Cyprus."

Chapter 29: 3-Way + 1

It took thirty minutes for Daisy Hallenbeck to discredit *The Guardian*'s tranche of documents. Ruby Parker then informed the CIA in Langley. Langley put the fake documents – which *The Guardian* had no further use for – together with Mike Rasmussen's confession, and ordered the immediate detention of ten officials in CIA Istanbul, including Nedrick Sullivan, on the grounds of 'serious professional misconduct'. A list of criminal charges followed an hour later.

In Turkey, after informal communications between Ruby Parker and her long time Turkish counterpart, a secretive old woman called Afife Türkpençe – and with evidence amassed and presented by Special Agent Hulusi Erkekli - Colonel Tuncel Alasya was arrested on charges of 'conspiring to endanger state security'. An hour afterwards, the thirty-five members of JBL were unexpectedly 'rescued' by an unnamed Kurdish militia group and driven away from Anamur in the direction of the Syrian border, a development confirmed by US spy satellites. By now, the American airlift operation was halfway to its destination, but, after a frantic barrage of communiqués between Washington, London and Ankara, it was called off, and the plane, plus its fighter escorts, turned around. The whole process, from Daisy coming down from the roof, to the abandonment of the emancipation mission, took ninety-seven minutes. Luckily, a lot of the most important pieces had been in place beforehand.

The next day, Mordred found himself sitting in Ruby Parker's office again, with Phyllis on his right. After the usual, 'Well done, John's, they settled down to discussing the finer points of the case.

"The chief conspirators," Ruby Parker told him, "were Nedrick Sullivan, Walter Doyle and Tuncel Alasya. The aim was to break NATO up by provoking Turkey's expulsion, and thus permanently change the face of continental Europe. Incredibly, all three were acting from what they considered patriotic motives. Nedrick Sullivan even managed to enlist several of his fellow countrymen and women."

"The Americans' motives are the ones I least understand," John said.

"Well," she went on, "Sullivan's motive for wanting to dismantle NATO lay in his firm conviction that America can manage defensively on its own, and that the other partners aren't pulling their financial weight. Doyle expected an expelled Turkey to take revenge by releasing hundreds of thousands of Libyan, Syrian and African migrants northwards into central Western Europe. The aim here was to 'flood' – his word – the EU with Muslim migrants, thereby impacting its ability to compete with Britain post-Brexit; levelling the playing field, as he saw it. Tuncel Alasya wanted the same thing, but for different reasons. A more Muslim Europe, broadly receptive to Ankara as the centre of a new Ottoman Empire. He wanted to play the supposedly trump card Erdoğan himself has always kept in reserve and tried to use as leverage to get his own way."

"Essentially, they all bought into the right-wing fallacy of migration spelling economic disaster," Mordred said.

"What none of them realised," Ruby Parker went on, "is that they were all being individually played by Russia. Each of the three thought he alone was conspiring with Moscow, although they knew Moscow had some influence over the others. Had they succeeded, the biggest loser of all would probably have been Turkey."

"So what were the Russians hoping to get out of it?" Phyllis asked. "Although I think I can guess."

"They were expecting the fear of Muslim migrants to provoke greater ties between the various branches of the Orthodox Church," Ruby Parker said, "and ultimately, as an organic outcrop of that, a new political union – a massive expansion of The Commonwealth of Independent States - based on anti-Muslim, anti-migrant paranoia. It would include Romania, Hungary, Estonia, Ukraine, Albania, Georgia, and – the jewel in the crown – Greece. The idea was that Greece would be easy to prise out of the EU if more help with immigration and an aggressively united front against Turkey was on the table, as it almost certainly would have been. Had the plan succeeded, Turkey would have found itself surrounded by hostile powers, having already endured a conflict with the USA from which it would inevitably have emerged battered, and possibly broken. Meanwhile, the migrant army it sent north would, over the course of one or two generations at most, have settled down and become loyal taxpayers, as virtually always happens."

"And the whole thing flopped," John said, "because the Russians couldn't source two working grenades and a functioning pistol. I'd call that funny."

"That's what you get with a kleptocracy," Phyllis said. "It's all about robbing your citizens. After a while, no one on any level does a particularly good job."

Ruby Parker frowned slightly. "Explain how that might work in this particular instance."

"Either someone in the Russian intelligence services decided the objective wasn't achievable," Phyllis said, "or he or she was paid to think that, and deliberately put a spanner in the works; or the Russians decided to source the required kit from 'unofficial suppliers', since using certified Russian merchandise would leave a trail. By 'unofficial suppliers', read 'gangsters', since in that setup, the line between state providers and criminal entrepreneurs tends to be hazy at best."

"That explanation works for me," John said after a pause.

"It works for me too," Ruby Parker said. "But you should also know that the reason Doyle's gun failed to work is that Preeti Akhtar-Bunsen, one of our younger MI7 operatives, posing – ironically – as an FCO cleaner, as part of the surveillance operation on Doyle, had discovered it in the bottom drawer of his desk. On my orders, she replaced the real bullets with dummies."

"Well… thank you," John said.

"In any case," she went on, "the whole thing was falling apart long before Doyle requested a pair of grenades and a firearm. It began when Daisy Hallenbeck refused to play ball. The tipping point was when you, John, called Mike Rasmussen out."

Phyllis folded her hands. "I'm assuming Angela Barnes had evidence, or even proof, of everything you've just outlined. She must have."

"That's the assumption the Russians were working on," Ruby Parker replied. "And that's why they ordered her killing. We're now fairly certain that the body that was autopsied in Cyprus wasn't hers; probably a murder-to-order, someone chosen solely because she looked like Angela. Our investigation into that is still ongoing. The corpses were switched in Britain. Doyle was in charge of her case from the very beginning – I say 'her': I mean, the fictional Angela who was killed in Iraq - because he put himself forward. As for what evidence Angela actually brought to Britain with her, we may never know what that was, although I still think she must have had something concrete, possibly physical documentation. She just hid it too well. Or Daniel Batsford did, though I doubt that. Once she was dead, he'd have had no interest in concealing anything she'd given him. Quite the reverse."

"Do we know who the assassin was yet?" John asked.

"A Russian by the name of 'Pavel Nikolayevich Alikhanov'," Ruby Parker replied. "Or so Walter Doyle says. We have no reason to disbelieve him, but nor have we anything in the way of independent confirmation. A 'serial killer', or so the man apparently described himself: as opposed to an international assassin. According to Doyle, he claimed to have written a secret online journal, due to be automatically released into the public domain later this year. So we may find out more about him at that point, assuming the Russian authorities don't get to it first, or Doyle's not fantasising."

"According to the papers, Doyle seems to be doing remarkably well," Phyllis said witheringly.

"He's in serious trouble right now," Ruby Parker said. "Assorted offences relating to the Prevention of Terrorism Act, including possession of explosives and attempted murder. He'll almost certainly be found guilty, but the sentences will probably run concurrently, and he could well build up a loyal following outside prison. *A patriot to the core* is how his memoirs will likely depict him. With time off for good behaviour, he could even be back at liberty within ten years, and then, as the law currently stands, there's nothing to stop him running for Parliament again. Who knows where this country will be then?"

Phyllis and John looked at each other. There was a long pause.

"Sorry to end on such a dispiriting note," Ruby Parker said at last, apparently noticing their discomfort. "Now, if you've no further questions, I suggest we call this meeting - "

John took a gift-wrapped tube from his inside jacket pocket. "We bought you this," he blurted out.

"It's a leaving present," Phyllis said emotionally. "Although obviously, we know that nothing..." She wiped her eyes. "No present could possibly... Sorry."

Ruby Parker peeled the paper off and half smiled. A maroon Che Guevara beret, with a gold star on the front. "I, er... Thank you. I won't put it - "

"There's a letter inside," John said hastily. "We couldn't actually decide what to get you, because, well, you know, you've meant more to us over the years than we could possibly get our tiny heads round, definitely in present-buying terms. So I called Vilma Cuesta, who we got to know during the Empire case. The beret was her idea, but somehow it seemed right. The star's pure brass, by the way, just so you know we haven't gone totally bonkers. Throw it in the bin, if you want. Anyway, she – Vilma - sent us a letter to put inside. We haven't read it obviously, and we're going to skulk out in a minute, so you can read it when we're not here. But I do know she's coming to stay in Britain for a while, starting the day you retire. She told me that on the phone: I didn't attempt to elicit it: she just came out with it. I didn't try to dissuade her, obviously, because it's none of my business, but nor did I encourage her: she was going to do it anyway. In any case, we had a nice chat, and she said we could remain friends after you retire, so if you're prevented by 'protocol' from ever speaking directly to us again, or vice-versa – you know how stuffy MI7 can be, but I think Stella will be different, though I don't one hundred per cent know her yet – we can do it through Vilma. I really hope you'll - "

"Thank you, both of you," she cut in. "It's a lovely present. And I appreciate your kind words."

They both knew what she meant. *Meeting over*.

Chapter 30: All Change Here

"I got the job," Phyllis said when they were in the corridor. "And I've been given the go-ahead to tell you."

He'd known the announcement was coming today, but he hadn't expected it so suddenly. "Wow!" he said. He saw a grand gesture was called for so he picked her up like a manly man and kissed her. "I knew you could do it! We need to go out and celebrate."

"I don't feel like celebrating." They got in the lift. "I know that sounds grumpy. Every new beginning... I don't know... We're at the end of a really fantastic era. We're getting older, for God's sake."

"I know." He pressed the button for the canteen. "Fun's end. Let's get a pot of tea and two bags of Wotsits or a Twix or something. You can have whatever you want. I'm paying."

"Are you really going to join Black?"

"So they told you, did they?"

"Come on, John. Apart from anything else, you just said, 'I think Stella will be different, though I don't one hundred per cent know her yet'."

"In my defence, I was nervous. Do you think RP liked our present?"

"I think her opinion of us went down yet another notch. Not what I was hoping for, but then I was hoping for the moon. Oh God, I hope she'll be all right."

"She's the Tyson Fury of retirees. Why wouldn't she be all right?"

"Because she's so bloody good at what she does, that's why. Put it like this. Can you imagine Alec having a private life? Yes. Or Ian, or Edna, or Suki? Yes, yes, yes. What about Ruby Parker? Well, no. What could you imagine her doing for a hobby? She's probably institutionalised, after all this time. She *is* the job. One day she's full-on in it; the next, bang, she's retired. And this is MI7. It's not like she can ever come back."

"I think she can."

"So you're rewriting the rules now. What makes you say that?"

He laughed. They got out of the lift. "It hasn't quite sunk in yet, has it? When she leaves, you're going to be one of the five or six most important people in this building. It's going to be MI8 from what I hear, so new rules, and you'll help make them. If you want to invite her back for a chinwag and a chunk of advice, then you probably can."

"Lady Parker of Brixton Hill. I'll probably have her back every week, for all the good *I'm* going to be."

"You'll just have to resist the temptation. Anyway, we've been through that. You're by far the best person for the job, and that's the end of the matter, so shut up."

She laughed.

The canteen was louder and much busier than usual. The news that MI7 was becoming MI8 had formally been announced at 9am, though nearly everyone already knew. Most people had been moved sideways. A few, like Alec, Phyllis, Edna, Annabel and John were being promoted. Edna to assistant Head of White, under Marcie Brown; Alec to Head of Grey, Annabel to join John in Black. The usual group sat at a long table, looking washed out. Mordred bought a pot of tea and two cream scones, Phyllis went to sit with Suki.

"Okay to join the wake?" he said, when he came over. He slapped Alec on the shoulder. "Congrats. And you, Edna."

"Cheers," Edna said, raising her Vimto.

"No more *Godzilla* or *Star Trek*," Alec said. "I've got to act like a grown-up now. On the plus side, it is more money, and I do get to order people around. People like Suki and Ian."

Suki laughed. "On the other hand, when we get things wrong, you have to carry the can."

"We should all go out for a drink," Phyllis said. "I'm sure it's allowed, just once."

"I second that," Ian said. He laughed. "Slight pay rise."

Somehow, today, there wasn't as much work to do as usual. Maybe it had been planned that way. They sat in the canteen for two hours, sharing the usual sorts of vaguely interesting anecdotes, making quips, just sitting enjoying each other's company. They never would go out for a drink together – Phyllis knew as well as anyone that it probably wasn't allowed – so this was as close as they'd ever get again. They felt sorry about the change, but optimistic about the future. Things would get better.

A week later, on her last day, Ruby Parker sat in her office and worked her way through a succession of files, trying to clear her inbox for Phyllis's sake. A variety of people kept coming to wish her farewell and say what a pleasure it had been working with her, several of them looking shaky. Her desk was covered with 'Good Luck!' cards, some signed by individuals, others by teams. Colin had sent her a little teddy bear with a heart attached.

When 5.30pm came, she shut down her computer, gathered all the cards and gifts and put them neatly in a carrier bag. She'd reposition them at home on the sideboard. She took one last look round her office, then got up and left the room.

She'd make a special point of signing out so she could say thank you in person to Colin. Then Kevin would take her home.

She didn't feel as emotional as she'd expected. John had done an excellent job on the Barnes case, and she was in the rare position – she knew it *was* rare, for this job – of leaving without any loose ends dangling. It could have been so different had she not had the good fortune to work with such a talented team.

She donned the mask she'd bought at reception, got in the lift and pressed 'ground'. It ascended and, three seconds later, opened on to the reception area. A huge crowd stood in solemn silence, apparently waiting for her, and burst into applause the moment she appeared.

She tried to look impassive. It wasn't what she'd wanted. There had been enough fuss with all the cards and gifts. She'd hoped to be able to leave without any more.

Yet she couldn't help marvelling. She'd never seen the place so packed. There were even people on the stairs and the first floor.

She signed out, and said thank you to Colin. She hoped he was a good lip-reader.

As she turned to go, someone called out, in a final gesture of perfect kitsch, *"Three cheers for Ruby Parker!"*

Despite the masks, the noise went up several decibels in a trio of pulses, and stayed there. But as far as she could tell, it was all perfectly controlled – that was the important thing - and probably sincere. No balloons or any of that nonsense, just dignified men and women in their work clothes, expressing their appreciation in the conventional manner. Afterwards, they'd almost certainly return to their desks, and carry on as if nothing had happened. Just as it should be.

Annabel held the door for her. She walked out of the building for the last time into the early summer evening, and the low drone and diesel smell of the city. The sun shone.

Kevin was waiting. He helped establish her on the car's back seat, got in, politely asked if she was comfortable, and pulled out.

As they crossed Lambeth Bridge, she suddenly noticed the conventional pile of fresh newspapers at her side. Someone must have requested them for her. For a moment, the gesture seemed redundant, but then she remembered: she had no intention of retiring from public life, not any more. Quite the opposite.

She put each individual newspaper to one side until she came to *Private Eye*. She opened it at page one - 'Eye Summer Quiz' - and began to read.

Books by James Ward

General Fiction
The House of Charles Swinter
The Weird Problem of Good
The Bright Fish
Hannah and Soraya's Fully Magic Generation-Y Snowflake Road Trip Across America

The Original Tales of MI7
Our Woman in Jamaica
The Kramski Case
The Girl from Kandahar
The Vengeance of San Gennaro

The John Mordred Tales of MI7 books
The Eastern Ukraine Question
The Social Magus
Encounter with ISIS
World War O
The New Europeans
Libya Story
Little War in London
The Square Mile Murder
The Ultimate Londoner
Death in a Half Foreign Country
The BBC Hunters
The Seductive Scent of Empire
Humankind 2.0
Ruby Parker's Last Orders

Poetry
The Latest Noel
Metals of the Future

Short Stories
An Evening at the Beach

Philosophy
21st Century Philosophy
A New Theory of Justice and Other Essays

CPSIA information can be obtained
at www.ICGtesting.com
Printed in the USA
LVHW032157240321
682338LV00010B/228